MW01059415

Facing Forward

For three days, I stayed in my apartment and refused to answer the phone. I hated everyone and everything, and I felt sure that this bitterness would be with me forever. I didn't want to see friends or talk to my family. I had to return to work, though, so I focused all of my energy on the kids. As the school year began to wind down, I realized I couldn't stay in New York any longer—it just wasn't the same. I wasn't the same. My whole existence had been turned on end. I needed to start over, but I didn't have the energy to tackle somewhere new so I decided to go home. I called my mom, and my embarrassment at having another messed-up relationship was quickly negated by her warm and practical approval. My emotions had been raging out of control, and some time with my level-headed mother was just what I needed.

As I drove past the familiar fronts of Smith's Hardware Store and McBride's farm stand, my anxiety gave way to exhaustion, and then I felt an intense longing to be in the comfort of home. I was mentally and physically drained when I pulled into the driveway of my mother's house, but when she ran out to greet me, the pain returned.

"What am I going to do?" I asked through my tears.

My mother released me from her protective grasp, looked me square in the eye and calmly said, "You, my dear, are going to get on with your life."

Wings

FACING FORWARD

by

Robyn Sheridan

A Wings ePress, Inc.

Contemporary Romance Novel

Wings ePress, Inc.

Edited by: Rosalie Franklin
Copy Edited by: Karen Babcock
Senior Editor: Anita York
Executive Editor: Marilyn Kapp
Cover Artist: Nick A. Sheridan

Wings ePress Books
http://www.wings-press.com

Copyright © 2009 by Robyn Sheridan
ISBN 978-1-59705-444-7

Published In the United States Of America

July 2009

Wings ePress Inc.
403 Wallace Court
Richmond, KY 40475

Dedication

For Mark, Alex, Nick and Gina. Thanks for your constant support and reminding me of what's really important in life.

Also, thanks to Mom, Dad, Vera, Joe, Di, Pam and Claire for always cheering me on.

For Sunny,

Thanks so much!

Robyn Ce

Prologue

I stood over the empty crib and slid my hand against the sheet hoping to feel some remnant of warmth. The coldness of the crib stung my hand, and the ache in my heart intensified. The past week had been a living nightmare. Each day I awoke hoping and praying that it had all been some terrible, terrible dream, and each day I came to the horrendous realization that it was all very real.

I bent over to smell the sheets and get some reassurance that Joe had indeed existed. The fresh, powdery aroma was waning, but it was still there. As long as I had the scent of him, he couldn't totally be gone. I closed my eyes and just breathed in and out, praying that I could get through another day. I grabbed his blanket and rubbed the silk edge against my cheek. I looked around the room and saw how perfect everything appeared. The only thing missing was him.

How could I miss someone so fiercely who had only been alive for six weeks, I wondered as I sat in the rocker. It was somewhat soothing to sit and hold his blanket in my arms, but the emptiness was still palpable. The door to the nursery opened and my mother peered in, but I just shook my head and she left without saying a word. I tried to fight back the tears that were building up, but was overcome and finally just let them flow. I had shed so many tears already, yet they seemed to be unending.

The door re-opened, and again my mother appeared. I shook my head once more, but instead of retreating, my mother said, "Jane, it has to be done."

"Not now," I replied.

"Jane, we are going to do this now. You can't move on until we do."

"Move on?" I asked indignantly through my tears. "Move on? My son is dead, and you want me to move on? You have no idea what I'm going through," I spat.

My mother was stoic in her response. "I realize that, Jane, but I know that I need to help you."

"Help me? Since when have you been so interested in helping me? You didn't help me when I lost my first baby. Why do you want to start now?"

"Jane, that was different."

"Different, how? Two of my babies are dead, and you think you can come in and make it all better. Well, it doesn't work like that," I said indignantly.

"Listen, I did the best that I could back then, and now I am only trying to help you. We are all in pain. We're all sad. Don't you think I miss him too?" she asked as she broke down sobbing.

I hated seeing her like this. It rattled me, but I didn't want to make her feel better either. I wanted everyone to be in as much as pain as I was. I clutched Joe's blanket tighter and said, "We all do."

We stood in silence for a few moments, and finally my mother said, "It's time." She opened Joe's closet and began to sort through his clothes.

I rose to help, but needed to steady myself. I walked over to my mother, but couldn't bear the finality that this signified. "I can't," I said quietly and I left with his blanket firmly clutched in my hand. I went to my room and placed it under my pillow.

One

I'd always had a glamorized version of myself as one of those strong women who, when faced with adversity, would turn it into something worthwhile. Years later I would realize that true strength sometimes only enables you to get out of bed in the morning. However, when I packed everything up and moved back home at the age of twenty-eight, strong wasn't a word I would use to describe myself. Scared, unsure, depressed—those were words that better seemed to suit me.

After three years in New York City, I was returning to my hometown of Wilmington, New Hampshire. It was postcard New England complete with stunning fall leaves, old churches and a large town square where community gatherings were held. I left there, full of excitement and optimism. I had completed my teaching degree and had gotten a job at P.S. 248 in Brooklyn. Not exactly an inner city school, but so much different from where I grew up. I quickly came to love the frantic pace of the city and the mix of the different cultures. My job was hard—harder than I had imagined. I had had this vision of changing the life of each child that I taught, but after that first year of teaching kindergarten, I was proud that almost all of the kids could follow basic directions, write their first and last names and most could sit still for short periods of time.

Near the end of that first year, I began dating Nick. He was the friend of a friend, and we met at a bar when a few people from work went out for drinks after a grueling week. His dark hair and almost black eyes, which were in sharp contrast to my green eyes and blonde hair, immediately attracted me. I was not interested in getting involved with anyone, but he wasn't about to let that stop him, so he came up and introduced himself.

Conversation came easily between us. Nick told me about his job. "I'm a paramedic. It's truly awful some days, but then when I'm able to help, it's incredible. I don't think I'll be able to do it forever. It's so physically and emotionally demanding, but for now I'm happy."

"I teach kindergarten. Some days it can be quite hazardous, too," I laughed.

We talked about our families. Nick grew up in a large Italian family, the youngest of five. "I have three sisters and one brother. Every Sunday, we all have dinner at my parents' house. It's crazy, but I wouldn't trade it for anything," he admitted.

I told him about my dad dying when I was twelve. "He was a firefighter, and he died in a house fire. My mom is a remarkable person. She raised my older sister and me by herself. They both still live in New Hampshire."

We continued to talk, and before I knew it, two hours had passed and most of our friends had scattered. When we realized the time, Nick said, "I've got an early morning, but I'd love to see you again."

I gave him my number, and I was excited, but cautious. On our first few dates, we explored the city together visiting museums and parks and soon discovered that we had a lot in common. We even became running partners with grand plans to do the New York City Marathon. After a few months, we had become a couple. We spent all of our free time together and our personalities, though different, provided a nice balance. I was more outgoing and emotional whereas Nick was reserved and even-keeled. We fit together quite well.

I met his parents at one of their typical Sunday dinners. The day was filled with loud voices, kids running everywhere, delicious food and lots of hugs. They were so different from my own family, and I instantly fell in love with them.

Shortly before I began my third year of school, Nick and I spent what had become our typical Sunday together. We ran five miles in the morning and then went for coffee and bagels around the corner. Nick watched some sort of sporting event on television while I went through my lesson plans for the week ahead and took a nap. I was sleeping soundly when Nick sat on the edge of the bed and smoothed my hair in an effort to wake me.

"What's up?" I asked while rubbing my eyes.

"I want to talk to you about something."

"Okay," I said as I sat up and propped my pillow behind me.

"You know I love you, right?" I nodded not sure of where this was going. "I want to take our relationship to the next level, and I was thinking that we should move in together."

This was not quite the proposal I was hoping for.

"Nick, I love you too, but I want more than just living together. You know what I've been through. I need a commitment. I want to get married."

"I am committed to you, Jane and I want to get married, but I also want the timing to be right. I'm up for raise soon, and I need to be more financially secure before we get married. I'm not going to hurt you. You have my word."

It was a difficult decision that I mulled over for a few weeks, but in the end I agreed to let Nick move into my one-bedroom apartment. Not much changed in our relationship until that Thursday in January. The flu was running rampant in school, and every kid in my class had a runny nose and cough. I didn't feel great that morning; by lunchtime, I had a temperature of one hundred and one. I left school early, and when I went home, I felt an odd sensation as I closed the door behind me. I heard Nick's voice coming from the bedroom, and I felt my heart beat out of control. When I opened the bedroom door, there was Nick and a woman I recognized as a co-worker of his in our bed. For a moment, we all just stared at each other, Nick and his playmate with a look a sheer panic at having been caught. I was so full of hurt and rage that it took me a minute to figure out what to do.

I stammered a few seconds and finally sputtered, "Get out both of you." I left the room, but was dizzy so I sat on the couch.

The woman came out first and opened her mouth to try and say something, but I just looked her in the eye and said, "Don't."

I sat there numbly trying to make sense out of the situation when Nick approached me.

"Jane, let me explain. There was a horrible car accident—a mother and her two kids were killed. I've never seen anything like it before. I couldn't take it. It just happened."

"I can't talk to you now, Nick. Just leave."

"Please, Jane, don't do this. I'm really sorry. God, I can't believe this is happening."

"I can't either," I replied bitterly.

"Let me fix this, please. I'll do anything. We can get married."

"Get married?" I asked in disbelief. I stood up to put some much-needed space between us. "You have sex with another woman in our bed, and you want to fix it by getting married? You are out of your mind. You need to leave. Get some things and get out. I'll call you in a few days and you can come get all of your stuff."

"Jane, please..." he begged.

I stared at him a moment as a tear escaped down my cheek. "You promised. You said you wouldn't hurt me."

"I'm so sorry, Jane."

"Shut up. Just stop talking and get out of here," I screamed. "Get out now."

For three days, I stayed in my apartment and refused to answer the phone. I hated everyone and everything, and I felt sure that this bitterness would be with me forever. I didn't want to see friends or talk to my family. I had to return to work, though, so I focused all of my energy on the kids. As the school year began to wind down, I realized I couldn't stay in New York any longer—it just wasn't the same. I wasn't the same. My whole existence had been turned on end. I needed to start over, but I didn't have the energy to tackle somewhere new so I decided to go home. I called my mom, and my embarrassment at having another messed-up relationship was quickly negated by her warm and practical approval. My emotions had been raging out of control, and some time with my level-headed mother was just what I needed.

As I drove past the familiar fronts of Smith's Hardware Store and McBride's farm stand, my anxiety gave way to exhaustion, and then I felt an intense longing to be in the comfort of home. I was mentally and physically drained when I pulled into the driveway of my mother's house, but when she ran out to greet me, the pain returned.

"What am I going to do?" I asked through my tears.

My mother released me from her protective grasp, looked me square in the eye and calmly said, "You, my dear, are going to get on with your life."

Two

My mother was an incredible source of strength during those first few weeks. She didn't ask many questions and just let me heal in my own time. She was a typical New Englander—hardworking and strong with her emotions in check. My dad, Joe, died when my parents had been married only fifteen years. My mom had to go back to work, and while there were times we could tell that her life was difficult, she never let it get her down. She was a true survivor, and I knew that I would have to follow her example to move past my hurt over Nick. She was not one to put up with a lot of drama.

I settled back in my old room, and while it was depressing to be living with my mother again at my age, the fact that my room was still the same as I left it didn't help. My mom was extremely frugal, and I knew she would never redecorate, so I offered to do it as thanks to her.

"Mom, let me do this for you. I have the time, and I really could use something to keep me busy until school starts."

"You know it's not necessary, Jane, but I would love it," she smiled. "I'm really enjoying having you here, so don't feel like you have to rush out and get a place of your own. It's nice to have the company." She paused, then added, "This house can be pretty quiet at times."

"Where has Grace been?" I asked. Grace was my older sister, who lived about twenty minutes away. I had called her a day or so after I got into town and hadn't heard back from her.

"I haven't talked to her in a while. Let's invite her over for dinner this week. Call her at work, if she's between patients she can usually talk for a few minutes."

Grace was a nurse at the county hospital. She had worked there for the past five years and did an amazing job working with premature babies in the neo-natal intensive care unit. We became very close after our dad died, but as we grew older, our interests and personalities took us in different directions. Grace was quiet, shy and a homebody. She had a small circle of friends, but they were true. I hung with the popular crowd, and when I needed help, it was Grace who came to my rescue. She had gotten me through one of the most difficult times in my life, and I was excited to re-connect with her. I didn't have any friends left in Wilmington and I was hoping to have one in my sister. I took my mother's advice and managed to reach her at work.

"I'm sorry I haven't gotten back to you. Work has been really busy, and I've been dating someone. I think it could be serious."

I had never heard such liveliness in my sister's voice, and I was thrilled. "I want to hear all about him— What night can you come over for dinner?"

"What about tomorrow? Do you think Mom would mind if I brought him too?"

"Mind? Are you kidding? Are you sure he's up for a face to face with me and Ruth?"

"I think he'll be fine with it. I'll see you tomorrow after work. And, Jane," she added softly. "I'm glad you're back."

My mom was very surprised to hear that Grace was bringing a date. "We talk every week, but I don't see her much. We had lunch on Mother's Day, but she never mentioned dating anyone. I'm glad she feels comfortable bringing him. I just hope he's a good guy."

"Me too." I added, "the Richards girls' track record hasn't exactly been stellar."

~ * ~

The night of the dinner, Mom and I set a lovely table. I picked up a beautiful bouquet of stargazer lilies and daisies that complemented the floral tablecloth my mother had chosen. Just as I was opening a bottle of Cabernet, I heard a knock at the front door and my sister call for us.

I turned the corner and was greeted by my sister's bright smile. I held her embrace for an extra few seconds to let her know how much I had missed her.

I held out my hand to introduce myself to her boyfriend, but he drew me in close and said, "Jane, I've heard all about you," as he kissed me on the cheek. "I'm Derek Meade."

"It's wonderful to meet you, Derek," I replied, stepping back to get a little space. He was older than I had imagined. His graying temples and sun-damaged face led me to guess that he was at least forty five—a good fifteen years older than Grace.

"Where's Mama Richards?" he asked.

"I'm Ruth Richards," my mother answered as she entered the room. She stuck out her hand and said, "Welcome to my home." She hugged Grace and said, "It's so good to see you, honey. It's been too long."

So this is the new guy in Grace's life, I thought to myself. He had only been here for two minutes, and already he made my skin crawl. I forced myself to put aside my uneasiness and suggested we go out to the patio and have a drink. It was a perfect New England summer evening. The light, cool breeze and a few sips of wine helped calm me down a bit as I tried to get the conversation moving.

"Grace, how did you and Derek meet?"

"He's a pharmaceutical rep, and he would come by every few weeks with cookies and cakes for the nurses. One day we struck up a conversation and decided to go out for dinner."

"I could tell she hadn't been on a date in awhile, so I thought I'd help her out," Derek added, laughing. Grace's face fell, so he quipped, "It was just a joke." He looked at me and said, "Your sister needs to lighten up a little."

I shot him a serious look and said, "I think she's fine just the way she is."

Then, my mother came out to the patio with a tray of stuffed mushrooms and baked Brie.

"That looks wonderful," I said trying to change the subject.

The discussion flowed a bit more smoothly after we each had a drink. As I poured another glass of wine for us, I tried to focus on my sister and find out what else besides Derek was going on in her life.

"So, Grace, what have you been up to?"

"I've been taking a painting class. I'm doing watercolors. I've always wanted to try it. I'm not that good, but it helps relieve the stress of work."

"Have you finished anything? I'd love to see some of your paintings," I added, glad that my sister was trying new things.

She told me about some new and old friends of hers, and we continued catching up with one another while my mother went to work on Derek. She was never a meddler in our lives and let us make our mistakes, but she was always there to pick up the pieces. However, tonight I could sense she was in the protector mode. While she had Derek alone, it looked as though she was trying to figure him out.

As my sister and I continued our conversation, I tried not to call Grace's attention to Derek for fear she might try to rescue him. I wanted Mom to have time to make her point.

"How are you holding up, Jane—you know after the whole Nick thing?"

"At first I was devastated. I couldn't believe he was capable of cheating on me. It made me sick, literally. I threw up for a week. I felt so stupid because I wanted to marry him. I make such bad choices where men are concerned."

"I know you've been hurt a lot, but you are not stupid. You're one of the strongest women I know. You were blessed with Mom's genes," Grace said proudly. "You're a survivor."

"Me? How about you? Nursing school and taking care of premature babies and their parents. That's something to be proud of, and I'm amazed at how much you have accomplished. I really admire you."

"I've missed you so much. I'm sorry about the way things went down with Nick, but I'm so happy you came home." She gave me a hug and said, "Let me save Derek from Mom. I don't want her to scare him off. I really like him, and I don't want her to mess this up."

Her comments left me with a pit in my stomach as we sat down to dinner. My mother made one of my favorite meals—beef tenderloin with garlic mashed potatoes and asparagus. My mom always made a special meal for us when we came home, and this was my standing first night at home dinner. The aroma of steak just off the grill replaced the pit in my stomach with a pang of hunger.

After a few bites, I was in heaven. "Mom, this meal is incredible. I forgot what a great cook you are. Before I go back to work, please give me some cooking lessons."

"Grace could use some too," Derek added. Again, Grace's face fell "What?" Derek asked. "So you're not the best cook in the world—maybe if you practiced."

I quickly changed the subject, "Are you from Wilmington, Derek?"

"No, I was raised outside of Chicago and moved here two years ago with my job. I like it here, though."

"Do you still have family in Chicago?"

"No, I was an only child and both of my parents are dead, so it's just me. I have a few cousins in Ohio and Michigan, but I pretty much keep to myself."

Grace seemed eager to take the spotlight off Derek and asked, "When do you start your new job, Jane?"

"The kids come back the day after Labor Day, but I'll start back in August. I want to meet my assistant and spend some time getting my room and lessons ready."

Derek spoke up. "I'd be happy to help you out. I have a flexible schedule."

Grace smiled at Derek "You are so thoughtful. I'm sure she'd love the help."

"Let me get these dishes cleared up," I said, trying to ignore his offer. "You three stay put, and I'll put on some coffee for dessert."

While I was cleaning up in the kitchen, my mind was racing, because while this guy wasn't outright awful, he definitely made some rude and belittling comments. I was anxious for them to leave so my mom and I could compare notes. Grace hadn't dated much, and I had hoped she wasn't getting in over her head, but then again I wasn't qualified to give relationship advice.

I was lost in my thoughts when Grace came into the kitchen and asked, "Jane, what do you think of Derek? Isn't he great? I really want you two to like each other."

"He's a little critical of you, don't you think?"

"Oh, he's just joking. He has a great sense of humor."

"I didn't think his comments were funny. You don't have to put up with it, you know."

"I don't mind, Jane. He's really good to me. Besides, I think he might be the one."

"Hey, what's keeping you two?" Derek asked.

I was startled to hear his voice and wondered how much he had heard.

"You know I don't like you away from me for too long." He pulled Grace to him and kissed her as if she had been gone for a year.

Trying to put an end to my discomfort, I grabbed the plates and said, "Grace, bring out the pie when you're done."

My mom, who was left alone at the dining room table, mouthed, "We have to talk to her." I nodded in agreement as Derek protectively led Grace back to the table.

The remainder of the evening went by without incident until Grace and Derek were saying good-bye.

"Thanks for dinner, Mom," Grace said as the two embraced. We'd walked them to the door when Grace said, "I forgot my purse. I'll be right back, Derek."

Derek was visibly irritated and said, "Be quick or I'll leave without you."

I shot him a questioning look, and he laughed nervously.

"I'm just kidding. She's just so forgetful, one of these days I'm going to have to teach her a lesson."

My mother had reached her limit with Derek and said quietly, but firmly, "She's not a child, Derek, and she does not need to be taught a lesson by you or anyone."

Just then, Grace returned and said to Derek, "I'm really sorry. I need to get better at remembering things."

"No problem," Derek quietly replied.

I hugged my sister and said, "Call me and we'll have lunch."

Grace smiled and replied, "I will. Thanks again for a nice evening."

My mother closed the door and said, "I need a drink."

I poured us both another glass of wine and waited for my mom to start talking because she looked like she might explode.

"Okay, is it me or there something slimy about that guy? He thinks he's subtle with those digs he gives Grace, and I can't believe she takes it! Any fool could tell that his comments hurt her feelings, but she just holds it in. Why does she let him get away with it?" she asked, knowing that neither of us had the answer to that question.

"I don't know. I've been so wrapped up in my own world that I haven't been the best sister. Have you met any other guys that she's dated?"

"No. She's mentioned dates on occasion, but this is the first man I've ever met."

"The last guy she told me about was Ethan, and she never told me any of the details of their breakup. I know she was very upset about it, but I had so much going on. I'm afraid I wasn't very good at listening. We need to talk to her," I said adamantly. "She seems pretty serious about him."

"I don't know if it will do any good. He mentioned marriage to me when the two of you were in the kitchen getting dessert. He knows Grace wants to be married and have a family more than anything and I'm afraid he's going to take advantage of that."

"Marriage?" I asked incredulously. "Tell me exactly what he said."

"We were talking about Dad dying, and I let him know that the three of us were very close and if anyone hurt one of my girls, they would have to answer to me. It seemed to go right over his head, and he said to me, 'When Grace and I have kids I am sure she'll be the same way.' Then I asked him if they had discussed marriage, and he said 'Not yet, but I know she'll say yes.' Can you believe the arrogance of this guy?"

I was determined to fix this for Grace. "I'm going to call her right now. She has no idea what she's getting herself into."

"Jane, you need to calm down," she said with a hint of annoyance. "She's a grown woman, and we can't run her life for her."

We sat in silence a moment, and finally I gave in and said, "Let's wait a little while and maybe she'll realize what a jerk he is and we won't have to get involved."

"Let's hope he's not shopping for an engagement ring."

Three

Thankfully, I had managed to avoid any further contact with Derek. I purposely asked my sister to join me for shopping trips and lunches during her days off in the hopes that Derek would be working then. I didn't ask many questions about their relationship—Grace seemed so happy that I began to wonder if I had overreacted to a bad first impression.

In three weeks, school would start, and I asked Grace to help me get some supplies I needed. We stopped for a sandwich at McMahon's deli, and I broke down and asked how she and Derek were getting along.

"I'm really happy, Jane. I know he isn't perfect, but he really cares about me. You know, I haven't had a relationship since Ethan and that was eight years ago."

"I know it's none of my business, but what happened with you two? I know we weren't close back then, but you seemed so happy with him."

"I was happy. We started out as friends. We had the same anatomy class and were study partners. He was so supportive and always found something positive to say to me. We started spending more time together. He got me into hiking and I lost twenty pounds. I felt so good about myself and I started to fall in love with him. I thought he loved me too, but..."

"What happened?" I asked gently.

"We were getting along great, but when he came back to school after Christmas break he was different. He was still kind, but he was distant. I thought it was the stress of school, but then one day he told me he needed us to have some time apart. I was devastated because it seemed to come out of nowhere."

"Just like that? You had no idea that anything was going on?" I asked.

"Maybe I was naïve, but, no, I didn't. Finally after two weeks, I got a letter from him. He apologized for leading me on and explained that he had a fiancée and they were getting married in the summer. He said that he transferred to a school back home because he truly loved me and he couldn't bear to be near me and not be with me. He asked me to forgive him and told me to have a good life."

"That was it?"

"That was the last I heard from him."

"Wow, I never would have guessed. Grace, I wish you had confided in me earlier."

"It was so hard for me. I was humiliated and couldn't talk about it. How could he just walk away? I've never loved anyone like that, and it took me a long time to get over him, Jane."

"I know exactly how you feel." A stab of pain at my own betrayals returned like a chronic ache. "Let's hope that things start changing for the Richards girls in the man department," I added.

"I think my luck has turned around. Derek loves me." I just smiled and tried to swallow the lump in my throat.

~ * ~

The week before school began I decided it was time to get back into the work mode and decorate my room. There was so much to do, and when my assistant walked in to help, I was thrilled. "Hi, I'm Jane Richards. I'm so glad to meet you."

"Hi, Jane. I'm Mattie Pritchard. It looks like we have some work to get done here."

As we worked hanging up posters and bulletin boards, we learned about each other.

"Have you been teaching long?" she asked.

"I just finished a job in Brooklyn. I taught there for three years, and I learned a lot. How about you— Have you always worked in education?"

"I was a teacher many years ago, but pretty much retired after I had my boys. When they were grown, I realized that I missed being around little kids. I didn't want a full-time career again so I applied for the assistant teacher position, and I've been here for the past eight years. Why did you leave New York? Are you from here?"

I decided it was time to move on past my breakup with Nick and replied, "I was ready for a change and didn't want to start someplace new, so I came home. My mom and sister still live here."

"I take it you're not married. Can I give you some advice? Watch out for Sylvia. She's the secretary here, and she'll try to fix you up with her son. He's thirty-eight and still lives at home."

I laughed, "Thanks for the warning. How about you? Are you married?"

"For thirty-six years. My husband Jim is a great guy. Our sons are both on their own, and Jim travels a lot so that was another reason I wanted to go back to work."

"Where do your sons live?" I asked.

"Jamie is married and lives about forty minutes away. My granddaughter is two and absolutely perfect. Matt lives in Manhattan. He's an investment broker and may never settle down." She added, "I don't care. As long as he's happy."

I immediately loved Mattie. She was energetic, optimistic, and I appreciated the bits of helpful information she passed along. I also met a few teachers who were new like me, and right away I hit it off with Jillian Lane who taught kindergarten in the room next to mine. This was her first year teaching, and she was anxious to get the first day out of the way.

"I can't believe how nervous I am. I haven't slept in days," she complained.

"Once it gets here you'll be fine. Why don't we go out on Friday to celebrate the end of our first week?" I asked, feeling proud of myself for initiating plans for a night out.

Mattie and I continued to get our room ready, and when most of the work had been done, I suggested to Mattie we sit down and review the list of kids in our class and see if any of them had special needs or circumstances.

"Let's see. We have twenty kids," I began when I felt someone staring at me.

Mattie and I looked up at the same time; she asked, "Can I help you?"

Derek smiled as he leaned against the door way. "I'm here for her," he said slyly.

"Derek, what are you doing here?" I asked, not bothering to introduce him to Mattie.

"I told you I was available to help in any way. Here I am."

"We really don't need any help. You should have called, and I could have saved you a trip," I added, hoping to let him know that I did not want surprise visits from him.

"No problem. I was in the area, and besides, I haven't seen you since our dinner," he replied, implying a level of familiarity that made me very uncomfortable.

"Well, we're in the middle of something and have to finish. Thanks anyway," I said in form of dismissal.

Derek just stood there a minute burning me with an intense stare that went through me like an ice pick. He finally left without uttering another word, and I shuddered.

"Who was that?" Mattie asked with a confused look on her face.

"That was Derek—my sister's new boyfriend." Mattie got a concerned look on her face. "I know—you don't have to say anything—but my sister is falling for him, and I'm afraid she is making a huge mistake."

"If she were my sister, I'd have to say something. There's something about him that makes me uneasy. Maybe it's just me."

"Oh, it's not you, but right now I need to get through the first week of school, so let's finish working." I went back to the list. "Okay, we've got twelve boys and eight girls. That ought to keep us hopping. Luke has asthma, and Karl is allergic to dairy. Sophie's parents are divorced, mom has custody, and dad's new wife is not allowed to pick her up. That's lovely. Can you believe a five-year-old has to deal with this?"

"It gets worse, Jane," Mattie said. "Emma Manning. Her mom died in a car accident. It was awful. It happened two years ago when Emma and her mom were out Christmas shopping and we had this brutal snowstorm that came out of nowhere. The weather turned so fast, and she lost control of her car. Annie died immediately, but little Emma didn't have a scratch on her. Her dad, Ted, is a great guy, but it's been rough on them. Emma is a fabulous little kid, no trouble at all, but then again... sometimes it's the quiet ones you have to worry about."

"Well, it looks like we're in for an interesting year. I didn't know I was going to need a psychology degree, too. And think, this is only kindergarten!"

~ * ~

On Monday morning, I was at school an hour early. I hardly slept the night before. My goal for the day was to meet all twenty kids and their parents and return twenty kids at the end of the day. It didn't seem like a lofty goal, but it was going to be a challenging one. At 9 a.m., the children began to trickle in. They were adorable with their new backpacks, clothes and haircuts. I hoped I would remember them this way later in the year whenever my patience was wearing thin.

Two of the boys cried when their parents left and were comforted by Sophie. I could tell she was going to be the mother of the class. Three of the boys had a hard time sitting still and would be a challenge, but I was up for it. The rest of the kids came right in as if they had done this every day of their lives. And then there was Emma. When her dad brought her to class, she held onto his leg and closed her eyes as tears escaped. Her dad looked weary, and I could tell it had been a tough morning for him. I called Mattie over and asked Emma if she would like to sit with her.

I did my best to assure Emma's dad that she would be all right. "She'll be fine. Just go, and if there are any concerns, we'll call you."

At snack time, I passed out cookies that I had made the night before and purposely sat at Emma's table to try to coax her out of her shell.

"Hi, Emma, do you like the cookies?" I asked softly
She smiled and nodded.

"What do you think you'll like best about kindergarten?"

Again, she smiled and said, "Having you for a teacher."

"And I think I'm going to like having you in my class, too."

~ * ~

At the end of the first week, I was extremely happy. Exhausted, but happy. The kids were sweet and funny, Mattie was so easy to work with and I had made some new friends. Things were definitely moving in the right direction. Maybe it was time to shake things up.

Four

On the drive back to my mom's house, I realized that the pain of my breakup with Nick was fading and my spirit was lighter. I had made the right decision when I moved back to Wilmington, but now I was ready to find a home of my own.

That evening I broached the subject with my mom. Not one to hold back, I said, "Mom, I think I'm ready to get my own place."

"Really?" she asked. A hint of disappointment passed over her face, but she quickly recovered and said, "You know I don't care how long you stay."

That was my mother's way of saying she would miss me.

"I know, but it's time. I won't be able to move before the end of the month so I'll be here for a few weeks at least. I'm just ready to start looking."

On Monday, I was anxious to meet up with Jillian and another new friend, Lauren Jameson. The three of us had bonded during our lunch period, and each day I looked forward to our chats.

"I'm ready to leave the nest, and I need some advice from you two," I announced.

Lauren spoke up. "You should check out that cute area just outside of the town square. A developer came in and built these loft apartments, and they've been putting in some cute shops and restaurants all within walking distance. My friend Trish just moved in there, and she loves it."

"Let's all go check them out this weekend, and then let's go do something fun like dinner and a club. Have you gone out anywhere since you moved here?" Jillian asked me.

"Just that night with the people from school and lunches with my sister."

"That's pathetic," Lauren said, and I immediately felt stung. I had been feeling so proud of myself, and that one comment was like a slap in the face.

Jillian caught my reaction and said, "It's not pathetic. You've been through a bad breakup. It takes a while to recover. Let's just go out and have a fun evening."

Lauren apologized, "I didn't mean anything by it."

"I'm still a bit sensitive I guess. I need to finish some stuff in my classroom," I said and left the lunchroom. I was fighting back tears and found the nearest bathroom. I felt like such a baby. As I dried my tears, I decided that I needed to keep moving forward. I was going to go out with them and have a good time.

~ * ~

Jillian and Lauren picked me up on Saturday afternoon, and we went to check on some apartments I had gotten information on during the week. We started at the area known as The Mill. There was a grocery store around the corner and a café across the street that sold coffee and bagels. The next block down there was a drugstore with an old-fashioned soda fountain and a fun-looking restaurant that served Thai food. The apartments were these modern lofts with cement walls and ceilings where you could see all of the pipes. It was so different from the typical New England home, and I loved it. There was no reason for me to look any further.

"I love it and I'll take it," I told the woman who was showing us the apartment.

"Great. Come down to the leasing office and we can take care of the paper work."

"Can we just look around a few more minutes so I can make a shopping list?" I asked.

"Sure, just lock the door when you leave. I'll have everything ready." With that, she left the three of us.

"Isn't this place great?" I asked, already knowing they were in total agreement with me.

"I am so jealous of you," said Lauren. "You're going to meet so many guys here. Just remember to share the leftovers."

"You, my friend, have a one-track mind," Jillian chided. "And so we don't break your train of thought, let's wrap things up here so we can get busy finding some of those men."

Despite my earlier determination to enjoy the evening, I suddenly became anxious, and for a minute, I felt a longing for Nick. Not him, exactly, but the comfort of being half of a couple. I started to back out of our plans, but Jillian was on to me.

"Listen, you are not going home to mommy. You have to get back in the dating world so why not let us help you? At least come to dinner, and we can talk about the club afterwards."

"Thanks," I replied as I gave Jillian a hug.

~ * ~

The next morning I joined my mom at the kitchen table for a cup of coffee. "I found a place at The Mill. I love it. I move in on the first of next month. Would you like to come see it with me? Let's call Grace. I want her to see it, too."

"Whoa, slow down." My mom laughed. "I haven't finished a cup of coffee yet."

"I'm sorry. I'm just excited. Things are going really well, and I can't wait to have my own place again. No offense, Mom. I'm just ready."

"None taken. Let's call Grace, and we'll all go see your new place and get some lunch."

I called my sister, who was unable to come with us, but she offered to help move, which I gladly accepted. On moving day, my mom and I were packing when Grace and Derek showed up. I was determined to be gracious because I really needed the help, and for Grace's sake, I wanted to give Derek every chance to redeem himself.

"Thank you both for helping. It would take me forever to do this without you. I didn't think I had a lot of stuff, but I guess I've accumulated some things since I came back."

"We're happy to, Jane. Derek insisted on helping, too," she added a bit too eagerly.

"I really appreciate it," I replied, giving Derek my most genuine smile. "Let's load up the truck and get this first trip out of the way."

"Why don't I stay here and keep packing?" my mother offered.

"That would be great. I think we can get all of my stuff moved in just two trips."

Derek drove the truck, and Grace and I followed in my car. I was happy to have her alone for the fifteen-minute ride.

"Grace, thanks again for helping. Moving back was the right thing to do. I'm so happy that we're getting to spend more time together."

"Me too," Grace replied. "I can't wait to see your place."

"I love it. And there is so much within walking distance, I can't wait to start exploring."

As we pulled into the parking lot, Derek backed the truck in a space next to my car.

"Come in first and let me show you the place," I suggested.

"Give me minute," Derek replied. "I want to check and make sure nothing opened or moved around too much."

"Thanks Derek, you've been a big help," I added, hoping I sounded sincere.

As Grace and I started to make our way into the apartment, a good-looking young guy in jogging shorts and no shirt ran by and waved. Grace and I giggled like schoolgirls, and I told her, "I think I'm going to like it here."

I opened the door and showed Grace around. "Here is the powder room, and the kitchen, dining and living room are kind of one big room."

"I love how open it is. It's so modern. Are the walls cement?"

"Yes. I love that. Come up the stairs and I'll show you the bedroom." Just then, Derek came in and was obviously angry.

"Grace, I want to talk to you... alone."

I searched Grace's face for a response and she nodded, dismissing me. "I'll just be upstairs."

I stayed by the door to try to overhear, and it turned out that I didn't have to strain too hard at all. Derek clearly didn't care who heard him.

"I saw the way you looked at that guy," he said accusingly.

"What guy?" Grace asked timidly.

"The half-naked guy who ran past you and your sister. You should have seen your face. Did you think I wouldn't notice?" he asked, his voice getting louder.

"We were just joking, Derek. I'm not, not..." She stammered to find the right words.

"You're not what? Not turned on by that guy? Not wishing I looked like that? What is it, Grace? Tell me."

"Derek, stop. I love you. Don't you know that?" she cried.

Derek kept badgering her. "You have a funny way of showing it. Do you think that he would give you more than a second look? Keep it up, Grace. Keep it up, and you'll be sorry."

I couldn't stand to hear my sister being bullied this way so I ran down the stairs to her defense. "Hold on, Derek. Don't threaten my sister. I was the one who was looking at that guy, and I made a joke to Grace. You are making something out of nothing."

Derek backed down a little and said, "This is between me and Grace." He turned to her and said, "We'll finish this later," before he went out to the truck.

"Grace, are you all right?" I asked quietly.

"I don't want to discuss it, Jane. I don't want Derek to overhear us talking about him."

"What do you mean? He acted like a jealous lunatic. Are you going to let him get away with that?"

"Jane, I can handle it," she said firmly, and she left me to join Derek outside.

I was shaking and sat down on a box to regain my composure. I was so angry, but not just with Derek. I was mad at my sister for being so weak, and I was mad at myself for being so critical of her. After a few minutes, I went outside, and we emptied all of the boxes from the truck as if nothing had happened. By the late afternoon, we managed to get all of my stuff moved in and my bed set up so that I could spend the night in my new home. I was exhausted and suddenly starving, so I offered to take everyone out to dinner.

Derek spoke up. "I need to get home and get some work done. Thanks anyway. Grace, are you coming, or are you hoping your boyfriend will jog by again?"

Grace looked up with empty eyes as if she intended to respond, but just nodded and said to me, "I'll talk to you during the week."

As the door closed, my mother immediately asked, "What was that about?"

"Let's go eat and I'll tell you all the nasty details."

"Great," my mom replied sarcastically. "I can't wait."

We slowly walked the two blocks to an Italian restaurant that had caught my eye. After we had placed our order for a large veggie pizza and two draft beers, I began to replay the incident for my mom. "Grace and I were going into the apartment and a cute guy jogged by and waved. I joked that I was going to like living here, but Derek apparently was watching us and went ballistic on Grace. He was yelling at her as if he was jealous of this guy."

My mother sighed and took a sip of her beer. "What did Grace say? Did she defend herself?"

"No, she tried to explain, but he wouldn't listen. She was pitiful, Mom. She started crying and I finally had heard enough, so I told Derek it was me that had made a joke about the guy. He backed down a bit and told Grace they would finish later—not talk about it later. I'm scared for her."

My mother rubbed her forehead and, for an instant, looked older than her years. My anger began to resurface, and I was ready to take on Derek myself.

"I'm going to talk some sense into her. This is crazy. She needs to stand up for herself, and I'm going to make sure she does."

My mother, annoyed at both the situation and my impatience said, "Jane, we can't ambush her. She's an adult, and we need to treat her like one. I'll call her and arrange a time for the three of us to meet. And then, you and I need to plan how we're going to approach her on this. I want to be sure that this doesn't backfire on us."

Five

A few days later, there was a message on my machine from my mom asking me to call her. I sorted through my mail and took a shower before I settled on the couch and dialed her number. "Do we have a plan?" I asked after we exchanged greetings.

"I spoke to Grace, and we're going to meet for dinner next Thursday at The Villager. I though it might be better to talk in a public place. It will help us keep the emotions under control."

I smiled, thinking that my mother was all about keeping the emotions in check whereas I was all about getting it out into the open.

She continued, "I thought we would start out by telling her that we're concerned about the way Derek treats her."

"You mean we can't just come out and say that Derek is a jerk and she shouldn't take his bullshit anymore?" I asked, only half kidding.

"Jane, we have to be careful. We can end up alienating Grace if we're too harsh. That's the last thing I want to do."

"You're right," I agreed. "I'll look up some web sites on helping victims of abuse. Maybe there will be some advice on what to say and what not to say."

"Let's talk in a few days and finalize our plan."

~ * ~

At school, thankfully, my life had settled into a comfortable routine. Jillian was becoming a close friend. She was cheerful and optimistic—the kind of person who made you feel better just by being in the room. I had enjoyed the night out with her and Lauren, but was definitely more at ease with Jillian. She respected my feelings and was learning when to give me a gentle push forward. Mattie was easygoing yet hardworking, and the kids adored her. She had some strong opinions, but I got a kick out of hearing her stories.

"Jane, everything seems to be going smoothly with our class. You run a tight ship with these kids. I like that," Mattie said.

"It makes my job a lot easier if I do. I love these kids and want them to do well, but I can't stand chaos. It helps me as much as it does them. The kids all seem to be adjusting well, too. How about Emma? Do you think she's happy here?" I asked.

"I think she's getting along just fine. She's starting to open up a bit with the other kids. She just needs some time."

"There's just something about her." I paused to find the right words. "She kind of makes your heart melt. I think about all she's been through, and yet, she's still such a sweet girl. I give her dad a lot of credit."

"Ted's a great guy. I wish he'd find somebody. Kids shouldn't have to grow up without a mother," she said sadly.

"I know. It was hard growing up without my dad. My sister took it the hardest, though. They were so close. It's almost like she never got over it."

"Is she still dating that guy?" she asked with motherly concern.

"Unfortunately, yes," I answered in a defeated tone. "My mother and I are having dinner with her next week, and we're hoping to have somewhat of an intervention."

"Is it that bad?" she asked.

"It's awful. He's rude and demeaning, and she doesn't stand up to him. I can't let her make the biggest mistake of her life."

"You have to say something. Better to hurt her feelings now and avoid problems later."

"You're right, Mattie, but I'm dreading the whole evening."

~ * ~

The night of our dinner, my mom and I agreed to meet half an hour before we told Grace to get there. When I arrived, the maitre d asked, "Are you meeting someone?"

"Yes, my mother," I replied. "That's her at the corner table."

She was lost in thought as I sat down at the table, and she jumped in surprise. I leaned over to kiss her cheek.

"Sorry, Mom, I didn't mean to sneak up on you."

"I'm so nervous, the least little things have been rattling me today," she replied.

"It's going to go fine," I tried to assure us both. "Let's order a bottle of wine and when Grace gets here, we'll gradually bring the conversation around to Derek. Then we'll tell her that we're concerned about the way that he treats her and we fear that it's going to get worse."

"Just keep it as calm as possible. I don't want her getting hysterical or feel like she's being ganged up on. She's so sensitive, Jane. If only she were stronger..." My mother looked up and said, "There's Grace. Oh, no—Derek is with her. I told her we wanted to talk to her alone."

Grace was beaming, a smile that lit up her whole face as she and Derek joined us at the table.

"Derek, we weren't expecting you," I said pointedly.

"I didn't want to be away from Grace this evening, and I figured you wouldn't mind if I joined you. Besides, we have something we want to tell you."

My heart began to race, and I felt dizzy. *No, No, No, this couldn't be happening,* I thought to myself. *Please don't let them announce their engagement.*

Grace held out her left hand and blurted out, "We're getting married."

I watched the color drain from my mother's face as she took in the news.

I had to say something. "Wow, that was kind of sudden, wasn't it?" I asked. Derek sat back in the chair with a smug look on his face.

"I was getting ready to come here, and Derek showed up at my apartment with flowers, champagne and a ring. Isn't it beautiful?" she asked as she held her ring out for my inspection. "He came in and said, 'You and I are getting married.' I was shocked and thrilled. It was the most romantic moment of my life," she added softly as she reached for Derek's hand.

My mother still looked like someone had punched her in the stomach, but after a moment of awkward silence she spoke. "I'm extremely surprised. I didn't even know you were talking about marriage," she said flatly.

"Mom, aren't you happy for us?" Grace asked with a tremble in her voice.

"I'm just taken back a bit. I have some concerns, but I would rather talk to you about them at a more private time."

"Hey, anything you have to say," Derek commanded, "say it now. Grace and I are getting married, and there's nothing you can do about it."

"Derek, please," Grace implored.

"Please, what. I know your family hates me, but they should be happy I'm taking you off of their hands."

My mother and I exchanged panicked looks. This was escalating quickly, and we needed to defuse the situation immediately.

"We are happy for you Grace. We just weren't expecting this kind of news right now," my mother countered. "Congratulations, honey."

Grace began to cry and sobbed, "This was supposed to be the happiest day of my life," as she ran to the restroom.

Derek stared at us both with a look of disgust on his face. I jumped up and said, "I'm going to talk to her."

I slowly walked to the bathroom, not sure of what I was going to say. I opened the door and saw Grace sitting in front of the mirror trying to wipe away her black tears. I sat down next to her and said, "Grace, I'm sorry if I hurt you. I didn't mean to. I'm worried about you marrying Derek."

"I know he's not perfect, but I love him and I want to marry him. You know that all I ever wanted was to be married and have kids, and now you and Mom are trying to sabotage my happiness. You have ruined the best day of my life."

"Grace, I just don't want you to marry Derek because you think you might never have another chance. He treats you badly, and I think you deserve better."

"Better than what? Nick?" she asked.

Her words were like a slap in the face, but I kept my cool. "You're right, Grace, Nick was a jerk, but when I found out what he was really like I threw him out. I would have never gotten involved with him if I had known he was going to cheat on me."

"Derek would never cheat on me. He loves me and he wants to have kids with me. This is my decision—if you can't be supportive of me then don't come to the wedding. God, Jane, I wanted you to be my maid of honor. Why don't you want me to be happy?" she pleaded.

"I want to see you happy. I really do, but this guy is trouble and I want you to get out while you can." I had finally said it. I waited for a response.

Grace was silent a moment. She stood, looked me in the eye and said, "I love him, and if you love me, you will never speak badly of Derek again."

She left the bathroom, and I sat there dumbfounded. I got up, splashed water on my face, and dried it. When I left the restroom, Derek was waiting for me.

"Jane, jealousy does not become you," he said smiling. I was immediately fearful as he brought his face closer to mine. "I know you want me, but I met Grace first. So sorry." He laughed. I tried to go around him, but he kept me cornered. "I'll tell you this only once. Stay out of our lives. If I get angry, your sister will pay," he said confidently.

I was shaking as I went back to the table. Mom, Derek, and Grace sat in silence when Derek spoke up and said, "I think we should go home and celebrate ourselves, Grace, if you know what I mean." He kissed her with such intensity, it was embarrassing for the rest of us.

I didn't want Grace to leave, but just said, "Grace, call me so I can help with the wedding plans."

She smiled weakly and said, "Thank you."

Derek led her out of the restaurant, and my mother lost it.

"I'm just sick about this, Jane. I don't know anything about Derek, and what I do know is extremely upsetting. He is rude and condescending, and we know nothing about his family life or his friends. Has Grace even met any of his friends or family? What can she be thinking?" she asked, not expecting an answer.

I began to get nervous because I had never seen my mother this upset. I reached for her hands and gently rubbed them. I wanted to fix this mess. I wanted to save both Grace and my mother from this pain, but realized that I was powerless.

"Mom, I don't know what else we can do."

She looked up at me with tears in her eyes and just nodded.

Six

The holidays were usually my favorite time of year, but this year I was dreading them. I had only spoken to Grace on the phone in the weeks since our dinner, and our conversations were short and strained. We were both hurting and instead of being able to comfort one another, there was a wall between us. I also missed having a man around and desperately wanted someone to share my life with. I needed a shoulder to lean on, and I was feeling very much alone.

School was my refuge. I loved being with the children each day. They were so smart and full of life. They made me laugh, and I was grateful for each one of them. I had been conducting parent-teacher conferences, and it was intriguing to find out more about the parents of my kids.

On the last day of school before the Thanksgiving holiday, I had the last of my parent meetings with Emma's dad, Ted. When he arrived, I shook his hand and said, "It's nice to see you again, Dr. Manning."

"Please call me Ted," he replied.

"Then you must call me Jane. Have a seat. Let me first say that Emma is a pleasure. She is so well behaved. She is still very quiet, though, and I'd like us to work on that."

"Does she interact with the other kids?" he asked quietly.

"Yes, but she is reluctant to join in the group on her own. She has to be coaxed a bit," I answered.

"Is this something I should be worried about? I hate to sound ignorant, but this is my first child, and I'm at a loss with certain things. These are the things a mom is supposed to know how to deal with," he said wistfully.

"No, no. I didn't mean to worry you. She's a lovely child. I just know that she's been through a lot, and I want to help her."

"Thanks—it's been quite the challenge. When Annie died, I was caught completely off guard. Not only did I lose a wife, but I had to be both mother and father to Emma. Annie was a stay-at-home mom, and she knew everything about taking care of Emma. In an instant she was gone, and here I was left with a toddler who was missing her mother as much as I was."

I swallowed the lump in my throat. "How did you get through it?" I asked softly.

"My mom came and stayed with us for three months, and eventually I got a routine together. But there's always something to worry about."

My heart was breaking for him. I wanted to reach out but reminded myself that he was the parent of one of my students. "Please don't worry about Emma at school. She's very close to Mattie, and I'll make sure that she's all right here."

"Mattie and Jim have been so good to us. I was extremely grateful that Emma was in her class."

"And just so you know, she is really bright. Look at this," I said, pulling out an evaluation I had done on

Emma. "I tested her, and she is already reading at a first grade level."

He smiled, and said, "Annie was adamant about reading to Emma from the time she was born, and that was the one tradition that I made sure I kept up with."

"It's paid off because she is extremely capable of expressing herself. We'll just work on getting her to be a little more outgoing."

He looked relieved and said, "Jane, thank you for everything. This is new territory for me, and I appreciate all the help I can get."

"Feel free to call me at any time if you're worried or have questions."

"I will." He stood and looked at his watch. "I'm sorry I kept you so long. You must have some place to go."

"Actually, I'm just headed home."

He paused a moment. "Emma is with my in-laws, and I don't have any plans. Would you like to have dinner? Or is that against the rules?" he asked awkwardly.

"I would love the company, but it probably wouldn't be a good idea," I said feeling somewhat disappointed.

"I didn't mean to put you on the spot. It's very quiet without Emma around. I need to go running anyway," he said quickly.

"I'm a runner, too. Do you ever race?" I asked hopefully.

"I'm going to run the 10K on New Year's Day. Are you interested?"

That was a loaded question. "Sure, can you send me the information?" I asked hoping I didn't seem overly enthusiastic.

"I'll email it to you. It starts and ends in the town square, and there are booths and games for the kids. It's a fun time and even better in the snow."

"I'm looking forward to it. Have a nice Thanksgiving."

"You, too, Jane. And thanks again."

When Ted left, I was full of mixed emotions—annoyed at myself for not being more professional, yet excited by the attraction. He had such a warm demeanor, and I wanted to get to know him better, but knew it was dangerous territory. I had made so many bad choices. I didn't need to make another.

~ * ~

Thanksgiving Day was quiet. Mom and I invited Grace and Derek to dinner as a peace offering, but they declined the dinner invitation and stopped over for dessert. I was fearful of losing contact with Grace, so I said, "Let's spend Christmas together—the four of us." Grace smiled and looked hopefully at Derek.

"I'd like that. Derek?" she asked tentatively.

"Sure, that's fine. Anyway we're going to be one big happy family very soon."

I tried not to let my feelings show as Grace jumped up and hugged Derek. "And speaking of the wedding, Jane, I was wondering if you would be my maid of honor?"

Tears brimmed in my eyes. "I would love to," I said quietly, and I rose to hug her. Drops fell from my eyes as I prayed silently for something to stop this wedding.

Seven

We had the first snowfall of the year, and I took my class outside to play. We caught snowflakes on our tongue and made a miniature snowman. This instantly lifted my spirits, and I decided to forget about our blah Thanksgiving and focus on enjoying the Christmas season. The kindergarten was putting on a holiday play, and the children in my class were snowflakes. Several of the moms had come in to help make the costumes, and we were practicing our rendition of "Winter Wonderland." I was very proud of my kids and extremely excited to see their big performance. I invited my mom and Grace, who helped me get the kids ready that evening.

"Thank you both for helping. I'm so nervous. You'd think I was putting on a Broadway production," I said, laughing.

"It'll be fine, Jane. Just enjoy the moment," my mother replied with a smile.

It was show time, and so I clapped my hands three times, which was the signal to my class to stop talking and listen to me. "All right, kids. It is time for our play. I

46

know you will all do a great job out there, and I am very proud of each and every one of you. Let's do our best and have fun," I cheered.

The show went great. The kids were adorable, and my class of snowflakes brought tears to my eyes. They sang their hearts out, and this was one of those moments that reminded me of why I became a teacher. We had a small reception of cookies and milk to celebrate. I tried to speak to each family for a moment or two. I spotted Ted and Emma with a couple that I surmised were her grandparents. I made my way over and gave Emma a hug.

"You did a wonderful job, sweetheart." I looked at Ted and said, "It's nice to see you again."

"You too," he replied with a slight grin. "I'd like you to meet Emma's grandparents, Liz and David Bowden. This is Jane Richards, Emma's teacher."

I shook their hands and said, "It is so nice to meet you. Emma is one of my favorite students."

"We are pretty fond of her, too," Liz replied.

"Dad, I want to show Grandma and Grandpa my pictures that are hanging in the hall. We'll be right back," said Emma.

I was excited at the thought of having a few minutes to talk with Ted alone.

"Have you been training for the race?" he asked.

"As a matter of fact I have, and you better watch out. I'm in it to win," I said coyly.

"Ooh, is that a challenge, Miss Richards? Because I'm up for a bit of friendly competition. Maybe we could make a wager. The loser pays for dinner?" he suggested.

Before I could answer, Emma came running up and said, "Daddy, Grandma and Grandpa want to take me for ice cream. Can I go?"

"We'll drop her at the house when we're done. Is that all right, Ted?" David asked.

"Sure, and thank you both for coming. It meant a lot to both of us," Ted said sincerely. He hugged Liz and shook David's hand as they left with Emma.

"Annie's parents have been very good to me since she died. At first, I thought it would be awkward, but they've gone out of their way to make sure that I feel a part of the family. My parents live in Boston and they visit a lot, but it's been extremely helpful to have David and Liz close by."

"It's nice to live near family. That's what brought me back to Wilmington."

"I'm glad it did," Ted replied raising his eyebrows ever so slightly.

I looked around and realized that several of the families had gone and there were only about fifteen people left. "It looks like it's time to wrap things up here. I'm on cleanup duty, so I'd better get to work."

"I can help," Ted offered.

"Thanks, but it's not a big deal. Besides, don't you need to be home for Emma?" I asked.

Ted laughed and said, "I forgot about her for a minute. There goes my father of the year award."

I smiled and said, "It was nice talking with you. I'll see you soon."

I found my mother and Grace and hugged them both. "What a fun night. Weren't the kids great? I'm so happy that you two were here tonight. Moving back was the best thing for me."

"Wow, where is all of this coming from?" my mother asked.

"I think it has something to do with that man that you were talking to," Grace responded. "Who is he?" she asked.

"Oh, Ted, he's the father of one of my students. We're both doing a 10K on New Year's Day, and we have a bit of a friendly rivalry going on."

Ever the realist, my mother asked, "What does his wife think of your friendly rivalry?"

"He's not married. His wife died in a car accident a few years ago. Besides, there is nothing going on between us. His daughter is one of my students," I emphasized.

"Too bad," Grace said with a smile. Our relationship was starting to warm up again, and I was trying to keep it going in a positive direction.

"I know," I said returning her grin, "but I need to find an uncomplicated relationship. Is there such a thing?"

Grace's expression hardened a bit, and I immediately regretted my words. Quickly I added, "Any relationship that isn't complicated probably isn't worth it."

Grace's face relaxed, and she said, "I'd better get going. Thanks for inviting me, Jane."

"I'm so happy you came. Thanks again."

My mother said, "I'll walk out with you, Grace. Nice job, Jane. It was a fun evening."

"Thanks, Mom. I'll talk to you soon."

I watched them leave the cafeteria and had started to pick up the empty plates and half-eaten cookies when Jillian joined me.

"Are you on clean up duty, too?" she asked.

"Yes, but I don't mind. Tonight was great, wasn't it? The kids did an amazing job."

"They really did. I'm glad it's over though. I'm exhausted. I hardly slept last night."

"Not me. I am full of energy," I said.

"Does your second wind have anything to do with that man I saw you talking to?" she asked.

I must have been pretty transparent when I was talking to Ted. "What man?" I asked nonchalantly.

"The tall man with the short blonde hair and the little girl."

I felt like a kid who had taken the last cookie. "Oh, that was Ted Manning. He's Emma's dad. We're both runners, and we were just talking about an upcoming race."

"Be careful," Jillian warned.

"Of what?" I asked. "Nothing is going on."

"Be sure it stays that way. You looked quite enthralled with him, and if you don't stop it now, you could be in some trouble."

"Whoa, nothing is going on," I repeated. "I know better than to get involved with a student's father."

"I just worry about you, Jane. You're vulnerable right now, and I don't want you to get into a bad situation."

"Jillian, you are a good friend. Thanks for looking out for me. I'm not going to get involved with Ted Manning," I stated resolutely.

~ * ~

Later that night, I lay in bed recalling my conversations with both Ted and Jillian. I knew that it would be wrong in so many ways for me to pursue a relationship with Ted, but my heart felt otherwise.

Eight

By the time school let out for the Christmas holiday, I think I was as excited as the kids were. Being with the children had done so much to raise my spirits, and now I was actually looking forward to Christmas. I was running four days a week, and I was feeling fit and happy. Mom and I were going to my aunt Rose's house on Christmas Eve, and then I was going to spend the night at her house. Grace was going to spend the night, too, and it brought back memories of Christmas when we were kids.

I spent the Saturday before Christmas finishing my shopping. I wanted to get something special for my mother and Grace. I settled on a leather purse for Mom. She had been admiring it in the window of the boutique down the street from my house, and I knew she would never allow herself the extravagance. I returned to the gift store a few shops down to get my sister a silver Italian charm bracelet with a sister charm on it. I wandered in and just loved the warm cinnamon smell that came from the candles they always had burning in this shop. I started to browse as I remembered that I had not gotten anything for Derek. This was the last thing I needed to buy, and I was at a loss. I looked at the men's section and wondered if he played golf or had a favorite sports team. I always thought that whenever Grace or I married, that the other would be a good friend with our future spouse. I could barely stand to be in the same room with Derek. They had some nice silk ties and comfortable looking bedroom slippers. Either of those would be safe, so I turned to get the sales woman's attention, and I literally bumped right into Ted Manning.

"Oh, I'm glad it's only you," I gushed as I bent down to pick up the slipper display that I had knocked over.

"It's nice to see you, too," he said, smiling.

"Gosh, that came out wrong. I'm glad that I ran into a person I know, rather than a stranger. You know what I mean—don't you?"

"Yes, I do, and I'm happy we bumped into each other. Are you buying something special?" he asked.

"Oh, the slippers," I said slowly trying to tell if he was maybe a little jealous that I was buying a gift for a man. "Which would you prefer? The cranberry silk tie or the brown slippers?" I asked, being a little more playful than I knew I should have been.

"Well," Ted answered, "they're both nice, but not very personal."

"Good," I replied. Again, I waited to see if I could detect even a hint of relief, and Ted smiled faintly. "They're for my sister's boyfriend and let's just say we aren't very close."

"Either of those should do the trick."

"How about you? Have you finished all of your shopping or are you too busy training?" I asked, not the least bit embarrassed at my flirtatiousness.

"I have one more gift to get. It's for a very special woman. Maybe you can help me pick something out." I felt an instant disappointment, and after a second he added, "It's for Emma's grandmother, Liz."

Now it was my turn to be toyed with. "Sure, let me get this tie and the bracelet for my sister and we can find a gift for her." I made my purchases and asked, "What kind of gift were you thinking about?"

"Actually I was thinking about the jewelry box that was in the window. It's hard to find a gift that let's her know how much she is appreciated."

"I'm sure she knows," I replied softly. "Let's look."

The saleswoman treated us as if we were a couple, and neither of us said anything to set her straight. While they wrapped Ted's package, we stood awkwardly for a moment, and I asked "What are your plans for the holiday?"

"We're spending Christmas Eve with Liz and David and their kids, and then that night we will drive to my parents' house. They live north of Boston. I don't want to be alone on Christmas morning." He stopped for a moment as if he were lost in his thoughts, and then was embarrassed for letting his guard down.

Without thinking, I touched his arm in a gesture of comfort, but did not know what to say. Thankfully, the saleswoman, who had finished wrapping the gift, interrupted us and I said, "Tell Emma I said Merry Christmas."

"I will and, Jane... you have a Merry Christmas, too."

I left the store in a state of confusion. Why was I so attracted to this man? Was it really that bad to date a student's father? Maybe he wasn't as great as he seemed. I couldn't bear to have another bad relationship. All I knew was that I was happy to have two weeks off to just contemplate the direction my life was headed. Plus, I couldn't wait until the race on New Year's Day so I could see Ted again.

~ * ~

Christmas Eve was so much fun. I visited with aunts, uncles and cousins, and I was reminded of how much I loved my family. I had lost touch with them when I lived in New York, and I was glad for the opportunity to spend time with everyone.

That night Grace met us at church for midnight mass. I grabbed Grace's arm and walked up the stairs to the vestibule of the church. "I'm so excited that we're spending the night together. I feel like a kid again."

Grace smiled, and we took our seats. The ritual and traditions of the service were soothing, and my thoughts drifted to my dad. He would sing so loudly in church. I was thoroughly embarrassed back then, but would have loved to hear his off-key singing now. I put my arm around my mother and gave her a gentle hug as I wiped a tear off my cheek. My emotions were on overload, and I was very sleepy by the time the mass was over.

Once back at home, I got a second wind and suggested, "Why don't we get our pajamas on and have cookies and hot chocolate?"

"The holidays really do bring out the kid in you," my mom replied.

"It's been such a great day, I hate for it to end. Grace, are you in?"

"Sure," she answered, and ten minutes later we all met in the kitchen. I got the plate of Christmas cookies that I had put together earlier that day, and my mother made the hot chocolate.

"Grace, get the whipped cream out of the fridge," I said as I got the Christmas mugs from the tray in the dining room.

My mom poured the hot chocolate, and we all went to the family room to eat, drink and enjoy the Christmas tree.

"It's such a treat to have you both here tonight. I would hate to wake up alone at Christmas," my mother said as she took a bite of her cookie.

My thoughts immediately went to Ted. I hoped he was having a nice Christmas. I was counting the days until the race and was actually nervous about seeing him again.

"Hello, Jane. Are you with us?" my sister asked.

"What? Sorry, I was just thinking about something. What were you talking about?"

"It wasn't important. What were you thinking about?" Grace asked with a smile on her face.

My mother yawned and said, "I'm going to go to bed and let you girls talk. It's been a long day. See you in the morning."

When she was out of the room, Grace continued to question me. "So, maybe I should ask who you were thinking about."

"Nobody, really. I was thinking about the race that I'm running on New Year's Day, and I hope the weather holds up. That's all."

"Derek and I would love to come see you, but I'll be working both days over the New Year's holiday. Derek isn't much into holidays, so it doesn't matter to me that I'll be working."

"What about Christmas? What did you two do tonight?" I asked.

"We just had a quiet dinner at my place. Derek doesn't like Christmas at all. It brings back bad memories," Grace replied.

"From when he was a kid?" I asked, hoping not to sound too eager. This was the first bit of personal information I was getting about Derek, and I wanted to know all that Grace would volunteer.

"He grew up with very little money. His father abandoned him and his mom when Derek was eight years old. I don't think his mother was any better."

"Wow, I'm sorry. Is his mom still alive?" I asked.

"No, she died when Derek was in his twenties. She was an alcoholic, and she destroyed her liver." Grace then immediately looked panicked and pleaded, "Please don't ever mention what I just told you. Derek is a very private person, and he would be very upset if you knew about his family. I shouldn't have said anything. Please forget what I told you." Grace began to shift in her seat.

"Don't worry. I'll never say anything to Derek. I'm just sad for him that he had such a lousy childhood."

"I'm hoping that when we're married, he'll start to like the holidays again. Once we have kids and he gets the chance to be a good father, he'll come around. I saved up to buy him something special. I really think he's going to love it."

"I'm sure he will. I won't ask what it is so we can both be surprised." I tried unsuccessfully to stifle a yawn and looked at my watch. "It's late. I think I'm going to turn in." I stood and gave my sister a hug.

"See you in the morning, Jane. And thanks for keeping that stuff about Derek to yourself."

"You're welcome. Merry Christmas, Grace."

~ * ~

The next morning the three of us worked preparing our family's usual Christmas meal of turkey with all of the fixings. "What time will Derek be here, Grace?" my mother asked.

"I'm going to call him and check."

Grace went into the family room to use the phone in private, and my mom and I continued to work. In just a few minutes, Grace returned, and it was obvious that she had been crying.

"What's wrong, Grace?" my mother asked with a look of concern.

"Nothing. Derek... um, Derek doesn't think he's going to come over today," she said softly.

"What? Are you kidding? It's Christmas. How could he do that to you?" I asked, letting my temper get the best of me.

"He doesn't like the holidays," Grace reminded me. "It's fine, really. I'll stop by and see him later."

"Are you sure you're all right?" my mother asked.

"Yes, I'm sure. I'm going to take a shower." Grace left the room and I turned to my mother, who just shook her head.

"I wish she would just open her eyes and see how terribly Derek treats her. How could he not be with her on Christmas?" she asked.

I thought for a minute and said, "I'm going to call him and tell him we want him to come to dinner, too. Maybe we can guilt him into it."

"How are you going to call him? Do you know his number?" she asked.

"One word," I smiled. "Redial."

I sat on the sofa and hit the redial button. I waited nervously for the phone to ring, and when his answering machine picked up, I quickly composed my thoughts so I could leave him a message.

"Derek, this is Jane. Grace said that you might not join us for dinner today, and I just wanted to ask you to reconsider. Both Mom and I would like you to come. Please have dinner with us. It would mean a lot to all of us. Get here around three o'clock, okay? We would like all of our family to be together on Christmas." I shuddered as I threw in that last line. My sister was important to me, and I wanted her to be happy on Christmas—and if that meant Derek had dinner with us, then I could survive being nice to him for one day.

At three on the dot, the doorbell rang. I volunteered to get the door. There with a bottle of wine and a box of candy stood my future brother-in-law with a sly smile. "Thank you for coming, Derek."

"I'd do anything for you, Jane," he said as he slipped his arm around my waist. His touch revolted me, and I jerked myself free.

"Grace, there's someone here to see you," I announced, ignoring Derek's comment.

Grace came to the door, and her face broke into a wide smile. "Oh, Derek. I'm so happy to see you." She threw her arms around his neck and hugged him tightly. "Thank you so much. It means everything to me that you showed up."

"Well, I couldn't disappoint your sister," he said, smiling at me.

Grace looked crestfallen. "What do you mean?" she asked looking at me.

"I called Derek and asked him to reconsider coming to dinner. I couldn't bear to see you so upset," I confessed.

"Oh," she said quietly.

"What? I'm here aren't I? Do you want me to go back home?" Derek asked her with a hint of impatience in his voice.

"No, I'm glad you're here. Merry Christmas, Derek," she said. "Let's open that bottle of wine and start our celebration."

We had drinks and dinner and, although it was strained, we all managed to make conversation. We talked about our jobs, and Grace told us about a set of quadruplets that had been born the week before.

"Are they all okay?" I asked tentatively.

Grace frowned. "One of them didn't make it, but the other three are fighters. They should be just fine. The parents are having a tough time of it. Even though they have three other children, it's still hard when you lose one."

My mother shifted in her seat and said, "Do you mind if we talk about a more pleasant topic?"

"Sorry, sometimes it all comes flooding back to me," I said as Grace reached over and took my hand.

Even Derek, though he didn't understand why, realized that we needed to move the conversation in another direction and asked, "What's going on in your class these days?"

"The children in Jane's class were the best snowflakes ever in the holiday play," Grace boasted.

Our dinner continued in a very pleasant manner, and after we finished clearing the dishes, I put on some Christmas music and we spent the next hour opening presents. Grace waited to give Derek his gift. He appeared a bit uncomfortable with us watching for his reaction as he opened an expensive silver watch. He was silent for a moment, and then he looked at Grace and smiled.

"Thank you," he said quietly. He then stood up and left the room. We were all a bit puzzled, and Grace went after him.

I looked at my mom and shrugged my shoulders, because I surely didn't know what was going on. We sat in silence for a few minutes, and then we heard the door open and a car start. Grace came back and said, "Derek had to go."

"Is everything all right?" my mother asked.

"I don't know," Grace replied, leaving me to wonder if life would ever be all right for Grace again.

Nine

The week after Christmas seemed to fly by, and other than training for the race, I didn't do much of anything. My mind didn't get much rest, though. Each encounter with Grace and Derek left me more distraught over their impending marriage and Christmas was the worst. The sadness in Grace's face continued to haunt me, and I had no idea what to do about it. It made me so sad.

I tried to focus my energy on my running, and that led to a whole other set of obsessive thoughts all centering on Ted Manning. I went back and forth between chastising myself for wanting to pursue him and rationalizing that a relationship with Ted would have no impact on my ethics as Emma's teacher. My mind was working over time, and I hoped that seeing Ted at the race would put my fantasies about him to rest.

I had no plans for New Year's Eve, and I was feeling sorry for myself. I tried to convince myself that with the race early the next morning I couldn't go out and party, but a diversion would have been welcome. Grace was working and my mom was going to a party at church.

Jillian invited me to a party, but as pitiful as it felt to spend New Year's Eve alone—the thought of going to a party with a bunch of strangers was worse.

So, I decided to make the most of my evening alone, and I ventured out to the shopping area around the corner in search of something different to eat. There were not a lot of people out. It was a clear night, and though it was cold, the forecast was for clear skies the next day, which would make the race much more pleasant. I had never run in the snow and was glad that I didn't have to start. The stores had closed for the most part, but the bookstore was still open. It had a coffee shop inside, and I wasn't very hungry yet, so I stopped in for a hot chocolate and a bit of browsing. I loved to read, but hadn't picked up a book other than a textbook since school started. I got my drink and slowly made my way over to a display of new fiction. After a few moments, I picked up two novels and decided to look for a few magazines. I found some and sat down to peruse them while I finished my hot chocolate. I had been sitting for a while when I felt someone staring at me and I looked up to see Ted Manning gazing at me from across the aisle. I smiled as he walked over and sat in the chair next to mine.

"Hi there, Miss Richards."

"Hi there, yourself. Big plans for New Year's?" I asked.

"This is about the high point of my night unfortunately. Emma is staying with my parents so I'm on my own. The house was so quiet, I couldn't stand it anymore so I went out for a drive and ended up here. How about you?" he asked.

"Pretty much the same exciting plans that you have. I'm not much in the party mood, I guess. Besides, we have a big day tomorrow or did you forget?"

"Oh, I didn't forget," he said with a playful grin. "Have you been training?"

"I sure have. You better be ready for some stiff competition tomorrow."

"I believe we made a bet. Loser buys dinner, or did you forget?" he asked.

"We didn't shake on it so it's not really a bet."

"Oh, really. Well, do we have a bet?" he asked as he extended his hand to me.

"You're on, Dr. Manning."

"What do you say we do a little carbo loading for the race? There's a great Italian place not far from here. Would you like to join me for dinner?" he asked.

"I'm not sure," I said. "What if..."

"What if what? Someone sees us? We're just two friends having a pre-race dinner," he said with the look of an innocent child.

I hesitated because although my heart had already said yes, my head was giving me conflicting views. I couldn't handle another failed relationship. The hurt would be too much, yet I wasn't able to say no.

"We'll take separate cars. It's just dinner. What are you afraid of?" he asked.

"That did it," I smiled. "I'm never one to shy away from a challenge. Where is this place?"

Ted gave me directions, and I told him I'd see him there. I paid for my books and ran home to get my car and freshen up. I quickly went into the bathroom and brushed my hair and my teeth and did a fast makeup job. I thought about changing my clothes, but decided not to. I didn't want to seem too interested. I grabbed my keys and locked the door behind me. As I got closer to the restaurant, I began to get nervous. My stomach was fluttering and my mouth felt dry. I parked the car, took a moment to calm myself down, and went in.

Ted was waiting for me in the lobby and said, "Thanks for meeting me, Jane. This will be a nice way to ring in the New Year."

We were seated at a table in the corner. It was small and dark with a stone fireplace on the far wall. It was a casual place and still had some empty tables. I did a scan of the room to see if I recognized anyone, and Ted laughed as he realized what I was up to.

"Is the coast clear?" he asked.

"As a matter of fact it is," I stated in my most professional voice. "Now, let's get down to business and order some food because I'm starving."

We placed our orders, and after our drinks arrived I had relaxed a bit and sat back in my chair. Ted immediately picked up it and asked, "Calmed down?"

I played coy and said, "I don't know what you're talking about. So how was your Christmas?"

"It was fine. Emma had a good time. We spent a lot of time with family, and it was helpful. In fact, Emma stayed in Massachusetts with my parents. How about you?"

"We spent Christmas Eve with my aunt and uncle and their family. It was a lot of fun, and then we had a quiet Christmas at my mom's."

"I'm glad it's over. The holidays are always tough," he said quietly. "But, now it's onto a new year. I always like this holiday. It's so optimistic. A fresh beginning."

"Aren't you philosophical?" I asked in a teasing voice.

"Sorry, I didn't mean to be so intense."

"Actually, I enjoy your outlook. It's been a crazy year, and I'm looking forward to the New Year, too."

"What was so crazy about it?" Ted asked. "If it's not too personal," he added.

"I had a bad breakup and left my life in New York to come home. It's been sort of a roller coaster year."

"I've had one of those myself. The year after Annie died, I never thought life would be normal again."

"Is it normal yet?" I asked.

"Well... I guess it is. It's not what normal used to be, but it never will be. But you know what? We're happy and we're making it, so I guess we have achieved some degree of normalcy."

I raised my glass and said, "Here's to normalcy."

"And to new friends," Ted added as we clinked glasses.

We were never at a loss for conversation during dinner, bouncing back and forth between subjects and during dessert I asked about Emma. "When is she coming home? You must miss her."

"I do. It's amazing. She has brought so much joy to my life. When Annie died, I didn't know what to do with her. Now I don't know what I'd do without her."

"You're doing a great job with Emma. She's becoming a more outgoing and confident kid every day."

"You've been a big help, Jane."

There was a comfortable silence, and I finally said, "I should be going. I have a big race in the morning."

"Let me get the check," Ted offered.

"Let's split it," I replied.

"Please let me pay."

I started to protest, and Ted said, "Please, I'd like to do this."

"All right, but then you're going to have to buy me dinner again after I beat you in the race," I countered.

"I'll manage," he smiled.

After he paid the bill, he walked me out to my car. It was awkward for a minute, so I said, "Thank you for the dinner and the company. It was nice to spend time with a friend."

"Yes, it was," Ted replied. "I'll see you bright and early."

I smiled and said, "I'm looking forward to it."

Ten

I had a difficult time getting to sleep. I kept replaying the dinner conversation in my head and came to realize that I had been denying my attraction to Ted. There was something about him. He was so warm and open. He had been through so much in such a short period of time, but he didn't let it get him down. He had experienced loss, yet Ted remained strong, and that was very enticing.

The lack of sleep didn't impair my competitive nature, however. I arrived at the race and was performing my pre-race stretching routine with one eye out for Ted. He snuck up behind me, and I jumped as he asked, "Are you ready?"

"Well if I wasn't awake before, I am now. Good morning."

"Are you tired? Did you stay out too late last night?" he asked wryly.

"Aren't you witty this morning?" I retorted.

"I try. So are you ready to take a beating?"

"Is that a threat, Dr. Manning?"

"I'm just looking forward to you buying me dinner, that's all," he replied.

"I've been training, so you may not want to be overconfident. I can't believe how many people are here. Is it usually this crowded?" I asked.

"It's pretty popular. New Englanders don't let weather get in the way of our running, you know."

"I see that. And speaking of which, it's cold out here. I'm ready to get started," I said.

"It's almost time. They'll start us in groups based on our number. I'd like to stay and start with you... if that's okay?" he asked.

"Sure, I'd really like that. I'm so nervous."

"Don't be. Let's just have fun," Ted said as we made our way to the start line. We ran at a nice pace, and Ted stayed with me the entire time. We chatted a little and he encouraged me when I needed it. Once I got going, I felt great. The sun was shining and there was no wind—it was a perfect winter day, and I was enjoying myself tremendously. I looked over at a sign and realized that we were almost finished.

"One more mile to go and we're done," I said enthusiastically. "Let's pick up the pace," I challenged.

"Show me what you've got," Ted countered, and with that we ran hard, and when the finish line came into view, my adrenaline went into full gear. I started to pull ahead of Ted and crossed the finish line before him. I looked back and saw him jogging across the finish line with a huge smile on his face.

He ran over to me and said, "I guess I'm buying dinner."

"You let me win, didn't you?" I asked breathlessly.

"I had to do something to ensure another dinner with you," he said sincerely.

"If you won, I'd have to take you out," I said.

"Yes, but I thought you might chicken out and buy me a gift certificate or something. I want to make sure we have dinner together," he said.

"You certainly have put some thought into this, haven't you?" I asked, grateful that he had.

"Maybe."

We stopped for some water and collected our race shirts, oblivious to the crowd of runners and spectators. We stood in silence, neither one of us seeming to want to say goodbye just yet. After a minute, I said, "I'm starting to fade. I think I'll head home."

"Me, too. I'll be in touch about your victory dinner."

He doesn't have my number, I thought to my self. *Do I give it to him and keep this thing going or do I end it right here and now?* I didn't want to end it, so I asked, "Do you have my number?"

He grinned and said, "Are you offering?"

"I intend to collect on my bet. My car is right over there. Let me get paper to write on."

We walked over, and I opened my car door and scribbled my number on a piece of paper. "Here's my cell number," I said, handing him the note.

"I'll be in touch," he said.

I sat in my car for a while with my eyes closed when I was startled by the ringing of my cell phone.

"Hello?" I answered.

"So, are you free for dinner tonight?" Ted asked.

"Wow, you work fast."

"Emma comes home tomorrow, so I'm all by my lonesome tonight," he said trying to sound pitiful.

I hesitated and said, "I want to, but..."

"But what? We're having dinner to celebrate your victory," he countered. "Come on, Jane. We'll go somewhere out of the way. I promise."

"You are persistent, I'll give you that," I said smiling. "Soooo... What time and where should we meet?" I asked hesitantly.

"Why don't I pick you up?"

"Oh, I don't know," I said suddenly anxious about saying yes.

"Jane, you can walk to the coffee shop right?" he asked.

"Yes, why?"

"Meet me there at seven, and then I'll drive us to dinner."

"Fine," I said. "I'll be there."

"And, one more thing," Ted added.

"Yes, Dr. Manning?"

"Thank you for saying yes."

~ * ~

I was useless for the rest of the day. I tried to nap, but was too excited to sleep. I tried to go over my lesson plans, but I couldn't concentrate so I took a long, hot bath. It was extremely relaxing and I was finally able to unwind a bit. I wanted to talk to someone about Ted, but did not know who to call. I wanted to call Jillian, but I didn't want to put her in an awkward position at work. I decided to try Grace.

"Hello?" she answered.

"Grace, I'm glad you answered. Do you have a few minutes to talk?"

"I'm actually on a break for about five more minutes. What's up?"

"I met this guy and I'm not sure I'm doing the right thing," I said.

"What's the problem? Is he married or something?" she asked.

"No, it's not that." I hesitated. "He's the father of one of my students," I said quietly.

"Ooooh, that's a tough one. Is there a rule against it at your school?" she asked.

"I'm sure there is. I didn't pay much attention to that part of my contract. The last thing I was thinking about was another relationship, but this man is special, Grace. He's a widower, he's warm and kind, and he runs. I know I shouldn't be, but I'm attracted to him."

"Have you gone out with him yet?"

"We ran a race together today and we're having dinner tonight. He lost the bet. I'm so confused."

"It's only one date. Be cautious and see how it goes. Maybe you won't hit it off. I've got to get back to work, so call me tomorrow, okay?"

"Sure. I'll talk to you later."

I hung up and sighed. *Maybe we won't hit it off.*

Eleven

The remainder of the day dragged on, and my mind was muddled—I couldn't even decide what to wear to dinner that evening. Time passed so slowly; I was relieved when it was finally time to start getting ready. I ended up wearing a wraparound dress and black leather boots. Nothing too sensual, but it fit well and definitely accentuated my small waist and long legs. I left my hair down and put some extra effort into my makeup job. The natural look took a good bit of time to master, and I realized that it was almost time to meet Ted. I grabbed my coat and began my stroll to the coffee shop.

Ted was waiting at the door for me, and my heart began to race at the sight of him. "Hi, Ted. Have you been waiting long?" I asked.

"Just a minute or so. Let's get going. I don't know about you, but I've been starving all day."

He escorted me to his car, and again I glanced around to make sure we hadn't been spotted.

"I think we made it out of there safely," Ted kidded. "Don't worry. We're going to a place that's about thirty minutes from here. No one will recognize us," he assured me.

"I'm not usually the paranoid type. It's just that I don't want to give anyone the wrong impression. The gossip mill in these small towns can be pretty powerful."

"I respect your feelings, and we'll be ultra-discreet. I hope you like this restaurant. I've never been myself, but a few patients have talked about it and I thought it might be nice."

"I'm fairly easygoing in the food department. Keep me fed, and I'm a happy girl."

Ted laughed and we talked some more about the race. Before long, we arrived at Hugo's, a stylish-looking restaurant. I felt like I was inside a cozy ski lodge with stack stone walls, several fireplaces and wooden beams across the ceiling. It was dimly lit, but there was a comforting atmosphere.

The smoke from the grill stung my eyes a bit, but charcoal smell of the steaks caused my stomach to growl loudly, and before I could wonder if Ted heard it too, he said, "Sounds like we'd better get you fed."

I laughed, "So much for my manners. Let's eat."

We sat in a booth with a starched white tablecloth facing each other, and my mind began to wander as the waitress told us about the specials. I had to be crazy to jeopardize everything. My job, my sanity. I was just feeling normal again, and here I was about to put myself in another precarious position. I took a quiet deep breath and told myself to calm down. This wasn't even a date technically. It was the payoff of a bet and nothing more.

"Do any of the specials appeal to you, Jane?" Ted asked when the waitress had finally stopped talking.

I quickly recovered and said, "Let me have some time to look at the menu."

"How about a glass of wine?" Ted asked.

"Sure. Why don't you pick out something for me," I suggested.

After he ordered the wine, Ted looked at me and asked, "So, are you back?"

"What?"

"You seemed to wander off while the waitress was telling us her specials. Is everything okay?" he asked.

"Yes." I smiled. "I guess the exhaustion of the race is starting to catch up with me."

"I want you to relax and enjoy yourself."

"I will. Thanks, Ted."

Ted and I traded stories throughout dinner about our college experiences and first jobs. During dessert, he told me about meeting Annie and some of the places they'd visited. He talked nostalgically without any bitterness.

When I remarked on that, he said, "I had five great years with her, and together we had Emma. I want to show Emma that bad things happen, but you can still be happy. I can't let sadness destroy either one of us. Annie wouldn't have wanted that. Enough about me. Tell me more about you."

"There isn't much to tell really. Just the boring life of a kindergarten teacher," I replied.

"Do you miss New York?" he asked.

"Sure, the cultural experiences there are unmatched. There is so much to see and do there. I miss that aspect, but I needed to leave."

"Ah, the bad breakup?" he inquired.

"Yes, it left me a bit shell-shocked, and I needed the comfort and familiarity of home. It's been a good move for me."

"I for one am happy you made the move," he said. Then he added, "Emma loves having you for a teacher."

I returned his smile and said, "She's delightful. And this was a nice evening, thank you."

Ted paid the check and escorted me back to his car. He put a mellow jazz station on the radio, and I gave into my exhaustion and closed my eyes. I felt the car come to a stop, and when I opened my eyes, we were right by the coffee shop.

"Hey, sleepyhead. Which way is home?" Ted asked.

"Oh, my gosh. I'm so embarrassed. Turn left at the light. I live in the apartments at The Mill. Turn right here. There it is, number 1612."

I yawned and said, "I'm so sorry. The wine and the race really wiped me out. I had a lovely time, though. Thank you."

"Let me walk you to your door," Ted offered.

"Really that's not necessary," I replied.

"It's late and I insist."

We walked up to the door, and Ted waited while I found my keys in my purse. I opened the door and stood awkwardly for a moment, then Ted leaned over and softly kissed my cheek, sending a ripple of electricity through my body.

"Thank you, Jane. It's been such a long time since I have enjoyed an evening out this much."

"Good night, Ted," I responded in a whisper and went into my apartment and shut the door behind me. "What am I doing?" I wondered to myself.

Twelve

Two days later I returned to work, and was both disappointed and relieved that I had not heard from Ted. Between the stresses of having to do a reading evaluation on each of my students in the next two weeks and the mental strain of Grace's impending wedding, I did not have the time to dwell on the situation with Ted.

The wedding was in three weeks, and I put aside my feelings about Derek in the hopes that Grace's wedding day would be the most special day of her life. It was going to be a small wedding—Saturday afternoon Mass followed by dinner and dancing. Grace kept me so busy with fittings and table arrangements that Ted Manning had disappeared from my mind, only to be brought back via an email.

"Jane, enjoyed losing the bet. Care to wager another?"

It was a bit cryptic, but I figured he was being careful since it was my work email. I responded, *"Sister getting married first of February. All bets off until then."*

The time flew by, and the day before the wedding was upon us. The rehearsal had gone off without a hitch. There was a sincerity about Derek that gave me a glimmer of hope that maybe he would be a good husband to Grace. Grace was positively glowing, and I was grateful that her wedding day was turning out to be everything she had dreamed of.

The morning of the wedding we gathered at my mom's to get dressed. I was the only attendant, as Derek had only wanted a best man. He had chosen Stephen, a friend from college, to stand up for him. I had not had time to really talk with Stephen and was hoping at the wedding to learn a little bit more about Derek.

While Grace was in the shower, I went to see if my mother wanted another cup of coffee, and when I opened the door to her bedroom, I found her lying on her bed.

"Sorry, Mom. I didn't mean to disturb you. Are you crying?"

She wiped her face with a tissue, but made no attempt to cover up her distress. "I don't know if I can do this, Jane."

I felt slightly dizzy and asked, "Do what?"

"Go to this wedding and act like I'm happy for Grace," she replied numbly.

I crawled onto the bed beside my mother and rested my head on her shoulder. "We have no choice."

"I wish your dad was here," she said, choking back a sob.

In all the years, my mom had never openly admitted to missing my father. I felt my heart shatter like a piece of fine crystal. "I'll take care of you, Mom. I promise. We'll get through this together."

We lay there silently for awhile, and finally I said, "Let's get ready."

My mother sat up, but then buried her face in her hands.

"Mom, we need to do this for Grace."

"You're right," she said, and slowly she climbed out of bed and made her way to the bathroom. I went to check on Grace, who was busy getting dressed. She chatted nervously as we both applied our makeup. I did my best to act upbeat, and when we were both ready, I stood back and took a long look at Grace. She was absolutely radiant, and I felt tears welling up.

"Grace, you are stunning."

She was embarrassed by my compliment and said, "All brides look good on their wedding day."

"No. You are breathtakingly beautiful. Derek is a lucky man and don't you forget that. You are a wonderful person, and I'm so proud of the woman that you have become."

A tear slid down Grace's face, and she chided me for making her cry. "Now look what you've done. Enough... this is the happiest day of my life and we are not going to spend time crying."

I smiled and said, "Let's go see if the car is here."

The ride to the church was quiet. We each seemed to be lost in our own thoughts. The ride in the limousine brought me back to the day of my dad's funeral. I had been so overwhelmed. All the people who wanted to hug and comfort me made me so scared. My mother was rock solid, yet so unavailable to Grace and me. I remember riding to the gravesite; I'd grabbed Grace's hand and held it tightly in my grip the entire ride. I reached over and grabbed her hand again, and Grace's eyes met mine. I wanted to say something profound, something to mark this momentous occasion in Grace's life, but could only manage a smile.

When we arrived at the church, my last hope of not having the wedding was dashed when the coordinator met us at the door and said, "Your handsome groom is waiting for you."

The music began, and as I walked down the aisle, I looked straight ahead and tried to avoid Derek's eyes. As I took my place on the altar, I looked up and Derek gave me a wink that caused my stomach to lurch. From anyone else, the subtle gesture would have been warmly received, but my new brother-in-law was a different story.

The wedding march began, and there stood my mother and Grace, both radiating warmth and beauty. My mother looked ten years younger. Her silver mane had been styled into a delicate bob and her blue eyes were accentuated by her violet beaded dress. Grace's dress sparkled in the candlelight reflecting off the myriad of crystals that had been painstakingly hand-sewn. As they approached the altar, my tears could no longer be contained. As I wiped my eyes, I looked over at Derek and watched as he swallowed the lump in his throat. There was genuine affection in his gaze as my mother and Grace stood before him. They both hugged my mother before she sat, and I noticed Derek whispering something in her ear. My mother nodded and took her seat.

The ceremony was lovely with very traditional vows and music, and before my eyes Grace became Mrs. Derek

Meade. Sadness clouded over me as we exited the church, but I was determined to keep my feelings hidden. The best man and I traveled to the reception in the limousine with Grace and Derek, and we toasted them with a glass of champagne. I tried to keep the conversation lively and upbeat. I asked Stephen, the best man, about Derek and how long they had known each other.

"We went to college in Chicago together. We were roommates our senior year. I was shocked when you tracked me down and asked me to be your best man, Derek. How long has it been, anyway?" he asked, looking to Derek for an answer.

Obviously irritated, Derek replied, "It hasn't been that long. Besides, you didn't have anything else to do, did you?"

Stephen laughed. "Even after all these years, you still know me, Derek. I've missed your sense of humor."

What a pair, I thought to myself.

Once at the reception, I relaxed and let myself enjoy the evening. Seeing Grace beaming while dancing and chatting lifted my spirits. The guests all seemed to have fun, and toward the end of the evening, I wanted to find Grace to see if she needed any assistance before she and Derek left for their wedding night celebration. Derek was standing at the bar, and it was quite obvious that he had been drinking a great deal. His eyes were red and glassy, and he was leaning on the counter of the bar as if it was keeping him upright.

"Derek, have you seen Grace?" I asked.

"Jane, Jane, Janey," he sang. "If only I had met you first."

I did everything in my power not to slap him across the face. I leaned in and with a forced smile said, "Listen, you bastard. Don't ever say anything like that again. You hurt my sister and I'll come after you, you son of a bitch," I hissed.

Derek laughed as I made my way into the rest room. I locked myself in a stall and cried silently, trying not to ruin my makeup. I finally composed myself and after checking with the mirror, I went back to the party to find my mom. I noticed a small group of people standing in a circle on the dance floor.

I made my way into the circle, and there was Derek lying on the ground, pale and sweaty. I turned to a friend of Grace's and asked, "What happened?"

"Derek passed out. A little too much party, I guess," she replied with a snicker.

What a great start to married life, I thought to myself. I stepped back and saw Stephen and Grace help Derek to a chair as I searched for my mother.

I found her sitting alone, nursing a drink. As I sat, I said, "Well, that's one way to end a party."

My mother sighed and said, "You know what he said to me on the altar?" she asked. Not waiting for a response, she continued, "He said that he would do his best to take care of Grace. If this is his best, then Grace is in deep trouble."

Thirteen

Ted and I exchanged emails over the next several weeks, and though I kept them light and impersonal, I looked forward to hearing from him. I began to check for his messages three to four times a day and realized that I needed to change my focus. After school ended for the day, I visited Jillian in her classroom.

"Are you up for dinner tonight? I could use some girl talk."

"Sure," she replied. "I feel like we haven't really talked in a long time. Let's go to that Thai place on Juniper. It's so miserable and cold out. I want something spicy to warm me up since I don't have a man to do that for me."

I laughed, and we made plans to meet in two hours. I cleaned up the painting center and put out worksheets for the next day. I straightened up the tables and chairs before I went home to freshen up. I arrived at the restaurant at 6:30 on the dot and scanned the room for Jillian. She waved to get my attention, and as soon as I was seated, she began talking about an Internet dating service that she was looking into.

"Isn't it weird to be meeting people on the computer?" I asked.

"Yes and no. Yes, I feel a bit desperate using a dating service, but the Internet helps me meet men who I would never have had the chance to meet before. This company is very reputable, and they do a thorough background check on all the applicants. The downer is that it's expensive. I'll only be able to afford to eat peanut butter and jelly if I decide to join."

"You're a brave soul, Jillian. I don't think I could do it," I said.

"I haven't done it yet. I'll keep you posted. What's going on with you? Have you met anyone at your new place?" she asked.

"I really haven't tried. Everything was so busy with the holidays and Grace's wedding. I literally didn't have the time, but now I think I'm ready."

"Good girl. We'll get you back in the dating world, yet. Ooooh, maybe we can join the dating service together," she added with a raise of her eyebrows.

We laughed and talked some more before ordering our dinner. When the server appeared with our meals, something caught my eye. I looked over to see Ted, Emma, and an attractive blonde who appeared to be in her late twenties. They were being seated at a table when Jillian asked what I was looking at.

"One of my students is here, that's all."

"We can't escape, can we? Just try not to look over there and maybe they won't notice us," she offered.

"I wouldn't mind really. Emma is such a sweetheart. It would be nice to say hello to her."

"Oh, my gosh. You are too nice. I'm off duty and intend to stay that way," she said as she took a sip of her wine.

We continued talking and eating, but once I saw Ted, I couldn't fully concentrate on Jillian. Why was I so flustered at seeing him with another woman? We weren't even dating. *And you can't date a student's father,* I chastised myself.

"Jane, did you hear anything I just said?" Jillian asked with mock indignation.

"I'm so sorry. I must be tired," I said as I unconsciously glanced over Jillian's shoulder at Ted's table.

"Why do you keep looking over at that table?" she asked as she turned to get a glimpse herself. "Now, I get it. That's the dad from the holiday play. Is there something going on between you two?" she asked with genuine concern.

"No, there is absolutely nothing between us," I said hoping that saying the words would influence my actions. "He's a widower, and this is his first experience with school, so I've been a bit more involved."

"Involved with him or the kid?"

"With Emma, of course. You're really making too much of this, Jillian," I said.

"Well, why don't you just go over there and pay them a visit?" When I didn't respond, she asked, "Is it because he's with another woman?"

"You are so off base, Jillian. Anyway, I'll see Emma tomorrow. Let's order some dessert," I said, trying to change the subject.

"Jane, you..." was all Jillian could say before Emma's tiny face appeared at our table.

"Hi, Miss Richards. My dad said I could say hi, but I can't bother you," she said with a slight frown.

"Oh, Emma. You would never bother me," I said as I motioned for her to sit on my lap. "This is Miss Lane," I said, nodding toward Jillian. "She teaches at our school, too. Miss Lane, this is Emma Manning."

"Hi, Emma. Nice to meet you," Jillian said using her best teacher manners.

"I know you. My friend Jonah is in your class," Emma responded.

"He sure is. I'll tell him that I saw you tonight," Jillian offered.

"How's your dinner, Emma?" I asked at the same time that Jillian asked who Emma was with.

I shot Jillian a look, yet Emma chose to answer her question first. "I'm here with my dad and someone who works at his office. She had a flat tire, and my dad is taking her home."

"What a nice guy your dad is," Jillian replied.

"I better get back," she said as she wriggled off of my lap. "See you tomorrow."

"Bye, sweetie," I said, and then I turned my attention to Jillian. "Why did you ask her about that woman? What if she says something to Ted?"

"I figured that you would want to know. And since you and Ted are on a first-name basis, I assume that you may be getting more involved than you should."

I was silent for a moment, and then said, "I admit, I am attracted to him, but I know that he's off limits. Really, I won't put myself in another bad relationship again."

Jillian smiled. "I'm sorry to be such a 'mother hen.' It's just that you've told me your horror stories with men, and I don't want to see you make another mistake. I'm sorry if I overstepped my boundaries."

"Jillian, you are such a good friend to me, and I do appreciate your concern. Thanks for keeping me honest."

"Any time, and now I believe I have officially turned into my mother," she added with a chuckle.

~ * ~

Once I was home, I took a long, hot bath. It was just what I needed to calm me down and help me sort out my feelings for Ted. I did have feelings toward him, but right now, it was only an attraction and nothing more. I vowed to stop all personal contact with him and concentrate solely on Emma and the other kids in my class. And maybe that Internet dating wasn't so bad after all.

I changed into warm, flannel pajamas and an old terry cloth bathrobe before I made myself a cup of hot tea. I was about to settle myself on the sofa when I heard a beeping sound that I recognized as my cell phone. I had a message. I searched my purse for the phone. I finally located it and listened.

"Jane, it's Ted. I'd really like to talk to you. Please call me."

He left his number, and I quickly found a pen and jotted it down. I flopped down on the sofa and realized that my earlier resolve was softening. *Maybe I'll just wait until tomorrow to call him,* I thought and chuckled aloud knowing that would never happen.

Fourteen

I sat for a few minutes trying to imagine what Ted wanted to talk about and reviewed the possible different scenarios in my head.

Did he just want to tell me something about Emma, or was it about us? Okay, so there really isn't an us, but maybe he wants there to be. Or maybe he doesn't. Enough, I told myself. *Just call him back.*

I took a deep breath and, with slightly shaking fingers, dialed Ted's number.

"Hi, Ted. It's Jane Richards," I blurted out before he even said hello.

"Hi, there," he said, ignoring my crazed greeting. "Thanks for calling me back."

"Sure. Is Emma all right?" I asked trying to sound more casual.

"Emma is fine, thanks. I just didn't get to speak with you at the restaurant, and I wanted to tell you about the woman we had dinner with."

I closed my eyes and said, "You don't owe me any explanations."

"I know that, but I want you to know that it was a woman who works at my office. She had a flat tire and I changed it for her. She picked Emma up at day care so I wouldn't be late, and since her husband was out of town, she offered to take us both to dinner to thank me."

He responded to my silence by asking, "Are you still there?"

"Yes, I'm still here. I'm glad you told me, but..."

"But what?" he countered.

"It's really none of my business," I answered.

"I want it to be your business, Jane."

I was silent a moment, wishing I could get my thoughts in order more quickly. "Ted, what are we doing?" I asked.

"We're not doing anything, yet, but I'd like to change that," he said waiting for my response.

I felt a rush, and my heart began to beat faster. Again, I was silent.

"Are you going to let me just hang here?" he asked.

"No, no. I'm sorry. I would love to get to know you better, but ethically this would be trouble for me."

"I don't have a problem with it," he countered.

"It's not you that I'm worried about. My principal and the other parents—they might have something to say about it."

"Hell, it's only kindergarten. How could Emma or the other kids be affected by our dating? This is ridiculous."

I had no response. I heard Ted take a breath, and he said, "I'm sorry. I don't want you to compromise yourself for me. It's just that I haven't been this attracted to another woman since Annie died," he admitted softly.

I felt myself weaken inside and said, "I'm sorry, too. And flattered."

"But this time flattery won't get me anywhere, will it?" he asked.

My heart was screaming, *yes, yes,* but in the end my conscience spoke. "I have feelings for you and would love to explore them further, but it would be wrong to start something now while Emma is in my class," I said, sincerely hoping that stating it aloud would hold me accountable.

"What about when the school year is over? That's only a few months away. What do you think?" he asked with a hint of anticipation in his voice.

My head started to spin. "Just put everything on hold until the summer?" I asked.

"Let's get to know one another. We can be friends first," he stated quietly. "Who knows," he added, "maybe we won't even like each other."

I laughed and said, "Speak for yourself. I, for one, am a very likable person." I thought for a moment, and asked, "Seriously, Ted, do you think this is wise?"

He sighed and said, "Wisdom is overrated. This time I'm listening to my heart, and it's telling me not to miss this opportunity."

"I hope we aren't getting ourselves into something we might regret."

"I'd only regret not getting to know you better. Good night, 'friend.' I'll be in touch."

"Good night, Ted," I whispered as I hung up the phone.

I dissolved into the sofa and immediately wanted my mother. I didn't want to tell her about Ted, but I needed her comfort and stability. I dialed her number and was surprised to hear a busy signal. *Who could she be talking to at this hour?* I wondered. I stood and warmed my tea in the microwave before trying my mother's number again. This time the phone rang and I was greeted by my mom's hello.

"Hi, Mom. It's Jane. I was just thinking about you and wanted to check in."

"Hi, Jane. Is everything all right?"

"Sure. It's been a long week and I'm ready for the weekend. Do you want to have dinner on Friday?" I asked.

"Well, I..." She paused a second and continued, "I have plans."

She sounded vague. That was not like my mother at all. "What are you doing?" I asked.

"Well, I believe I'm going on a date. A gentleman from church just called and invited me to dinner."

"And you said yes, I take it?"

"I did," she replied in somewhat disbelief.

"Well, then, you are definitely going on a date," I squealed. "This is so exciting. What's his name?"

"Lawrence McDermott. He's someone that I met through the seniors' group."

"Where is he taking you? What are you going to wear? You should get a new outfit," I gushed.

"Jane, slow down. It's just dinner. And I am not going to go out of my way to impress him. I'm too old to be playing the dating game. He can take me or leave me," she stated with utter practicality.

I laughed. "Sorry I got so carried away. You are a little excited though, aren't you?" I asked.

"Yes. And nervous," she admitted. "I haven't been on a date in years."

"You'll have a great time. If nothing else, it will be an evening out. How about if I come by after school on Friday and help you get ready?"

"That's not necessary, Jane."

"I know it's not necessary, Mom, but would you like me to come over?"

"Yes," she replied with a hint of relief in her voice. "I would like that very much. Maybe I'll go shopping tomorrow and pick up a new outfit. I've been needing new clothes anyway."

I smiled and said, "I'll see you Friday afternoon, Mom. Love you."

"You, too. Good night, Jane."

How fun. This was just what I needed to keep my mind off Ted. I just hoped it would do the trick.

Fifteen

The day of my mother's big date had arrived, and that day in school I was a bit preoccupied, which Mattie noticed instantly. "Jane, is anything wrong?" she asked as we straightened up the room while the kids were at art.

I smiled and said, "I'm fine, actually. Sorry. I've been a bit distracted today. Actually, though it's a good distraction. My mother has a date tonight and I'm very excited and a bit nervous for her."

"How nice. Do you know the man?"

"No. It's someone that she knows from church. I am hoping to at least get a peek at him tonight," I said with a slight mischievous grin.

"Do you have any other plans this weekend?"

"Unfortunately, not. I may call my sister. I haven't seen her since the wedding."

"I hope she is enjoying married life," Mattie said softly.

"Me, too. I guess no news is good news."

~ * ~

After the last bell rang, I wasted no time in getting over to my mom's house. I knocked softly and let myself in.

"Mom, it's me," I called out, hoping not to frighten her.

"I'm upstairs, come up," she answered.

I made my way to her bedroom, where I found her sitting among a pile of clothes. I stifled a laugh because I had never seen any part of my mother's house in such disarray.

"Wow, what's going on here?" I asked.

"I can't believe it, but I can't decide what to wear. I am a grown woman and I can't make a simple decision about my clothing. I'm ready to call Lawrence and tell him I'm sick and can't make it," she said.

I was extremely glad that I had come over. "Hold on, Mom. You are not going to cancel on him. I'll help you pick out an outfit. Where are you going to dinner?"

"The Harbor Town Inn. It's very nice."

"Is it casual or more upscale?"

"It's definitely one of the finer restaurants in town," she replied. "I bought a new outfit," she said as she pulled it out of the pile on her bed and added, "but I'm not sure."

I examined the long black skirt and the periwinkle sweater set. The sweater had a hint of sparkle to it, and I knew she would look stunning in it. "Mom, this outfit is great. Let's go through your jewelry and find some earrings to finish the look."

I found a pair of crystal earrings and a bracelet that had been my grandmother's, and we agreed that it made her outfit complete. "That wasn't so bad. You are going to look fabulous. How much time do you have before he gets here?" I asked.

She glanced at the clock on her nightstand and replied with a groan, "An hour and a half."

"Let's go have a cup of tea, and I'll help you kill some time until then."

"Great idea. Let me clean up this mess and you go get the tea started."

She joined me a few minutes later, and I couldn't resist letting my mother know that I was pleased that she was dating again. "Mom, I'm really happy that you're going out tonight. I hate that you're alone."

"I've gotten used to being alone, Jane, but I am looking forward to this evening."

"Maybe this will be the first of many," I smiled.

"Don't get carried away. I am very content with my life as it is. When your dad died, I lost the only man I ever loved. That kind of love doesn't come around twice in a lifetime."

I was pleasantly surprised at how my mother was opening up to me, and I didn't want it to end. "I'm not sure I'll ever have a relationship like that. The two times I thought I had found the right guy, it all came crashing down on me."

"I know you've been hurt, but you'll find the right man, Jane. And when you do, that pain will be replaced with strength. Everything happens for a reason, honey."

"Thanks, Mom. I love you."

"I love you, too, kiddo. Now, let's get me ready for my date."

My mom dressed, and I helped with her makeup and hair. "You look fabulous," I told her. I couldn't help smiling. Moments like this made me even more grateful that I had moved back home. The doorbell rang, and I asked, "Do you want me to get it, or do you want me to hang out up here? I can let myself out, if you like," I offered.

"You are a part of my life, so he might as well meet you now. Any man who can't handle that won't cut it for long. And, you can wipe that smile off your face. Let's not scare him off intentionally."

We walked downstairs, and my mother answered the door. A tall, rugged-looking older gentleman with a head full of white hair stood there with a bouquet of peach-colored roses.

"Hello, Lawrence," she said softly. "Come in."

"Hello, Ruth," he replied as he glanced my way.

"I'm Ruth's daughter, Jane. It's nice to meet you," I said as I extended my hand to him.

"Lawrence Mc Dermott. Ruth, these are for you," he said as he simultaneously shook my hand and gave my mother the flowers.

"Thank you, Lawrence. That was very thoughtful. Have a seat," she said as she motioned to the sofa.

I grabbed my coat, ready to make a quick exit.

"I need to get going, Mom. Enjoy your evening," I said, kissing her cheek. "Lawrence, good to meet you."

"You, too, Jane," he called after me as my mother walked me to the door.

"Call me," I whispered.

My mother admonished me with her eyes and said, "I'll see you soon."

I left there with a smile stuck on my face for the entire ride home. When I was settled, I called my sister's cell phone. I was disappointed to get her voice mail, but left a message. "Hi, Grace. Did you know Mom had a date tonight with a very handsome, older gentleman? They were so cute together. Call me. I miss talking to you. Bye."

My exhilaration from earlier was gone, and now I was bored and hungry. I looked in the refrigerator and nothing appealed to me. I found a bag of popcorn and was getting ready to put it in the microwave, when I heard my cell phone ring. I hoped it was Grace as I fished it out of my purse.

"Hello," I answered.

"Hi, Jane. It's Ted Manning. Are you busy?"

I felt a thrill just hearing his voice, but tried to sound casual. "No, I'm not busy. In fact, I was just getting ready to microwave a bag of popcorn for dinner. Exciting life I lead, isn't it?"

"Emma is spending the night with her grandparents, and I was wondering if you would like to share a pizza with me?"

I hesitated, but the truth was I dying to see him again. I wasn't sure where this intense desire was coming from, but I wanted to spend time with Ted. I didn't want to think about the ramifications, but I did, and so to be clear I asked, "Just friends, right?"

"Of course," he replied smugly.

"You'll be on your best behavior?" I asked.

"Do you really have to ask?" he asked pretending to be hurt.

"Yes, I do. So will you behave tonight if I agree to a pizza?"

"Yes, Miss Richards. So, are we having pizza or not?"

"Pizza it is. What time?" I asked as my doorbell rang. "Ted, hold on. Someone is at my door."

I looked through the peephole and there was Ted with a huge, satisfied smile on his face.

Sixteen

I opened the door and said, "Now that's service. Come in, Ted."

Ted had three pizza boxes and a bottle of red wine in his arms. "Let me take something," I offered as he handed me the wine. "Put the pizzas down right here on the coffee table. How many people are we expecting? There's enough pizza here for ten people."

"Well, I wasn't sure what you liked on your pizza, so I got one plain, one half pepperoni, half sausage, and one veggie. I tried to cover all of my pizza options," he said, still smiling.

"Pretty pleased with yourself, aren't you, Dr. Manning? What would you have done if I wasn't home or if I said no?" I asked playfully.

"I guess Emma and I would be eating a lot of pizza. However, since you were home and you said yes, let's eat. I'm starved."

I got two dishes from the cupboard along with two wine glasses. I handed Ted an opener, and he poured two glasses for us.

"Does the fireplace work?" he asked.

"Yes, there's some wood out on the patio. I haven't had a fire yet and would love to have one tonight."

In a few minutes, he had started a roaring fire. Ted said, "That feels better. It's freezing out, and I just heard that we are in for some snow this weekend."

"I love the snow. When we were little, I remember how Grace and I would spend hours outside building snowmen and snow forts. Snow days were the best. I wouldn't mind one of those this year," I said longingly.

Ted nodded and asked, "Do you mind if I start eating? I haven't eaten since noon."

"Not at all. Let's see what you've got here," I said as we opened the boxes. I chose a slice of veggie pizza and took a bite. It was hot and spicy, and it was much better than a bag of popcorn. "This pizza is great. Where did you get it?"

"Down off of Main there's this little hole in the wall called Luca's and it's fabulous. I'll have to take you there some time. They have the best meatballs I ever tasted," he raved.

I smiled in response, and when I could take the silence no more, I asked, "How was your week?"

"It was a great week. No major emergencies. I really love what I do. I get to know some of the nicest people. When Annie died, you would not believe all of the things that the patients did for me. I didn't have to cook for three months."

I felt a sting at the mention of Annie's name and wondered if I measured up. I quickly changed my train of thought, and hoped my expression didn't betray my lack of self-confidence. "I'm sorry to always bring up Annie. I need to work on that," he whispered.

I instantly felt ashamed at my jealousy and replied, "Please don't be sorry. Annie is a part of who you are, and she always will be. I'm sure talking about Annie is good for Emma, too. Now give me another slice of pizza," I commanded.

Ted obliged and asked, "What made you want to be a teacher?"

"When I was in high school I had a teacher who helped me through a very bad time, and she was my inspiration. Plus, I love kids, especially kindergarten age. They are so ready to learn, and they absorb information so fast. The best part is that they are loving and not afraid to show it. I get so many hugs each day. That alone makes my job worth it."

"I love how Emma comes home and tells me about all of the stuff that goes on in class. Some of the kids sound like real firecrackers." He laughed.

"Oh, they are. Especially in the beginning. I had one boy who kept trying to escape. He packed up, put on his coat, and when Mattie and I weren't looking, he left. I heard the door and immediately went after him and was chasing him down the hall when out of nowhere Mr. Samuels, the principal, appeared and scooped him up. For the next two weeks I kept a chair in front of the door just to slow him down a little."

"One day, Emma told me you were at your wits' end."

I chuckled. "They see and hear everything. When I brought him back to class, I told him that. I can't believe she remembered. Just know that they tell me about what goes on at home, too. I always tell parents that I'll believe fifty percent of what the kids tell me about home and they should believe fifty percent of what their child tells them about school."

"I never thought about that. I'm going to have to clean up my act. I bet you get a lot of laughs teaching those kids," he said.

"I do. It's not always easy, but it's very rewarding."

"One of the things I love about my practice is getting to know the families. I've been doing this for almost ten years now, and I've seen kids grow up and now some of the teenagers are grown and getting married. I can't wait until their kids start coming into the office," he said with genuine excitement in his voice.

"I'm sure being in a town like Wilmington is perfect for that. A smaller town where you can really get to know people. When I was in New York, it was difficult to have that community feel. I liked the hurried pace of the city, but after a while it became tiring."

"Is that why you left?" he asked cautiously.

"That and the end of a very bad relationship. I think I had always wanted to come back home, and my circumstances helped accelerate the process." Not wanting to go into any more detail about my relationship with Nick, I stood and cleared our plates. Ted brought the pizza boxes over to the kitchen counter.

We cleaned up in comfortable silence, and Ted asked, "Would you like another glass of wine?"

I hesitated a moment and then said, "Sure. I can sleep in tomorrow. Are you up for a game of Scrabble?"

"Scrabble, huh? Want to make another bet?" he challenged.

"How about we just play for fun," I offered as I went to the hall closet and pulled out the box.

We set up the game, and I found myself staring at Ted. His blonde hair was kept very short and he had a slight stubble on his face. I thought about how his face would feel against mine and was immediately torn from my daydream by Ted's voice.

"Jane, it's your turn. Are you okay?" he asked.

"Oh, I'm fine. I was just a little distracted. The wine is making me sleepy. Sorry," I added as I placed my word on the board. "Chalk—that's six points. It will be interesting to see how many words of mine relate to kindergarten."

"Occupational hazard, I guess," Ted replied. "So do you see much of your family?" he asked.

"I see my mom quite a bit. She's my rock. Always there to pick up the pieces. She's very practical and composed. When my dad died, she really made the best of a bad situation. I'm hoping to be just like her when I grow up," I said as I placed another word down.

Ted was arranging some letters and asked, "How about your sister? Are you close with her?"

"We are closer now that I moved back. There are four years between us, so when she was in college I was in my self-absorbed teen years and when she moved back home, I went off to college and then to New York."

"How was the wedding?"

"It was interesting. Let's just say, I'm not a big fan of my new brother-in-law."

"Too bad."

"What about you? Brothers and sisters?" I asked.

"I am the oldest of four. I have two brothers and a sister. She's the baby of the family."

"So, your parents kept trying for the girl, huh?"

"Well, having a lot of kids was the thing to do back then. We had one family in our church and they had ten kids," he said. "Can you imagine?"

"Well, I have twenty kids each day, but I am relieved to turn them over to their parents at the end of the day. It's exhausting," I said trying to stifle a yawn. "Does anyone live here?"

"My brother, Thomas, lives about thirty minutes away with his wife, and my other brother, Taylor, and my sister Theresa live in Boston near my parents."

"Your parents like names that start with T," I teased.

"I told Annie that I didn't care what we named our kids, but we would not have them all start with the same letter. I refused to do that to them."

"You all have nice names, though. My sister and I have two of the plainest names ever—Jane and Grace. How boring is that?"

"They are beautiful names, very classic."

"That's us—classic," I said trying to suppress another yawn.

"You're exhausted. Let me get out of here so you can get some sleep," Ted offered.

"I'm sorry. By the time Friday gets here, I'm wiped out. I enjoyed the evening, though," I said as I stood to get his coat.

Ted put on his jacket and gloves, and I walked him over to the door. "Thanks for the pizza. It was a nice surprise," I said.

"It was my pleasure. I'll see you soon," he said as he reached for the door handle. He stopped and turned to me and kissed me softly on the lips. I pulled back and looked deep into his eyes. Impulsively, I reached out to him, and he kissed me so long and hard, it took my breath away.

"Good night, Jane," he said as he opened the door and left.

I sighed and leaned against the door as I closed it. *I am in trouble*, I thought to myself.

Seventeen

I don't think I slept at all that night. Ted's kiss had stirred up a desire deep within me, and I could no longer deny that there was something between us. Now I had to decide on the best way to handle our relationship. I was surely violating an ethics agreement by dating a student's father, but I was unsure as to what to do now that we had clearly opened the door to our feelings. I sat with my morning cup of coffee, just staring out into space, when the ringing of the telephone startled me.

"Hello," I answered.

"Hi, Jane. It's Mom. I thought you'd be camped out on my doorstep waiting to hear all of the details about my big date."

I threw my head back against the sofa and closed my eyes as I realized I had completely forgotten about my mother and her evening out. I quickly recovered and said, "I didn't want to seem overly anxious, but I'm dying to hear so tell me all about it."

"I had a very nice time. I had forgotten how much fun it was to be taken out for dinner and dancing," she gushed.

I loved hearing my mother sound so animated. "Ooh. Dinner and dancing. Go on," I encouraged. "Don't leave anything out."

"After you left, we drove to the restaurant. I thought it would be awkward, but Lawrence was very easy to talk to. We had a lovely dinner, and then he surprised me by taking me to a dance club where they cater to an older crowd. The band played all of the old songs, and I can't remember the last time I danced so much."

"That's so great, Mom. Did you go any place else?"

"Yes, we went for coffee and talked until one in the morning. Can you imagine?" she asked as if she didn't believe it herself.

"So, when will you be seeing him again?"

"He called me this morning and asked if he could take me to breakfast after Mass on Sunday."

"Did you say yes?"

"I did," she replied with a hint of satisfaction, and then as if she was suddenly brought back to her practical reality she added, "but don't get carried away. It's just breakfast."

"You got it, Mom. I was wondering if you've talked to Grace. I haven't talked to her lately and was hoping we could get together this weekend."

"I had left several messages for her, and she finally called me this morning. She and Derek are coming over for dinner tonight. Can you join us?"

"I'd love to. What time?"

"Seven."

"Great. I'll bring some wine, okay?" I asked.

"Thanks, Jane. I'll see you tonight."

"Hey, Mom. Will Lawrence be coming, too?" I asked kidding.

"Now, Jane. What did I tell you?" she asked, trying to sound annoyed, but not succeeding.

I laughed and said, "I'm just having a little fun with you. I'll be there at seven... and tell Lawrence I'd like to know what his intentions are. Bye, Mom."

"I heard that," she said as I hung up the phone.

I stood up and was headed for the shower when my cell phone rang, and this time I recognized the number as Ted's. I took a deep breath and answered the phone, "Hello, Ted."

"Hi, Jane. I can't seem to get you out of my mind so I thought I'd call," he said, waiting for a response from me.

"I know the feeling. I enjoyed being with you last night..."

"But?" he prodded.

"But, I have to be careful. I could lose my job."

"I know, and I'm sorry that you are in such a compromising situation, but, Jane, I can't just walk away from you. I care about you, and it's been so long since I've been excited to be with someone... I need this," he added.

I felt an ache in my soul. My previous relationships had all turned out to be one-sided, and while I felt somewhat unsettled at Ted's admission, it was also impossible to resist. "We need to be extremely discreet," I said in resignation. "Please, you have to promise me."

I heard Ted release a held breath, and he replied, "Of, course. I'd do anything to keep on seeing you, Jane. Our 'friendship' means a lot to me, and I will do whatever it takes to protect it."

"Thank you, Ted."

"Do you have any plans for tonight?" he asked hopefully.

"As a matter of fact, I do." Then I had a thought. "You aren't standing outside my door again, are you?"

Ted laughed. "No. I'm at home. I was just thinking that with Emma home, we can't get together, but maybe we can talk after she goes to bed. That is unless you have a hot date tonight," he challenged.

"No date, I'm afraid. Just dinner with my mom and sister. I am looking forward to it though."

"Is the brother-in-law coming, too?" he asked.

"Afraid so, but it's the only way to see my sister, so I can put up with him," I responded.

"Is he really that bad?"

"Oh, yeah. He's downright scary. It's hard to explain, but he has an evil side to him, and I'm worried for my sister. She's not a strong person," I added.

"Have you tried to talk to her about it? What does she think?" he asked with genuine interest.

"She knows he's not perfect, but she wants to be married and have kids more than anything. I think she felt like Derek was her last chance to have all that. It's very sad, but hopefully she is enjoying married life. I'll find out tonight."

"What about you?" he inquired. "Do you want to get married and have kids, too?"

I felt my eyes well up, and I was immediately grateful that Ted and I were talking on the phone and not in person. "Yes, I do. I'd love to have a lot of kids, but I need to find the right man first. Kids need a stable and loving home. I have seen how bad marriages can mess kids up, and I would never forgive myself if I hurt a child like that."

"I bet you've heard a lot of horror stories in your job."

"More than I ever imagined. Life can be pretty tragic, but I guess you know all about that." I paused and immediately regretted taking the conversation to such a depressing point. "I'm sorry, Ted. I didn't mean to be such a downer."

"I've been through some tough times, but I like to think there's a purpose for everything. Plus I don't want to always be thought of as that poor guy who lost his wife. I made the decision that I would be an example to Emma and show her that people can get through bad periods."

"Wow, are you always this positive?" I asked.

"I really try. It's doesn't always work, but I do try. One thing I learned is that life is short, and I want to enjoy myself as best I can so I try not to dwell on the negative."

"That's a great quality and quite the lesson you're giving Emma. What will you two do tonight?"

"I rented a movie for her, and I'll probably fall asleep on the couch. Another wild night in the Manning household."

"Well, I hope that my night is low key, too. I never know how these family dinners are going to turn out. My sister's husband is very unpredictable," I said.

"What does she see in him?" he asked.

"I wish I knew, but hopefully I'll be pleasantly surprised and they'll be just like every other newly married couple—happy and in love."

"Just like in the movies, huh?"

"If only life were that easy. I'm not sure even your positive attitude could help these two," not knowing how true those words would be.

Eighteen

I arrived at my mom's house right at seven and did not see Grace or Derek's car. I was glad to have a few moments to chat with my mother alone before they got there. I knocked and let myself in. "Mom, it's me Jane," I called out.

"In the kitchen, honey."

The homey warmth of cinnamon and apples greeted me, and before I even said hello, I peeked in the oven and confirmed that we were indeed being treated to Ruth's famous apple pie.

"That pie smells fabulous. I can't wait for dessert."

"Hello to you, too," she said giving me a wink.

"Sorry, Mom. It's been a long time since I had your pie, and you know how much I love it." I put a bottle of wine on the counter and gave her a huge hug. "How was your day? Still basking in the glow of your big evening?"

My mother smiled, and then as if coming to her senses, she said, "Now, enough of that. I just went on a date. It's not as if I'm getting married or anything. I suppose you told your sister all about it."

"I wanted to, but I can never get her on the phone. I hope they get here soon. I'm starved."

"Grace called, and they are running a little late. They should be here in ten minutes. You can help me mash the potatoes."

I grabbed an apron that was hanging in the pantry and put it on so I wouldn't end up wearing any of the dinner. While I poured the water out of the pot, my mother lifted the steaming roast out of the pan and as we set about finishing up the dinner, I noticed headlights shining into the dining room.

"I think they're here."

"Great," my mom replied, and we both went to the foyer to meet them.

I grabbed Grace and gave her a hug. "I'm so happy to see you." I put my arm around her shoulder and led her into the living room. "Hi, Derek," I said and tried to give him a light hug, but he pulled me in and held me for an uncomfortable few seconds. I managed to separate myself from him. I linked my arm with Grace's and said, "Dinner is just about ready. Let's put it on the table."

I studied Grace, and her face looked a bit drawn and tired. "You okay?" I whispered.

Grace smiled and said, "Sure. Just tired. I've been working a lot."

We gathered around the table and filled our plates in silence, and when I could stand it no more I asked, "What have you two been up to since you've been back from your honeymoon?"

"I've been working a lot and Derek has been redoing the den. Tell them about the remodeling project you're taking on."

"It's nothing really. I'm just building some shelves. I know that Grace loves to read, and I wanted her to have a place to keep her books," he said with downcast eyes.

"That's quite an impressive undertaking, Derek," my mother offered. "What other things have you built?"

"Just some small furniture. I used to have a job in a cabinetmaker's shop when I was a teenager, and I learned a lot," he replied as he shifted uncomfortably in his seat.

"I can't wait to see it. Grace, have you settled into your home yet?"

"Pretty much. Derek has been very thoughtful and has really gone out of his way to make me feel like it's my home, too."

"It is your home, Grace. I hate it when you act so weak. We're married and it's our home," Derek said stingingly.

"Sorry, Derek," Grace said simply.

This is not going well, I thought to myself. *We need a neutral subject.* Before I could say anything my mother rose and said, "Let me warm up this gravy," leaving me to deal with these two.

"Tell me about St. Thomas. I've never been."

Grace perked up and responded, "It is beautiful. The water is so clear you can see the bottom of the ocean. We went snorkeling, and the fish and coral are just breathtaking. Derek is certified in Scuba diving, and he had a great time, didn't you?"

"Yes," he answered tersely.

I tried to keep the conversation flowing and asked, "How long have you been certified, Derek? Do you get to dive much?"

"I did it in college, but only dove in lakes so there wasn't much to see. St. Thomas has some great reefs and I had fun exploring them. Do you dive, Jane?"

"No, I'm a bit claustrophobic, so I don't think I'd enjoy it. I have been snorkeling in Mexico and I loved it."

"You'd love diving, I bet," Derek said visibly more upbeat. "I bet you wouldn't feel claustrophobic at all. Once you get the hang of it, it feels very liberating. I could teach you," he offered hopefully.

My mother had settled herself back in her chair and asked, "Teach whom what?"

"I want to teach Jane how to scuba dive," Derek replied confidently.

My mother couldn't hide the confused look on her face. "I didn't know you wanted to learn to scuba dive, Jane?" she challenged.

"I don't," I replied uncomfortably looking from Grace to Derek, who both had forlorn expressions. "I mean, maybe one day. I appreciate the offer, Derek. I really do. Maybe Grace and I could take some lessons together. That might be fun. What do you think?" I asked Grace.

She relaxed a little and managed a smile. "I'd like that. It could be something you and I can do on vacations together, Derek. I'd love you to teach me how to ski, too. Derek is an expert skier, aren't you?" Grace boasted.

"Grace, you're being embarrassing."

"I'm just proud of you, and I want everyone to know what a great guy you are," she said sheepishly.

"Stop it, Grace. I don't need you to sell me to your family," he said as he stood and left the table.

"I'm sorry. Derek has been under a lot of stress at work, and he isn't himself."

We heard the front door slam and the sound of a car engine starting. I stood and looked out the dining room window.

"He's leaving, Grace. I can't believe he left with out saying a word. What—?"

My mother interrupted my tirade with, "Jane, enough. Grace, has this happened before?" she inquired calmly.

"No, he's gotten mad, but he's never walked out. I'm sure he just needed to blow off some steam and he'll be back soon," she said as if trying to convince herself, too.

My mother pulled up a chair next to Grace and said, "The first year of marriage is the hardest, kiddo."

"I know, Mom. He really is a good man. I just wish..." She stopped talking and started to cry. "Excuse me," she said as she walked toward the bathroom.

"Oh, Jane. This is awful. I thought maybe things would get better after they were married, but it doesn't seem that way," my mother lamented.

"Let me clear the table, and I'll make some tea. Hopefully Derek will return soon and we can put this behind us."

"You get the tea and I'll wash the dishes. I can't sit still right now."

We each gathered some plates and brought them into the kitchen. While we were working, Grace returned and asked, "Has Derek called?"

"No, hon," I answered. "Give him some time. He'll be back, soon."

We finished cleaning and I brought tea into the family room and handed Grace and my mother a cup.

"Why don't you call him, Grace?" I suggested.

Grace took a deep breath and grabbed the receiver from the table next to her. Slowly she dialed, and we watched while she waited for Derek to answer. She shook her head as she hung up the phone.

"Jane, would you mind giving me a ride home?" she asked numbly.

"Sure, but maybe you should just come home with me. I can sleep on the pull out sofa, and you can have my bed," I offered.

"No, I need to go home."

"Just for tonight, Grace."

"No, Jane," she said forcefully. "I can call a cab," she said.

"Don't do that. I'll get my coat and keys," I said wondering why she was so resolute in her defense of Derek, yet so meek when dealing directly with him.

I kissed my mother good-bye, and I overheard her tell Grace, "Call me if you need me. I'm always here for you, Grace."

I swallowed hard and went out to warm up the car. A moment later, Grace joined me. We rode in silence with Grace giving me directions, as I had not been to her house before. After ten minutes, she pointed to a cute brick ranch with Derek's truck parked in the driveway. I pulled in and turned off the engine.

"Maybe I should come in and talk to Derek with you."

"No, Jane. That would only make things worse," she said as she reached for the door.

"Wait, Grace. I'm worried about you. Derek scares me."

"Jane, please. I'll be fine. I need to go. The last thing I need is for Derek to think we are sitting out here discussing him."

"What else would we be discussing? He left you stranded at dinner," I stated disbelievingly.

"I embarrassed him, Jane, and I have to learn to respect his privacy. He is my husband, and I owe him that much. I have to go."

I watched her walk up to her front door and hoped to get a glimpse of Derek, but she went inside and disappeared from view. I sat there for a minute before starting the car and driving off. I guess the honeymoon was officially over.

Nineteen

Waiting for spring in New Hampshire seems like an eternity. April could be the longest month of the year, and though it had just started, I was ready for some warmer temperatures that usually surfaced toward the end of the month. I had not talked to Grace in the two weeks since our fateful dinner. I left her messages, but they had gone unreturned.

Ted and I spoke on the phone a few times a week, but had not spent any more time together. Jillian and I had made plans to go out on Saturday night, and on this exciting Friday, I was shopping for some much needed groceries. I was deciding which type of apple I wanted when I felt someone next to me. I was greeted by Emma's toothless grin.

"Hi there, Emma. Doing some shopping?" I asked playfully.

"Yes. Me and my dad are getting some things because we are having a special dinner tonight."

Just then, Ted joined us, pushing a cart with steaks and a bottle of wine. "Miss Richards, nice to see you again."

"Hello, Dr. Manning. I hear you're having an important dinner tonight," I said hoping the hint of jealousy I was feeling wasn't evident.

Ted replied, "Yes, we are having a very lovely lady join us tonight and I really wanted to make a good impression on her." He flashed me a self-satisfied smile.

"How nice for you," I replied, returning his amused expression.

"Yes," he continued. "She's visiting from out of town and she's staying an entire week."

Now, I was thrown a bit, and my face must have given me away as Ted went on, "Maybe she can come to the school and have lunch with you, Emma, and then she can meet Miss Richards."

"Grandma and I already talked about it. She's coming to have lunch with me on Monday," Emma stated knowingly.

I felt relief wash over me, but then I immediately felt a bit childish.

"I guess she set me straight," Ted said smugly.

"When does your grandma get here, Emma?" I inquired.

"She should be at our house when we get there, right Dad?" she asked.

Ted smiled and responded, "As soon as we get these groceries, we're going to go right home. My mom hasn't seen us since the holidays and she's coming for a visit."

"I can't wait to meet her, Emma. I'd better let you two get on with your shopping. I wouldn't want you to be late meeting your visitor."

Emma grabbed me around the waist, and I returned her hug.

"See you Monday, kiddo. Have a fun time with your grandmother. Goodbye, Dr. Manning."

~ * ~

I spent a quiet evening at home and was watching a movie that I had wanted to see when my phone rang. It was Ted, and I immediately started in questioning him about his guest. "Did your visitor arrive safely?"

"As a matter of fact she did and she is busy putting Emma to bed, so I have some time to talk. I need to see you, Jane."

"You certainly are direct," I laughed. "Did you have anything in mind?"

"Oh, I have a lot in mind where you are concerned, but I'd like to take you out to dinner tomorrow."

"I have plans, Ted. Jillian and I are going out," I said not disguising my regret.

"Can't you cancel?" he asked hopefully. "It's not easy for me to get away without Emma, and while my mom is here, I can spend my free time with you. Come on, what do you say? You know you want to..." he cajoled.

"You are as bad as my kindergarteners. Yes, I want to see you, but doesn't your mom want to be with you?" I asked.

"Sure, but she also comes to give me a break, and she would be thrilled to know that I'm dating again."

"I thought we were going to keep things quiet?" I asked in a panic.

"Relax, Jane. I haven't said a word to her or anyone. I made you a promise, and I am good to my word. She will just be happy that I'm going out, and she won't even ask about the details. So what do you say? Dinner tomorrow at a nice, out-of-the-way location?"

"Let me talk to Jillian, and I'll see what I can do."

I dialed Jillian's number and asked, "Would you mind terribly if I cancelled on you tomorrow?"

"That depends," she countered. "Do you have a better offer, or are you chickening out?"

"A better offer, but it's with a guy."

"Now, we're talking. Of course, I don't mind. Who is he? Give me the scoop."

"It's just someone I've met," I hedged, not wanting to bring Jillian into the web Ted and I were creating. "There are no juicy details to report, yet, but you will be the first to know if there are any."

"I'll be waiting anxiously. I'm glad for you, Jane. I was concerned that you might be getting involved with your student's father. That would have been nothing but trouble."

I winced at her words, but managed to reply, "You're right, and thanks for being such an understanding friend."

I hung up, and though I knew it was wrong, I didn't waste any time in dialing Ted's number.

"You win. I changed my plans."

Ted replied suggestively, "I'd like to think that we both won. I'll pick you up at seven."

"Where are we going?"

"Don't worry about the details. I'll take care of everything, and I promise we won't run into anybody we know."

"You know I am a bit of a control freak, but I'll trust you. How should I dress?"

"Casual is fine. Emma is calling me so I'd better go. See you tomorrow, Jane."

"Good night, Ted."

I sat back, closed my eyes, and tried to ignore Jillian's warning that kept replaying in my head. Instead I went to my closet and concentrated on finding just the right outfit for my date with Ted.

Twenty

I woke the next day full of energy and took a long run. I busied myself running errands and even got a manicure and pedicure. It was somewhat of an extravagance on my teacher's salary, but I was in such a fabulous mood and I wanted to treat myself. I took a long bubble bath and called Grace at home while I was enjoying my soak.

Derek answered, and after we said our hellos I asked, "Can I speak to Grace?"

"She can't come to the phone right now. What do you need, Jane?"

"I don't need anything, Derek. I just miss my sister and I wanted to talk to her. When would be a good time to call her?"

"I don't know, Jane. We are so busy," he said curtly.

In the background, I heard Grace ask Derek who was on the phone.

"It's your sister," I heard him say to her before returning his attention to me. "I guess Grace can talk after all," he said dryly.

"Hi, Jane. What's up?" Grace asked quietly.

"Nothing, I just wanted to talk. How are you?"

"I'm fine. Working a lot. What about you?" she asked sounding a little more at ease.

"Work is great, and my social life has picked up. I've been seeing that guy I told you about?"

"The father?" she asked.

"Yes. Grace, I really need someone to talk to about this. Can you meet me for lunch tomorrow?"

"I have to work, but you could come to the hospital and meet me in the cafeteria. The food is terrible, but it's the best I can do."

"I'll pick something up and bring it to you. What time?" I asked.

"Meet me at one. I'll wait outside the cafeteria, and we can sit in one of the lounges. You have to fill me in on Mom's new man, too. We never got a chance to talk about it," she said softly.

"We'll catch up tomorrow. See you then."

"Bye, Jane."

I was totally wired up when I got off the phone with Grace, and I couldn't decide what to wear. Finally, I chose a black pair of pants and a silk print blouse with a slightly revealing neckline and long, flowing sleeves. I pulled my hair up into a clip and then decided I looked too formal so I let it hang loose with my bangs brushed to the side. I had just finished putting the final touches on my lipstick when I heard the doorbell. My heart began to race, so I inhaled deeply and slowly exhaled as I opened the door. There stood Ted looking incredibly handsome with his cheeks slightly red from the cold, holding a bouquet of pink tulips.

"Come in," I said motioning to him.

He shut the door and gently grabbed my arm and pulled me to him. He gazed into my eyes for a moment as he touched my cheek, and then he kissed me, slowly and intensely, leaving me wanting more.

"I've been waiting all day for that," he said as he released me. "These are for you," he said handing me the flowers.

I composed myself while I went to the kitchen to put them in a vase.

"How did you manage to find tulips at this time of year? They're gorgeous," I gushed.

"I have my sources," he replied. "Are you ready to go?"

"Just let me get my coat."

I locked the door, and the cold air helped cool me down as we headed outside. Ted was very much the gentleman, and I felt very pampered as he helped me into his car. As we began our ride, I became more curious as to our destination.

"So, are you going to tell me where we're going?" I asked.

"Sure, we are going to Boston for lobster," he stated proudly.

"Wow, Boston. You certainly picked an out-of-the-way location." I laughed.

"I'm willing to do whatever it takes. Besides, Boston is one of my favorite cities and I wanted to share it with you. Do you like lobster?"

"I love it. When I was little, my dad and I would go to the wharf and pick up lobsters for the Fourth of July. It was one of our family traditions. We would go to the

Square after dinner and watch the fireworks. Did I tell you that my dad was a firefighter?"

"No, you didn't. Is that how he died?" Ted asked hesitantly.

"Yes, he was putting out a house fire. He went in to get a child, and he never came out." I paused a moment as I recalled how proud he was of his job. "He was a great guy—always smiling," I added as I wondered what my dad would think of Ted. They were very similar—strong men with optimistic outlooks on life. "I still miss him."

Ted reached over and held my hand as we rode the rest of the way in comfortable silence.

Twenty-one

The next day, I slept in, and after a long run in the park, I showered and dressed for lunch with my sister. I picked up some salads and sandwiches from a new, upscale market that had opened near the hospital and made my way through the unfamiliar hallways in search of the cafeteria. As I turned the corner, Grace was standing outside the cafeteria doors talking to a young woman who appeared to be another nurse.

"Hey, there," I said as I approached them.

"Hi, Jane," Grace said while giving me a hug. "Jane, this is my friend, Charlotte. Charlotte, this is my sister, Jane."

We exchanged greetings, and Grace said, "See you after lunch, Charlotte. Follow me, Jane," she directed. "There's a small lounge just down the hall. There's never anyone in there so we can talk uninterrupted."

There was a small table in the corner. I set out all of the food, and we sat down. I looked at Grace and thought she looked haggard. "How are you, Grace? Are you getting enough rest?" I inquired.

"I'm fine. I have been working a lot and..."

"And what? Is it Derek?" I asked trying to control the panic in my voice.

"Yes, I mean no. It's just getting adjusted to married life. It's different than I imagined, and it's taking some getting used to."

"Can I do anything to help?"

"Thanks, but I need to handle things on my own. Besides, didn't you want to do the talking today?"

"Yes, but I'm concerned about you." I waited to see if Grace would open up with me, but she kept quiet, so I dropped the subject. "I'm so glad you could meet me for lunch. I really needed someone to talk to about this," I said taking a bite of my turkey club sandwich.

"I take it you two have been dating?" Grace asked.

I shrugged. "Sort of. We agreed to just get together as friends until the school year ends, but last night he took me to Boston for lobster and we walked and talked and... I had an amazing time, but I'm scared."

"Of getting caught?" she asked.

"Yes, but it's more than that. I mean, there's only six more weeks of school, and we are being very discreet. It's him—Ted. He's wonderful. He's kind and gentle and funny and he has such an optimistic outlook," I gushed.

"And the problem would be?"

"He frightens me, Grace," I admitted as I felt tears form.

"What are you afraid of?" she asked calmly as she handed me a napkin to dry my cheeks.

I took a deep breath and said, "Everything. I'm afraid that I won't measure up to his wife, I'm afraid Emma will hate me when she finds out her dad and I are dating, I'm afraid that I'm falling for him, I'm afraid that I'm going to get hurt again," I said, sobbing.

"Whoa, you've been on overload, haven't you? Just let it out," she encouraged.

I wept for a while and finally composed myself. Grace handed me a bottle of water she had retrieved from the vending machine, and I gratefully took a few sips.

"I'm so sorry. I can't believe I just fell apart like that."

"Don't be sorry. Let's talk about all of these things. First, what is bothering you the most?"

I closed my eyes and admitted, "I'm scared that I'm going to get hurt again."

"Oh, Jane," she said as she rose to hug me. "There are no guarantees in life. Sometimes you just have to take a chance." Grace returned to her seat and handed me more napkins.

"I know. It's just that Nick really broke my heart. I had confided in him about Michael, and he promised me that he would never hurt me. I believed him," I said sadly.

"You've had two very bad experiences, Jane, but you can't let that paralyze you. Have you told Ted anything about Nick or Michael?"

"No, he's knows I left New York because of a breakup, but we haven't discussed any details. We aren't at that stage, yet. We've only had a few dates, but last night was one of the best evenings I've ever had. I can really see this going somewhere, but I'm not sure I can do it."

"I think you just need to take things slowly and build trust between the two of you. You haven't slept with him yet, have you?" she asked cautiously.

"No, but I want to. I made a pledge to myself to wait until school is out, and I'm no longer Emma's teacher. But, I really want to." I laughed.

"Remember, take it easy and if it's meant to be, it will all work out. And as far as competing with his wife, you either have to deal with it or walk away. Her memory will always be with them, and you can't change that."

"I know that, but I guess I have no self-confidence."

"Jane, you are a very strong woman. You've just been burned, but you need to move forward. Just be yourself and listen to your heart and your head," she advised.

"You're right, it's just that Ted and I will be talking and Annie's name comes up and I get a pang of jealousy. Can you imagine? I'm jealous of a dead woman. You know, you are the only one I would ever admit that to."

"It's a natural reaction, Jane."

"I guess, but I still feel like a terrible person," I confessed.

"Take it from me, you are not a terrible person. You're just overwhelmed. Tell me more about your date last night."

"It was really sweet. He brought me flowers and took me a small restaurant in Boston on the water. We had lobster and champagne, and after dinner, we walked around Faneul Hall and listened to a jazz band while we had coffee and dessert. He's so open and easy to talk to, Grace. I've never met anyone like him before."

"He sounds special, Jane," she agreed.

"Then he drove me around town and showed me where he went to high school and the house he grew up in. He is so eager to share himself with me. It's all so new and different," I confided.

"Did you make plans to see him again?" she asked.

"He's going to call later. He wants to come by my apartment tonight after he puts Emma to bed. His mother is visiting, and he can leave her to baby-sit."

"Be careful," she cautioned. "Sounds like it will be an opportunity to take this to the next level."

"I know. I need to discuss my feelings about waiting with Ted so he knows where I stand." I sighed and said, "I feel so much better, Grace. Thank you. I really needed this. Can I do anything for you?" I asked.

"I'm fine. Really. It's like Mom said, 'The first year is the toughest.' Everything will work out." Then she added cryptically, "Hopefully sooner than later."

Twenty-two

My time with Grace gave me a lot to think about. I was waiting for Ted to arrive and was trying to compose my thoughts. I felt very clear and confident about how I wanted our relationship to progress and hoped to convey my feelings to Ted in a rational and tearless manner.

The doorbell rang, and a wave of exhilaration swept over me. I opened the door and invited Ted in. He handed me a bottle of wine before removing his coat. I put the bottle down and he pulled me to him and kissed me. His kisses left me weak and breathless. I stepped back and said, "I'm glad you're here."

"Me, too," he replied as he reached for me and kissed me again before folding me into him. I felt very secure in his arms, and although I instantly recalled that feeling of euphoria that often accompanies new relationships, I still held back. I wondered if I would ever be totally comfortable with Ted.

"Let me get some wine glasses. The stereo is in the corner of the living room, Ted. Why don't you put something on?"

I returned with glasses in hand and recognized the bluesy jazz sounds of one of my favorite stations. "Great music choice," I smiled. "Did you do anything fun with your mom and Emma today?"

"We did. We went to the aquarium in Newport. It was a gorgeous day out and it was perfect for a drive. Have you ever been?" he asked.

"To Newport? Yes, but not the aquarium. I miss going to museums and places like that. I'll have to check it out."

"Maybe we could go together," he offered.

"Maybe," I replied, returning his playful tone. I took a sip of wine and relaxed into the couch.

"What did you do today?" he asked.

"I went running and took care of some errands and then I had lunch with my sister."

"How is she? Are you still concerned about her?"

I decided that I was ready to start confiding in Ted about certain aspects of my life to build some more trust between us. "I'm extremely worried. She looks awful— tired and worn. I thought newlyweds were supposed to be glowing."

"Is she sick?" he asked with genuine concern.

"I asked her and she is a nurse, so I don't think it's physical. I think it's him. He's awful."

"You mean her husband?"

"I'm sorry, yes, her husband. His name is Derek, and he treats her terribly. The last time we all had dinner at my mother's house, he left her there. Can you believe it? He got mad and just left without saying anything to us," I said angrily.

"Has he done that before?" he asked.

"Left her? No, but he's very condescending and he makes mean remarks to her. It seems like he enjoys having the control—the upper hand. You know what I mean?"

"It sounds like he's abusive to her. Does she realize it?"

"Sort of. I know that's a stupid answer, but it's almost as if she knows his behavior is wrong, but she makes excuses for him. The night of dinner, she said that she embarrassed him and that was why he left her."

"She blames herself for his behavior. That is sad. What does your mother have to say?" Ted asked.

"She and I have talked about it many times, but we're really unable to do anything. It's so difficult," I sighed.

"Do you think he's hurting her, I mean physically?"

"I don't think so. I don't know, really. I haven't seen any signs of it."

"I'm so sorry, Jane. I wish I could do something to help."

"You are," I smiled. "Just having someone to talk with about it helps."

"I'm here whenever you need me," he said as he reached over and pulled me toward him.

He held me for a long time and just stroked my hair. I succumbed to his embrace and closed my eyes as I let myself accept his comfort. Then he gently pulled back and lifted my chin toward him. He brushed his lips against mine. I stared into his eyes as he took my face in his hands and kissed me again, this time with deep desire. Arousal stirred in me and I returned his kisses just as passionately.

Ted leaned back pulling me on top of him, and I realized I needed to stop now or I'd regret it.

I pulled away and said, "Ted, I can't."

He looked confused and asked, "Can't what?"

"I can't move this fast. I need us to slow down."

"It was just a kiss, Jane," he said coyly.

"Yes, I know, but it could have very easily turned into something more."

"Like what?" he asked playing dumb.

"You know where we're headed, but I need to wait. I need to be sure."

"Sure of what?" Ted asked.

"Sure of myself. I've made some bad choices before, and I've jumped into relationships too quickly. I've been hurt a lot," I said quietly.

"I told you I'm not like that, Jane."

"I know, it's just that..."

"This guy in New York told you the same thing, right?" Ted asked, finishing my thought for me.

"Yes," I replied softly.

"I'm going to prove to you that I am different, Jane. I've been hurt, too. I know what it feels like to have your world come crashing down. I also know that the hurt doesn't last forever."

"I know that. I'm just scared, Ted."

"What happened in New York, Jane?"

I hesitated and finally admitted, "Nick and I were living together and had planned to get married. One day I came home early from work, and I found him in our bed with a woman he worked with."

"Ouch. That's horrible, Jane, but people get through much worse. In a minute, I lost everything. My wife, the mother of my child, my future... and I'm willing to put myself out there with you. You've got to get past this. I'm not a kid, anymore. I want someone in my life again and..." He hesitated and continued, "I'd like it to be you, but you have to try and trust me."

"You're right, and I want to pursue a relationship with you, but the other thing is my job. I am Emma's teacher, and for the next few weeks we need to be cautious. And after that kiss, I wasn't sure I could restrain myself."

"Really? Well, then my hope has been restored."

"I want to see what develops between us, Ted. Really, I do. Let's just spend this time getting to know each other, and then when school gets out..."

"When school gets out," he interrupted, "we're leaving caution behind us."

Twenty-three

Springtime in New Hampshire was like being reborn. After all the snow and cold, it was refreshing to be able to enjoy the outdoors. I was running on a regular basis, and at school, the kids and I were both enjoying the freedom of recess. As the school year was winding down, my workload increased. There were evaluations to be done, papers to be filled out, and though I would return to the same classroom, it had to be packed up for cleaning during the summer. Ted and I had fallen into somewhat of a routine. We spoke nightly, after Emma was in bed, and we learned a great deal about each other. We told each other stories from our childhood and college lives. We laughed a lot, and I felt myself truly opening up to him, but had yet to tell him about Michael. I had made that mistake with Nick and didn't know if I would ever be able to share that part of me with Ted.

In two weeks, Ted and I would be able to date openly, and while I was eagerly awaiting the freedom, I was a little sad that we would have let others into our world. The time we spent together was so perfect that part of me didn't want to see it end. I did realize, though, that we could not go on like that forever, but I was nervous about telling Emma. We had to proceed with caution where she was concerned.

I wanted to talk with Grace again. It had helped so much last time, and I wanted her advice on telling people about Ted and me. I had tried to call her several times, but she hadn't returned my calls. I decided to stop by my mom's house and see if she had spoken to Grace. I pulled in the driveway behind a car I didn't recognize. I knocked on the door, let myself in and called out to my mother. I heard her giggle and tried to suppress a smile as she appeared to fix her hair before she came out of the kitchen.

"Hi, Jane. What a nice surprise."

"Hi, Mom. I stopped by to see if you heard from Grace. Am I disturbing something?" I asked mischievously.

"No, you are not disturbing anything," she said with unconvincing indignation. "Lawrence is here for dinner. Come in the kitchen and say hello."

Lawrence was seated at the kitchen table with a glass of white wine. He stood to greet me and said, "Hello there, Jane. It's good to see you again."

"Hi, Lawrence. It's good to see you, too. I'm sorry to interrupt your dinner."

"You're not interrupting us at all. It's nice to have a few minutes to talk with you. How was your day?" he asked with genuine interest.

"It was fine thanks. I teach kindergarten and we have two weeks left, so the kids are bouncing off the wall. Do you work, Lawrence?"

"I'm retired, but I spend some time doing volunteer work. I deliver Meals on Wheels twice a month and I have three grandchildren that keep me busy," he replied.

"How nice. Are your kids close by?" I asked.

"My son and his wife live about fifteen minutes away in Manchester. My wife and I only had Randall."

"Well, then it's good that he's not far. I like being close to family, myself. Speaking of which, Mom have you spoken to Grace lately?"

"She usually calls me about once a week, so I actually haven't called her in a while. Why don't you try her now? I wanted to invite you both to dinner next Friday so that Grace could meet Lawrence."

I rose, grabbed the phone off the wall, and dialed Grace's cell phone. I was informed by a recording that the number I was trying to reach was disconnected. "That's strange," I said.

"What's strange?" my mother asked.

"Nothing, I must have dialed the wrong number. What's Grace's cell phone number?" My mother called it out and I redialed, but got the same message. "Her cell phone has been disconnected. She must have lost it or something. I've done that before. Do you think she's at work?"

"She should be. Why don't you try her there? I have the number in my book on the table by the phone in the living room."

I found the number and dialed.

"Hello, can I speak with Grace Richards? I mean, Meade. Grace Meade."

"I'm sorry. She no longer works here. Can I help you with something?"

"What do you mean she no longer works there?" I asked unbelievingly.

"She left last week. Is this a personal matter?"

"I'm sorry. Yes, it is. I'm Grace's sister, and I'm just confused. Did she transfer to another department?" I asked.

"I don't think so. I haven't been here long, but I think she quit. I wish I could be more help," she offered.

"Is there someone there who may have some more information? What about her friend... I can't remember her name. She's petite with short black hair."

"Do you mean Charlotte?" she asked.

"Yes, that's her name. Is she working today?"

"She is, but she's with a patient right now. Can I take your number and have her call you?"

"Yes, please."

I returned to the kitchen and my mother asked, "Did you get her?"

Deciding it would be better not to worry Mom until I had spoken with Charlotte and knew more, I said, "No, she wasn't at work. Why don't you call her at home later? Derek won't pull anything with you."

"Why? Has he been giving you trouble?" she asked with concern.

"He just gives me the creeps, that's all. Anyway, call me when you hear from her. I'm pretty tired, and I'm going to head on home."

"Are you sure, honey? There's plenty of food," my mom offered.

"Thanks, anyway. I'll be here Friday. Just let me know the details. See you then, Lawrence," I said as I gave my mom a hug.

I drove home with my cell phone on the console next to me, so I wouldn't miss Charlotte's call. As I pulled into my parking space, the ringing of the phone startled me.

"Hello?"

"Jane? This is Charlotte Jennings."

"Charlotte, thanks for calling me back. I'm concerned about Grace. What happened with work?"

"She quit last week. She said Derek needed her at home."

"Needed her? What did she mean by that?" I asked.

"She said that when she was working she didn't have enough time to focus on Derek. She's been strange ever since they got married."

"How do you mean?"

"Well..." Charlotte said then paused before adding, "She's been quiet, almost depressed. It's just not how you would expect a newlywed to act."

"Did you ever talk to her about it?" I asked.

"Not much. She stopped confiding in me after I tried to talk her out of marrying Derek. It upset her, and we started to grow apart after that."

"Why did you try to talk her out of marrying him?"

"Can I be frank?" she asked cautiously.

"Yes. I am not a fan of Derek's, so please tell me everything," I commanded.

"I don't trust him. You have to see the way he flirts with the women around here. It goes way beyond the typical salesman schmoozing. Even after they were engaged, he kept it up right in front of Grace. It's like he has no respect for her at all and she just makes excuses for him."

"I know what you mean. He constantly makes disparaging remarks about her," I added.

"I said that to Grace. I told her that I thought he treated her terribly and if he acted that way before they married, it would only get worse afterwards. She became very upset with me and said that I didn't understand Derek. After that, the subject of Derek was off limits. I came to the wedding because I didn't want to lose Grace as a friend, but it killed me to see her go through with it."

"Oh, believe me I felt the same way. Now, I'm scared that she's cutting herself off from everyone," I replied.

"I just hope it's not Derek who's trying to cut her off from all of us," Charlotte said ominously.

Twenty-four

I wasn't surprised that I never heard from Grace, but nonetheless I was worried. I kept the news from my mother until I was sure what, if anything, I was going to do about it. I was anxious to meet up with Ted and get his advice. We agreed to meet for an early dinner while Emma was with her grandparents. Ted chose an out-of-the-way place that looked rather shabby, but was supposed to have incredible seafood. I scanned the restaurant and saw that he was already seated. He rose, and as he tried to kiss me, I offered him my cheek.

"Sorry, I'm not totally at ease when we're out in public."

"Who cares?" he asked, obviously a bit irritated. "There's two weeks of school left. Nobody knows us here."

"I'm sorry, Ted," I said as I reached for his hand. "I've been a bit preoccupied with my sister, and it's had me on edge. Let's order, and I'll fill you in. I really want to talk to you about it."

We placed our order. When our drinks arrived, I took a sip and said, "That's better. How are you?"

"I'm great, but just impatient. These are going to be the longest two weeks of my life."

"I know, but the end is in sight. We're almost in the clear." I smiled.

"I know. I'll stop my whining. Tell me about your sister. What's going on?"

"She quit her job. It really has me worried. She didn't tell anyone she was doing this, and I can't get in touch with her and I'm so afraid that Derek is trying to isolate her from everyone."

"Jane, it can't be that bad. Do you know why she would quit her job?" he asked softly.

"I spoke to a friend of hers who said that Derek wanted her to stay home because she needed to devote more time to him. Grace told her friend that she wasn't being a good wife to Derek and she needed to quit her job," I said sadly.

"Maybe she's pregnant and he wants her to stay home to be a mom," he replied hopefully.

"She would have told me if she was pregnant. Plus she won't return any of my calls. And her cell phone has been disconnected. What should I do, Ted? I'm frightened for her."

"Right now, you need to relax. Try to call her at home again. Try when her husband is at work. If she doesn't answer, go to her house and find out what's going on. It's probably nothing."

"You're right. It's just that I don't trust Derek at all, and I'm worried that Grace is not standing up to him," I said wiping a tear from my eye.

Ted moved his chair closer to me and caressed my cheek. "It will be okay, Jane. I hate seeing you upset."

"I'm sorry to be such a wreck today. It's just that Grace and I have just sort of found each other again, and I feel like I'm losing her."

"I can go to her house with you. Would that help?"

"It might. I'm okay—just needed someone to talk to about it. Thanks for listening," I said.

"Jane, you don't have to thank me. I was hoping we were closer than that."

I smiled. "We are. I just want you to know that I appreciate you."

Just then, the waiter appeared with our salads and I was able to relax and enjoy the evening. When we were finished eating, Ted called and checked on Emma.

"She's not ready to be picked up, yet. Let's go for a walk. It's a beautiful night."

"Sure, that sounds great," I replied.

We strolled along the sidewalk, and Ted reached for my hand. Normally, I would have pulled away, but Ted was always telling me not to worry about being seen so I squeezed his hand and leaned into him as we walked.

"Let's walk down to the water," Ted suggested.

We walked in silence and stopped at the end of the boardwalk and rested against the railing. Ted leaned over and kissed me, and I returned his kisses freely. Ted held me for a moment as I rested my head against his chest, and I wished I could capture that feeling of utter contentment forever. I lifted my head to kiss him again, but felt someone looking at me. I turned; staring at me was my principal and boss, Philip Samuels, and his wife. They had apparently been shopping and must have noticed us as they left the store.

Ted followed my gaze and muttered, "Shit."

I was frozen a second and then smiled and waved. Philip didn't return the favor, but instead nodded his head in a form of dismissal as he and his wife walked off in the opposite direction.

I sat down on the bench and said, "I can't believe this. What am I going to do?" I cried. I thought a minute and said excitedly, "Maybe he doesn't know who you are. There are hundreds of kids at school, and surely he doesn't know all of the parents. This could be no big deal."

"Jane, Philip knows me. He's been a patient for years," Ted admitted.

"What? He's a patient of yours? Are you kidding me? I can't believe you never said anything. So, he knows Emma is in my class, then. What were you thinking, Ted?" I shrieked.

"Jane, calm down," Ted said as he reached for my arm.

I pulled away, "Calm down! My boss just caught me kissing the father of one of my students. Do you realize how much trouble I am in?" I buried my face in my hands and cried.

"Jane, it will be okay. I will talk to Philip and explain."

"Explain? Explain what? What we did was wrong—there's nothing to explain. I just hope he doesn't fire me. Why didn't you tell me he was a patient? I thought I could trust you," I said sadly.

"Oh, God, Jane. You can trust me. I never thought this would happen. I didn't mean to keep it from you. I was so happy to have you in my life, and I thought if you knew about Philip, you wouldn't continue seeing me. I'm sorry. It was totally selfish," he added dejectedly.

I was not ready to forgive him. "I need to go home, Ted. Please take me home."

We were silent on the ride home, and when we arrived at my apartment, Ted parked the car and closed his eyes as he leaned against the headrest. He took a deep breath and said, "Jane, just listen to me for a minute. I'm sorry I hurt you, but I'm not sorry that we are together. I love you, Jane."

I started to speak, and he put his fingers to my lips. "Let me finish. I never thought I'd fall in love again, but I did. I just knew we could have something special together and we would have missed out if I had told you about Philip. We'll get through this," he said. Without responding, I got out of the car and slowly made my way to my apartment.

Twenty-five

I felt like a child again. Scared—just wanting someone to come in and make it all better. I didn't sleep at all that night and left for work earlier than normal so that I could meet with Philip before the school day started. I couldn't teach an entire day with this hanging over my head. I was so early that Philip's secretary hadn't arrived, but I hoped that Philip would be in his office. The door was shut, and I knocked tentatively. Philip came to the door, and when he saw me, he said, "I've been expecting you."

I went in and was surprised to see Ted sitting there. "Have a seat," Philip offered. I sat down and immediately felt like crying, but I was determined to maintain my composure and take my punishment like an adult.

Philip said, "Ted and I were just getting started talking, Jane. Who would like to start?"

At the same time, Ted and I both said, "I would." I looked at Ted and said, "Let me. Philip, Ted and I have been dating for a few months now. I knew going in that it was wrong and I did it anyway."

"Philip, there's more to it than that. Circumstances kept bringing us together, and we realized that we have a lot in common. We agreed to be friends, but it's turning into more than that. Jane has always been adamant about not compromising her job, and I've been the one who has been pushing for more. If anyone is to blame, it's me," Ted said quietly.

"I'm a grown-up, Ted, and no one forced me to be with you. I will say that I have never done anything like this before. I never even dated a co-worker, Philip. You have to believe that I never allowed my relationship with Ted to affect any aspect of my job. I am a good teacher, and I did not let my personal life interfere with my job." I took a deep breath and let it out. I was relieved that I was able to communicate without falling apart.

"I realize that these things happen, but, Jane, you put me in a bad position and I can't let it go. Ted, I think I need to talk with Jane alone please," Philip said as he stood to let Ted out.

Ted rose and squeezed my shoulder as he left. Philip closed the door after him and sat in the chair next to me. "Jane, I have known Ted for years and I know that he is an upstanding kind of man. He has had a hard road and I am happy that he has found you, but you clearly violated our code of ethics. The fact that it is your first year with us makes it tougher. You have no track record with us, and though I believe you when you say that nothing like this has ever happened before..."

"I know. We have been really careful, and I'm sure no one from school has seen us together," I rationalized.

"That's not the point. The point is that you broke the rules, and as your boss, I need to take some sort of action.

I am just not certain what that is yet. Come see me at the end of the day and we'll talk again."

I wanted to ask if I was going to lose my job, but part of me felt it was better not to even put that idea out there. Ted was waiting in the hall for me, and I told him, "I have to come back after school."

"Should I talk to him some more?" Ted asked.

"No, I think we should let it go until Philip and I talk this afternoon."

"Jane, just so you know, I told Philip that I am serious about you. This is not some fling—I am in this relationship for the long haul, and I am not going anywhere. You need to know that, too." He turned to go and added, "I'll be waiting to hear from you."

Slowly I walked to my classroom. Mattie was with Emma. Emma ran up and hugged me, "Hi, Miss Richards. I got to ride to school with Mrs. Pritchard today, and I get to be her special helper until the other kids get here."

"How fun for you, kiddo," I said trying to get my head together for the day.

Mattie said, "Emma, take these to the library for me." When Emma left, she asked, "Ted called me last night to ask me to take her to school with me, but didn't elaborate. I saw him in the hall outside Philip's office. What's going on? Is something wrong with Emma?" she asked nervously.

"Emma's fine. Let's have lunch in the room today, and we'll talk in private."

~ * ~

I tried to be relaxed and focused that morning, and after we took the kids to the cafeteria, Mattie and I sat down to eat and talk. I took a bite of my tuna salad and realized that I was not hungry at all. I pushed my tray aside and dove right into the speech I had been preparing all morning. "Mattie, Ted Manning and I have been dating, and this weekend Philip saw us. The three of us met this morning, and I have to go see Philip again this afternoon to discuss my disciplinary action. I'm so sorry if I let you down. I know it was wrong. It just happened and if I could change it, I would. I don't think I short-changed any of the kids because of my relationship with Ted. Philip may ask you about it—just be honest." I wiped my eyes with a napkin and swallowed hard so that I would not start crying.

Mattie looked me in the eyes and asked, "Is it serious between you and Ted?"

I nodded and said, "We've been taking it slowly because of my job, but he told me he loves me."

"Do you love him?"

I thought a moment and said, "Yes, I do but..."

"Jane, that's all I need to know. Ted Manning deserves some happiness and so do you."

"That's it? That's all you have to say about it?" I asked disbelievingly.

"Yes, Jane. You've become like a daughter to me, and I want you to be happy. As far as your teaching ability goes, these kids are lucky to be in your class, and I'll tell that to Philip or anyone else who needs to hear it."

I rose and gave her a hug. "Thanks, Mattie. You're the best."

"Why don't you go fix your makeup so the kids don't ask what's wrong with you," she ordered. I did just what I was told, and for the rest of the day, I was much more relaxed. That is until dismissal time arrived and I had to make a return visit to the principal's office. The secretary told me to go in, and Philip asked me to close the door.

My hands became clammy, and I realized that I had never been this nervous before. Philip once again came and sat next to me. "Jane, I looked into this, and there really isn't anything that directly relates to your situation. It pretty much comes down to my judgment, and I feel that you definitely crossed the line. That being said, I did call your former boss and inquire as to whether or not you had mixed your school and private life, and I was assured that you exhibited the utmost decorum. Since there have been no other issues and since there are less than two weeks left in the school year, I am willing to be lenient. I have written this incident up, and it will be a part of your personnel record. If after three years, there are no major incidents of any kind, I will remove it. Fair enough?"

I couldn't hold back the tears any longer. "Thank you," I cried.

"And one more thing, Jane. I'd appreciate if you and Ted stayed away from each other until the last day of school."

"Definitely. And Philip—I won't let you down."

Twenty-six

That evening I knew I had to call Ted, but I kept putting it off. I needed to sort out my feelings. I was initially angry that he didn't tell me about Philip, but now that it had all worked out it didn't seem like such a big deal. Trust was such a big issue with me, and I wasn't sure I could fully trust Ted. Was I making too much out of this, or was it a warning? My confusion was interrupted by the telephone, and at once I knew it must be Ted.

"Hello?" I answered.

"Jane, I've been waiting for you to call," Ted said somberly.

"I'm sorry, Ted. I've just been trying to sort some things out. First, let me tell you that I did not get fired. Philip gave me a written reprimand that will be a part of my personnel record for the next three years. If I have no other problems at the end of three years, it will be removed."

"That's great, Jane. I'm so happy."

"Me, too. Today was one of the most nerve-wracking days of my life."

"Jane, I'm sorry for not telling you about Philip. I honestly didn't think anyone would ever find out about us. Plus, I wanted to be with you so badly, I wasn't thinking straight. Please tell me you understand," he begged.

I hesitated and then said, "I do understand, but I trusted you, and now I have doubts. The other law Philip laid down is that we are not to see each other until school is finished for the year. Frankly, I'm grateful for the time. I need to do some thinking."

Ted was silent, then said, "Jane, I'm sorry I hurt you, but I will do whatever it takes to earn your trust back."

"I'm so wary because I've been hurt before."

"I know you have and I'm sorry that I have caused you pain, but I am going to prove to you that I am one of the good guys. I will take care of you, Jane." Ted paused, then added, "If you'll let me."

~ * ~

The time away from Ted as well as a chat with an old friend from New York who was a counselor helped me clear my head. Ellen worked at the school in New York with me and was so objective and unemotional—it was just what I needed. She had pointed out that when Ted and I were able to go public with our relationship, I would get more of a sense of his character. Seeing Ted deal with people and situations would shed a lot of light on the kind of man he was. Her parting words were to take it slowly.

Ted and I still spoke on the phone nightly, and I was once again warming up to him. He had sent me a long, romantic note reiterating his commitment to me and our relationship, and by the end of the week, I was missing him terribly. I was looking forward to dinner at my mother's, and with everything that had been going on, I never followed up with Grace. My mother had spoken to her, and she and Derek were planning on attending.

I arrived at my mom's right on time and noticed that I was the first one there. I was glad and thought that maybe I could have some time alone to talk with my mother about Ted. I found my mother in the kitchen. The familiar aroma of freshly baked bread brought back memories of my childhood.

"Hi, Mom. That bread smells heavenly. It always makes me think of snow days. Whenever we had a day off, you made bread."

"I can't believe you remembered that," she said, smiling. "How about helping me with the salad?" she asked.

"Sure."

I assembled a pile of carrots, red onion and cucumbers and began chopping. "Mom, I want to tell you something."

"What's wrong?" she asked with a look of concern.

"Nothing's wrong. I've been dating someone, and I wanted to fill you in."

"Oh, is that all? You sounded so grim, you scared me. So, who is he and when can I meet him?" she asked.

"His name is Ted Manning, but it's complicated. His daughter is in my class."

I waited for a response, and when I didn't get one I asked, "Aren't you going to say anything?"

"Jane, you are a grown up and I assume you know the risks or you wouldn't have told me it was complicated."

"I do. I didn't plan for this to happen," I said softly.

"Is it serious between you two?"

"I think it will be. We are waiting until school gets out to go public, and we'll just see. He's a good man, and I'd like you to meet him soon."

Just then the doorbell rang. "That must be Lawrence," she said, and that was the end of our discussion for now. I felt somewhat lighter now that I had made my confession at home and at work, but had hoped my mother would give encouragement without any hint of judgment. I was wondering how old I would be before I stopped needing my mother's approval when Lawrence appeared with my mother back in the kitchen.

"Hi, Lawrence. It's great to see you again."

"Hello, Jane. I'm happy to see you, too."

"Hopefully, Grace will be here soon. Have you spoken to her lately?" she asked me.

"No. She hasn't returned my phone calls. Did she say anything to you?"

"About what?"

"She quit her job."

"She quit her job?" she repeated in disbelief.

"Yes. I tried to call her and I spoke to her friend, Charlotte, who told me that Grace quit to stay home and be a better wife to Derek."

My mother sat down, and Lawrence immediately came to her side.

"I'm sure it's fine, Ruth. Let's not jump to any conclusions."

Just then we heard the doorbell. The front door opened. We all went to greet Grace and Derek and I immediately noticed that Grace had lost weight. Normally it would have been a good thing for her to lose a few pounds, but she looked awful. There were bags under her eyes, and she just looked worn out. She needed a haircut and didn't have any makeup on. I was greatly troubled at seeing her like this and was unsure as to what to say.

After our greetings and introductions, we all sat in the living room and had a drink and some cheese and crackers. I figured I might as well jump in and asked, "Grace, did you really quit your job?"

She immediately looked panicked, and Derek asked, "How did you know? Are you checking up on us?"

"No, I'm not. I have been trying to get in touch with you, Grace," I said, trying to leave Derek out of the conversation. "Your cell phone has been disconnected, and you haven't returned any of my calls. I called the hospital, and Charlotte told me you quit."

"Sorry. Since I'm not working we cut some things out of our budget, and my cell phone was one of them," she said meekly.

"Why did you quit?" my mother asked pointedly.

"She quit because she wanted to be a good wife, that's why," Derek replied. "There's no mystery, here." He was obviously agitated as he stood and poured himself another glass of scotch.

A nervous-looking Grace tried to change the subject. "Lawrence, are you from Wilmington?"

I was lost in my own thoughts as I contemplated what to do about Grace. I needed to approach her and thought maybe we could talk while we did the dishes. We all sat down to dinner, and the conversation was strained, but pleasant. I noticed that Derek had three drinks before dinner and another during dinner. By the end of the meal, he was getting a bit sloppy. I stood to clear the table and said, "Mom, I'm going to put on some coffee. Grace and I will do the dishes."

The others returned to the living room, and while Grace and I were in the kitchen alone, I came right out and asked. "What is going on? Why did you quit your job?"

"I needed to devote more time to Derek. We were having some rough times, and I thought it would help if I could focus solely on Derek."

"Whose idea was it for you to quit?" I challenged.

"What difference does it make?"

"A lot. Did Derek want you to quit?" I pressed.

"Yes, but I was happy to do it, Jane. I want to make it work with him."

"But it's like he's cutting you off from all of us. Why didn't you return my calls?"

"I forgot. Really you are making too much of this. I promise I will get back to you promptly the next time you call."

"I want you to get your cell phone back. Get one, and I'll pay for it."

"Jane, it's not necessary. You need to stop now. Please." She looked desperate.

"Just promise me that you will keep in touch with me. Promise me, Grace. Promise or I'll say something to Derek." Now I was the one who was desperate.

Tears brimmed in her eyes, and she whispered, "I promise."

Twenty-seven

The last two weeks of school flew by. I had so much work to do in order to close out the school year, but with diligence and help from Mattie, I managed to get it all accomplished. I had to clean up my room and store everything for the summer, and that had to wait until all of the children were gone.

The last day of school finally arrived, and it was extremely bittersweet. I had grown to love the kids in my class, and letting them go was going to be tough. My eyes welled up any time I thought about it. Saying good-bye would be difficult, but I was so proud of all that they had accomplished. Many of them were reading and doing simple math. They worked so hard, and I was so pleased at their progress.

On that final Friday, we had a shortened day and spent most of it outside, playing four-square and blowing bubbles. When it was time for dismissal, I put on a brave face and fiercely hugged each of my babies before sending them off to summer vacation. One of the last to leave was Emma, who was crying softly while Mattie hugged her.

I said, "Let her stay, and I'll talk to her for a minute." Mattie escorted the last group of kids to their busses, and I went over to Emma and pulled her onto my lap. Her eyes were red and wet, and I gave her a tissue to dry them. "What's the matter, kiddo?" I asked gently.

"I'm sad. I don't want school to end," she said meekly.

"You know what? I'm a little sad, too, but I'm also excited. It's summer, and that means playing outside all day, going to the beach and no homework. That is the best of all, don't you think?" I cajoled.

She smiled and nodded her head. I looked up and there was Ted. Emma ran to him.

"Hey, Em. Is everything okay here?" he asked.

"We were just saying goodbye and talking about all of the fun things to do in the summer," I replied.

"I'm going to miss school, Daddy," Emma said.

Ted smiled and said, "I know you will, so I was thinking we should invite Miss Richards over for dinner tonight. What do you think?"

Emma squealed, "Oh, yes. This is going to be so much fun. Wait until I tell Jessie that Miss Richards is coming to my house for dinner."

"She hasn't said yes, yet. What do you think, Miss Richards? Are you up for dinner at the Manning household?" Under his breath he added, "I do believe our two-week separation is officially over."

I laughed and said, "Emma, I would be delighted to come to your house for dinner tonight."

Again, Ted whispered, "I'll call you later with the details."

"Great. Emma, I can't until dinner," I said as they gathered up Emma's things and headed out of the door.

Mattie returned, and I walked right up to her and gave her a hug. She laughed, and asked, "What was that for?"

"That was a thank you for all your help this year. You made my first year here a great one," I said as I went to my desk and retrieved a present for her. "This is for you."

She opened the card; inside was a gift certificate for dinner. She unwrapped the box, and inside was a framed picture of Mattie and the kids from our class. "Thank you, Jane. You were extremely generous. I'm already looking forward to next year."

We began packing up books and supplies, and after a few minutes Jillian came to the door and asked to speak with me. We went next door to her room, and she said, "Spill it. What's going on with you and Emma's father?"

"How did you know?" I asked nervously.

"Jane, I've known all along that you were interested in him, and I just overheard Emma talk to her dad about your going to their house for dinner tonight. Is this like a date?"

"No, it's just dinner, but..."

"But what?"

"I can talk about it now that the school year is officially over. Ted and I have been seeing each other."

"Get out! I had the feeling something was going on. I can't believe no one ever found out."

"Oh, but they did. Philip saw us together, and while I wasn't severely punished, I was reprimanded and will be watched like a hawk next year," I confessed.

"I can't believe you never told me, you rat," she teased.

"When Philip found out, it scared me, and after that Ted and I didn't see each other until today. Now that school is finished, it can be out in the open. Although, I'd appreciate it if you kept it quiet—I really don't want to be fodder for the rumor mill."

"You know you can count on me. So when can we get together?"

"What about Sunday? There are a couple of movies I really want to see."

"Sounds great. I'd better get this cleaning started, because I am ready to start my summer vacation."

~ * ~

Ted called me that afternoon with directions to his house and I tried to take a little nap, but was too restless. I was really nervous about dinner. I was nervous about Emma and how she would eventually react to Ted and me, but I was really nervous about going to Annie's house. I wondered what the house was like. Would there be photos of her everywhere? Would it be just like going to anyone else's house? Why was I so scared? I couldn't pinpoint what I was feeling exactly. I felt somewhat guilty, like I was intruding on Annie's world. I tried to keep those thoughts from my mind as I drove and forced myself to remain calm. I pulled up to a traditional, brick house with a small, but well maintained perennial bed blooming pink and purple. I parked and walked to the front door carrying the cupcakes I had bought for Emma. I was not above bribery at this point.

I rang the bell and was greeted by Emma's boisterous greeting, "I knew it was you!"

"You are so smart. You must have had a wonderful kindergarten teacher," I said.

"You were my teacher, silly." She giggled.

Ted appeared and said, "Come in."

I handed Emma the cupcakes and said, "These are for you."

She took them and ran into the kitchen. Ted glanced over his shoulder, and when Emma was out of sight, he kissed me and said, "I never thought this day would get here. Come to the kitchen, and I'll pour you a glass of wine."

I followed him and relaxed in the warmth of the kitchen. I sat at the large island while Ted poured me a glass of Chardonnay.

I tried to be casual as I looked around, but must have been obvious as Ted said, "Feel free to look around. Annie did a lot of the decorating, and I haven't changed much since she died."

Just then Emma bounded into the room and said, "Daddy, my room is ready. Can I show her now?"

"Sure, then come back and we'll all sit on the deck and relax a minute before I get the grill going."

Emma grabbed my hand and took me down a hall that was lined with photos of a woman that I surmised was Annie. She had a huge smile, and I wanted to stop and take them in, but I needed to focus on Emma and her room. It was pale pink complete with a pink bedspread, pillows and curtains.

"What an awesome room you have," I gushed. "I bet I know what your favorite color is?"

"Pink," she shouted. Emma proceeded to show me all of her stuffed animals and tell me their names, and then she showed me her pictures. "This is me when I was a baby and this is me and my mom and dad. These are my grandparents."

"You were so cute, but you're even cuter now," I said as I reached over and tickled her lightly on the tummy. "Let's go see if your dad needs any help with dinner."

We joined Ted on the deck. It was a clear, slightly cool evening, and Emma stayed right by my side as we enjoyed cheese and fruit followed by grilled tilapia for the adults and a burger for her. After our dessert of cupcakes, Emma got herself cleaned up and ready for bed while Ted and I did the dishes.

"I am so happy you are here, Jane," he said while pulling me into his arms.

I returned his embrace, but gently released myself from him and said, "Me, too. Let's just be careful around Emma. We need to bring her into this gradually, don't you think?"

"Once again, you are the voice of reason. I just don't know how long I can wait," he said, smiling.

We continued to wash and dry the dishes. Emma came in wearing a pink ruffled night gown with matching slippers. She came over and jumped up into my arms.

"Don't you look lovely?" I said, giving her a hug.

Ted held out his arms and said, "Time for bed, Em."

"Can't Miss Richards put me to bed?" she said with her lip just slightly pouting.

"How can I resist that face?" I asked and then proceeded to carry her to her room and drop her full force on her bed.

She laughed and said, "My dad does that, too."

I helped her get under the covers, sat on the edge of her bed, and gave her a kiss on the forehead.

"Good night, kiddo."

"Good night," she said softly. As I began to get up, she tugged my hand and said, "Stay with me for a while."

I sat back down and gently brushed the hair on the side of her head with my fingers. Emma's breathing became more rhythmic and I was about to leave when she said, "I wish you could be my mom."

I didn't know what to say, so I just responded, "Sweet dreams, Emma," and left.

I decided not to mention that last comment to Ted. He was waiting in the living room with two glasses of wine for us. He motioned for me to sit next to him, and when I did he kissed me—softly at first, then with more intensity. I pulled back and was totally uncomfortable and confused.

"I'm sorry. I think I'm just nervous about Emma coming out and catching us."

"She sleeps like a rock," he countered.

"I'm sure, but..."

"But, what? I'm ready to move forward, so I need you to be totally honest with me, Jane."

"I'm a little uncomfortable here. In Annie's house," I admitted. "That sounds so awful, but it's the truth. I feel like an intruder."

Ted sighed and said, "Annie's gone, Jane. This is my house, me and Emma. Just give it a little time, and I'm sure it will get easier. Now, I want to talk about something. Like I said before, I'm ready to move forward with you—us. I'd like us to go away for the weekend together. Just the two of us, and I want to go the weekend after next."

I was taken back a bit by his urgency, and asked, "Why the rush?"

"Why not?" he countered. "All we have been doing is waiting. I want to be with you, Jane. Just say yes. I'll take care of all of the details. All you have to do is show up."

What was I waiting for? I wondered. I looked into his eyes and said, "Yes."

Twenty-eight

By the time Jillian and I had dinner together, I had so much to tell her. We met at a cozy, hole in the wall called Ed's. It was basically a diner, but without the bright lights. We settled into a booth, placed our order and began talking as if we hadn't seen each other in weeks, not days.

"Now, start from the beginning and don't leave anything out," Jillian ordered.

"Well, there isn't a whole lot to tell. After we ran the 10K, we had dinner and then it was like we kept getting thrown together. We spent some time together and had every intention of just being friends, but it turned into more."

"So are you officially an item?" she asked.

I hesitated a second and said, "I guess so."

"You guess. You sound like you aren't sure."

"No, I'm sure. I'm just cautious. It's weird, but it was less complicated when we were meeting secretly and we were the only two people in our world. Ted and I had dinner with Emma on Friday, and it was strange."

"Does she know about you two?"

"No. As far as she's concerned, I was just there as her teacher, but Ted is ready to move ahead. We're going away in two weeks, and I'm a nervous wreck." I admitted.

"I take it you haven't slept with him yet."

"No, I wanted to wait until school was over and Emma was no longer my student. And now that summer is here, there's nothing to stop us."

"What are you afraid of?" she asked.

"It's just that I have made some bad choices before, and I don't know if I can take being hurt again," I admitted.

"Is Ted different from the other guys?"

"Yes, he is. He's confident and caring and he says he wants a future with me."

"Do you love him?" she asked gently.

"I think I do. He makes me feel safe, and I've never had that before."

"Just go with it, Jane. It sounds like he's a special man who would be lucky to have you in his life."

"You make it sound so simple, Jillian."

"It's never simple, Jane, but if you don't take a chance you could miss out on something wonderful."

~ * ~

Ted and I went sailing and to the movies and spent one afternoon just running errands. We no longer had to look over our shoulder when we went out together, and I started to feel like we were truly a couple. When Ted was going out he told Emma that he would be with me, but did not go into the details with her. She had asked to come with us, but Ted had explained to her that he was having some grown-up time, and she had been content with his explanation. Uneasiness still nagged at me where Emma was concerned, so I decided that I would take her out for the afternoon and spend some time alone with her.

I arrived at their house to pick Emma up, and before the babysitter could call her name she bounded into my arms and we were off. She talked virtually non-stop on the car ride to the restaurant and once we sere settled in seats, the first thing she asked was, "Are you going to marry my dad?"

I nearly spit the soda out of my mouth. "Why are you asking me that?"

"Because when he goes out with you he always spends a lot of time getting ready and he keeps asking me if he looks okay?"

I couldn't resist indulging Emma a bit and asked, "And what do you tell him?"

"I say yes he looks good, but he has on too much perfume."

I laughed, and in attempt to dodge the original question, I said, "Grown-ups are funny, aren't they? I don't know about you, but I am starving. What do you want to eat?"

We made our choices, and then we talked about our families. I told her, "My mom and sister live here. We're going to visit my mom after we have our lunch."

"What about your dad?" she asked.

"He died when I was eight years old."

"Did your mom get you a new dad?" she asked.

"No, but right now she has a nice gentleman friend, and I'm hoping they might get married some day."

"Because you want a new dad?"

"Well, no. I just don't want my mom to be lonely."

She seemed to be content with my answer, and we continued to chat about friends and our summer plans. When we finished, I took her on a ride and showed her where I went to school, and we stopped for ice cream at the shop where I worked in high school. Then we drove over to my mom's house. I had told her we would be coming by, and when we arrived she gave me a hug and kiss and bent down to meet Emma.

"Hi there, Emma. I'm Mrs. Richards, but why don't you call me Miss Ruth?" she said as she stuck her hand out to shake with Emma.

"Hi, Miss Ruth. Are you Miss Richards' mother?"

"I sure am. Come on in, and I'll show you some pictures of her when she was a baby."

Emma chuckled, and I smiled at how much Emma had grown since that first day of school. She was no longer that shy girl, and it was so great to see her so full of confidence.

We sat on the deck, and my mom brought out a photo album and a pitcher of lemonade. Emma cackled at the photos of me when I was a teenager, and it was fun for me to reminisce, until we came to a picture of me and Mike at our prom.

"Who's that?" Emma asked.

I hesitated, then replied, "That's an old friend from high school and me at a dance that you go to called a prom."

"Did you have fun?" she asked.

"Yes, I had a lot of fun," *but I sure paid for it afterward*, I thought, trying to shake the bad memories from my mind.

My mother picked up on my discomfort and said, "Would you like to see Jane's room?"

I smiled in appreciation, and off we went to see my room. We stayed a while longer, and when we were ready to go, my mom pulled me aside and said, "She's a lovely little girl, Jane. I hope it all works out for you."

I hugged her tightly and said, "Thanks, Mom. I love you."

She then bent down, and Emma grabbed her around the neck. "It was so much fun meeting you, Emma. I hope I see you again soon."

"Me, too, Miss Ruth."

I was exhausted from our day and Emma was dozing in the back seat, when suddenly her head popped up and she said, "It's okay if you marry my dad, Miss Richards."

I didn't answer and just wondered how long she would continue to feel that way.

Twenty-nine

The morning of our trip, I thought I would go crazy waiting for Ted to arrive and pick me up. He was supposed to be there at ten, and by nine I was packed, dressed and had cleaned out several drawers in my kitchen in order to make the time pass more quickly. I began to get concerned when he didn't show at 10:15 and at 10:30, I had the phone in my hands when I heard a knock at the door. Ted came in and kissed me, but I sensed something was wrong.

"Is everything all right?" I asked.

Distractedly he answered, "Um, yes. It's fine... It's just that Emma threw a fit when I left her this morning. I don't get it. She was so excited to see my mother, and they have all of these fun plans for the weekend, but when I left she went hysterical, crying, begging me not to leave her."

"Should we stay home?" I asked while I prayed silently he would say no.

"No. She's with my mom and she's going to be fine. I was just thrown by it. She's never acted that way before, and I wasn't sure what to do. My mom called me on the way over and said that Emma was calmed down and I should enjoy my weekend."

What a great start to the weekend, I thought selfishly. How could I enjoy myself knowing that we left Emma in hysterics?

Ted must have sensed my thoughts and said, "Don't worry about it. I shouldn't have mentioned it. Are you ready to go?"

"Yes, but only if you're sure."

"I've never been more sure of anything, Jane," he responded as he enveloped me in a warm embrace.

"I'm ready, then," I said as Ted grabbed my suitcase.

It was a glorious day, and I held my face up to the sun to capture its warmth before settling into the car. We began our drive, and I felt myself relax. I looked over at Ted and had the feeling that this relationship would be different. Things were going to be good.

As we drove, I asked, "Are you going to tell me where we are going?"

"I guess I can tell you. We're going to Newport. We're staying at an inn right on the water. One of my patients told me about it. I believe she used the words romantic and quaint."

I smiled and said, "I can't wait."

Ted reached over for my hand and said, "Neither can I."

We stopped for lunch at a waterside café, and afterward we went for a walk and admired some of the storefronts. All the while we talked and laughed as if we had been together for years.

I looked at Ted and said, "I am so happy."

He grabbed me and kissed me hungrily. The passion between us was escalating, and when we came up for air, he pulled way and said, "Let's get to that hotel room."

We drove for about another hour before pulling up to an elegant inn that resembled a white castle directly on the rugged coast line. It was secluded and quiet and it had a breathtaking view of the ocean and the handful of sail boats that were cruising along.

"This is gorgeous," I whispered to Ted as the bellman arrived to take our bags. Ted held my hand as we entered the lobby. After we signed in we were escorted to our room. It had a large, four-poster bed with a view through the French doors of the crystal blue waters and rocky shore. When the bellman left, I turned to Ted and said, "This is magnificent." He grabbed me and held me close.

"Jane, I have been waiting so long for this," he whispered. He pulled back and kissed me long and hard. Breathlessly he said, "I love you, Jane." Without waiting for a response, he covered my mouth with his as he laid me down on the bed. For a moment he stopped and looked into my eyes with such raw emotion a tear formed and slid down my cheek. He gently wiped it away and asked, "Do you want me to stop?"

In reply, I pulled him on top of me and gave myself to him.

~ * ~

When I woke, Ted was standing in the door way gazing at the sunset. I covered myself in the sheet and wrapped my arms around him from behind.

"Everything okay?" I asked tentatively.

He turned and smiled. "I don't think it could get much better."

I relaxed and said, "Me either. This is pretty perfect."

Suddenly serious, Ted said, "I meant it when I said that I love you, Jane. I never thought it would happen again, but it has."

Fear took hold, but only for a moment, and I allowed myself to share my feelings with him. "I love you, too," I said hesitantly. "It scares me, but I'm not going to let it stand in our way."

"Jane, I know you've been hurt, but I'm in this for the duration. I love you, and nothing is going to change that."

Thirty

On the last morning of our getaway, Ted and I were lying in bed when he turned to me and said, "Before I take you home, I want you to meet my mother."

Panic set in, and before I could say anything, he said, "Just hear me out. I'd like Emma to see us together and I'd like her to see you meet my mother, too. I want Emma to get used to this, and I think the sooner we start, the better. Besides, my mother will love you, too."

I took a deep breath and said, "I'm game, but do we have to leave right now?"

Ted answered me with a kiss.

~ * ~

My mood on the ride home was euphoric. I closed my eyes as I recalled how perfect this weekend had been. Ted and I laughed, shared stories and couldn't keep our hands off of each other. I couldn't recall when I had been so content.

"That must be some dream you're having," Ted teased.

"You were the main attraction," I replied with a wink.

"I hate to disturb you, but we are almost at my house."

Once again, my heart started to beat quickly. I reached for my purse, retrieved my makeup bag and started to apply some lipstick.

"You look great, Jane. Please don't worry."

"Easy for you to say," I shot back as I tried to steady my hand so that my makeup would not look like a child applied it.

Finally, we pulled into the driveway. Emma and a woman I surmised was Ted's mother were sitting on the steps finishing popsicles. When Emma saw the car, she threw her popsicle to the ground and ran to Ted, who scooped her up in his arms.

"Hi, there, Em. Boy did I miss you," Ted gushed.

"I missed you, too, Daddy. I'm so glad you're back."

"Aren't you going to say hello to Miss Richards?" he prodded.

"Hi," Emma said almost mutely.

Great, I thought to myself. *Please let me make a good impression on his mom.*

Ted's mother approached me and extended her hand. "You must be Jane. I'm Bonnie Manning."

She was a petite blonde, and I was surprised at how young she appeared.

"It's so nice to meet you. Did you and Emma have a fun weekend?" I asked trying to perpetuate the conversation.

"We did. I'm exhausted, but I love spending time with Emma. How about you? Did you two have a nice time?"

"Yes, we did," I replied trying to control the blushing I felt rising in my face.

She smiled and motioned for me to come into the house with her. Emma was talking non-stop with Ted as they followed us into the kitchen.

I wanted to make some contact with Emma, so I asked her, "What was your favorite part of the weekend?"

She stared at me before answering, and I wasn't sure she was going to respond, but then she said, "We went to the zoo."

"What was your favorite animal?"

"The elephants were really funny. They put on a show. I got a new bathing suit. Do you want to see it?"

"I'd love to," I replied thankfully.

I followed Emma into her room and was relieved to see that she was her old self again. I sat on her bed as she pulled out a two-piece, pink polka-dotted bathing suit.

"Pink," I squealed. "I love it. Would you like to go to the beach with me this week?"

Without hesitation, she replied, "Sure. I can swim by myself now. Wait until you see me."

I laughed, and Emma brought out more new clothes to show me. Bonnie appeared at the door.

"Emma, why don't put those things away and then come and have some lemonade with us. Jane, would you like some?"

"Yes, that would be nice."

Bonnie and I returned to the kitchen, and Ted was nowhere to be found. I began to get nervous as Bonnie poured my drink.

"Jane, I wanted to have a minute with you alone," she began. "I am not one to intrude on my children's lives, but I wanted you to know that I have not seen Ted this happy in a very long time. I'm glad you two have found each other."

I released the breath I had been holding, and said, "Thank you for saying that, Bonnie. It means more than you realize."

Just then Ted appeared and asked, "Would you like to stay for dinner?"

I was tempted, but wanted to end our weekend on a positive note, so I declined. "I don't mean to be rude, but I'm exhausted, and I'm sure your mom and Emma would like some time alone with you."

Ted began to protest, but he quickly relented, and he called for Emma to come and say goodbye to me. Emma came running and I gave her a big hug. When I turned to Bonnie, she surprised me with a quick embrace.

"Thank you, Bonnie," I said softly.

"I hope to see you again, soon, Jane."

~ * ~

Once in the car, Ted said, "My mom loves you. I can tell."

I laughed, and said, "She just met me. I'm just happy she was nice to me and Emma, too. I was nervous at first because Emma seemed to be upset with me."

"Don't worry about Emma. She's a kid—she'll adjust."

"I know, but she has feelings too, and they have to be considered."

"That's true, but if I'm happy, she'll be happy. It will all work out, Jane."

We pulled into the parking lot, and Ted walked me into my apartment. It was a little stuffy, so I opened a window to let the breeze in and sat down on the sofa. Ted joined me and took my face in his hands and said, "Thank you for a wonderful weekend, Jane."

He kissed me, and I could feel things about to escalate when he pulled back and said, "I'd better leave now."

I teasingly groaned and asked, "Are you sure?"

"Of course I'm not sure, but don't you worry. I'll be back."

I walked him to the door and said, "I'll talk to you later."

"You sure will." He kissed me lightly and brushed my cheek with his hand. He started to leave, and then turned to look me in the eyes and said, "I'm going to marry you, Jane."

And with that declaration, he was off.

Thirty-one

Ted's parting words struck a nerve with me. In one sense, it excited me that he was thinking about our future, yet it scared me that we were moving so fast. I didn't like feeling that Ted had all of the control in this relationship. I decided not to bring his comment up as we continued to see each other daily. A few days a week, I picked Emma up from her babysitter and we went to the beach or ran errands together. When we were alone, she was lively and animated, but when the three of us were together she could be sulky and temperamental. It mostly occurred when she was tired; Ted always handled her firmly, yet lovingly, and her bad moods never escalated into a full-blown tantrum.

We settled into a rhythm, and most nights the three of us ate dinner together. I preferred the evenings when we were at my place. I still felt like I was intruding on Annie's home. It was almost as if I had this irrational fear that she was going to show up at any time and demand to know what I was doing taking over her life. I didn't share that with Ted, but I really needed to talk to someone about it.

I stopped by to see my mom, hoping that she'd have some tidbits of wisdom for me. The warmth of the summer sun was offset by the breeze, making it a perfect day to sit out on the deck.

"So, Jane. What's going on? You sounded troubled when you called."

"You get right to the point, don't you?" I quipped. "Actually, I need a sounding board. Ted and I have been seeing a great deal of each other, and he has brought up the subject of marriage, and Emma sometimes acts like she hates me, and I feel like a trespasser in his house because every inch of it has memories of his dead wife."

My mother tried to hide her smile and with a deadpan look asked, "Is that all that's bothering you?"

I laughed, but tears started to form in my eyes.

"I'm sorry, honey. I didn't mean to make fun of you, but it sounds like you are on overload. If you still want to talk about it, I'm ready." I nodded my head, and she asked, "First, do you love Ted?"

"Yes, I do, but given my track record, I'm scared," I confessed.

"How is he different from the others?"

I reflected a moment and said, "He's got character. The fact that he raised Emma and continued on with his life after Annie died is amazing. He's a good father, and he's a wonderful person."

"It sounds like he's a special man. Can you imagine your life without him?" she asked gently.

"No, I can't but everything else is so complicated."

"Jane, life is complicated. You either go with it, or you miss out on a lot. It's sounds like you've got a rock-solid guy. As far as Emma goes, she'll adjust. Just love her and treat her as if she were your own. That's all you can do."

"I guess you're telling me to act like an adult," I said sheepishly.

"That's one way to put it," she said, appearing satisfied with herself. "Why don't the three of you come for dinner? I'll invite Grace, too."

"I think Lawrence should be included, as well."

I saw a faint blush pass across her face as she said, "If you insist."

Two nights later, Ted, Emma and I arrived at my mother's for dinner. Emma walked in like she owned the place and called out, "Miss Ruth, I'm here."

I laughed as my mother came running and said, "I'm so glad you're back, Emma."

Ted stepped forward, offered my mom a bouquet of lilies and said, "I'm Ted Manning. Thank you for having us."

She shook Ted's hand and said, "I'm Ruth and I'm glad you could make it. These flowers are lovely and they smell divine. Hi, Jane," she said as she tried to kiss my cheek. Emma, however, had grabbed her free hand and was pulling her into the kitchen.

"Emma," Ted cautioned, but Ruth waved his concerns away.

We followed along, and my mom said, "Why don't you two go out to the deck and have a drink with Lawrence. Emma and I are going to put these flowers in a vase and then I have something to help keep her occupied tonight." Emma let out a tiny squeal, and I led Ted out to the deck.

Lawrence stood to greet us, and I gave him a quick hug before I introduced him to Ted. The three of us sat with our drinks, and the two men quickly discovered their common interests in sailing and golf. While they chatted, I excused myself to see if my mom needed any help. I found them both coming downstairs with a box of my old dolls and their clothes.

"Miss Richards, look at what Ruth is letting me play with. She said these were yours when you were my age."

"How fun!" I exclaimed as I helped Emma take them out of the box. "Wait until Grace sees these. When is she supposed to get here?" I asked.

"They should be here any minute now. Emma, why don't you take that out to the deck?"

I helped her gather everything up, and we carried it out to a small table that my mom had set up just for Emma. My mother joined us and asked about our trip.

"We had a lovely weekend. We went to Newport, and the view was spectacular," I gushed.

"I've been trying to convince your mother to take a trip with me, and I've finally succeeded," Lawrence boasted. "We are going on a cruise to Canada next week."

I looked at my mother in amused disbelief. "How exciting. You've been holding out on me, Mom," I chided.

Just then, I looked up to see Grace and Derek. I was shocked at how old Grace looked. She had dark circles under her eyes, and she looked worn out. I stood and kissed Grace on the cheek and gave her a light hug because she seemed so fragile—like she might break if I held her too tight.

"Grace, I am so happy to see you. Grace, this is Ted Manning. Ted, this is my sister Grace and her husband Derek."

Grace smiled warmly as she greeted Ted, but Derek made no attempt to be discreet as he looked Ted up and down.

The first words out of Derek's mouth were, "So Ted, is that your BMW?"

Ted was taken aback, despite my earlier warnings about Derek.

"Yes, it is."

"Must be nice," Derek said as he walked over to the counter to get himself a drink.

Ted shot me look of disbelief. I smiled for Grace's sake and called Emma to come and meet her.

"Emma, show Grace the dolls Ruth took out for you to play with."

Grace pulled up a chair and sat with Emma as she animatedly described our school year and how we now were kind of like a family. I smiled at hearing her speak comfortably about our situation and went to the kitchen to help my mother.

I expected her to be busy at the stove, but she was sitting at the table just staring.

"You okay, Mom?" I asked hesitantly.

"She looks like hell, Jane," she whispered. "Grace is too thin, and those bags under her eyes make her look older than me. What is going on with those two?"

"I don't know, but let's try to get Grace alone and talk to her. Meanwhile, let's get dinner going."

"It's all ready. I'll put everything out, and you have everyone sit at the table."

We all assembled at the table to a feast of garlic chicken and roasted potatoes, while Emma had the kid-friendly version of chicken nuggets and French fries. The conversation was strained at first, but then we settled into comfortable discussion. That was until Derek had polished off his third drink and started to show his true self.

"Ted, you must be some guy to catch our Janey, here. She seemed to be a bit of an ice princess, if you know what I mean, but I guess you have what it takes to melt her, huh?"

Ruth stood and said, "Derek, I will not allow that kind of talk in my home."

"Whoa, sorry, Ruth. I didn't mean to ruffle your feathers. I guess you aren't getting any from the ice queen, are you, Larry?" he said, laughing. He stood and said, "I need to stretch my legs any way."

He was quite unsteady as he walked away from the table, and it caused me to wonder how much he had to drink before he got here. I heard the door to the deck slam. At least he wasn't going to try and drive.

Grace's head was lowered in humiliation. Ted and I were stunned and grateful that Emma had excused herself before Derek's scene. Lawrence put his hand on my mother's arm and said, "Why don't you ladies go sit in the living room? Ted, would you mind helping me?"

"Not at all," Ted replied.

I flashed them both an appreciative smile and said, "Let's go up to your room, Mom. I don't want to be interrupted."

We assembled in her room with my mom in her rocker and Grace and I at the edge of her bed. Grace immediately broke down crying.

"I'm so sorry I ruined everything," she sobbed.

"You didn't do anything wrong, Grace. Derek was totally out of line. What is going on with you two?"

"Nothing. We're fine."

"You most certainly are not fine," my mother shrieked. "Have you looked at yourself lately? You have dark circles under your eyes and you've lost so much weight. What is he doing to you, Grace? He acts vulgar and inappropriate, and you apologize. It's all so twisted." She sobbed as she buried her face in her hands to try and hide her tears.

I went to my mother and gently rubbed her back. "Grace, we're scared for you. We never see you or hear from you, and we feel like you're cutting yourself off from us. Tell us what's going on. We want to help."

"I'm fine. You're making too much out of this. Sometimes he drinks more than he should and he gets a little boisterous, but since when are you so perfect? I'm so tired of the constant criticism of my life. I'm going to go get Derek and leave," she said as she stood and headed for the door.

"Wait," I hollered after her, but she was already out of the door.

My mother let a small sob escape and then I really became frightened because she was always the strong one. I knelt down next to her and said, "Don't worry. I'll get to the bottom of this." Then I added, "I promise," without a clue as to what I would do next.

Thirty-two

I awoke the next morning feeling like I had been run over by a truck. I was exhausted, nauseated and depressed. Grace was in trouble, and I didn't know how to help her. I was lying in bed trying to gather up my stamina to get into the shower when the phone rang.

"Did I wake you?" Ted asked.

"No, but I'm still in bed. I didn't get much sleep last night."

"Are you still worried about your sister?"

"I'm frightened for her, Ted. It's like she's Derek's prisoner, but she's so brainwashed that she doesn't even realize it."

"She needs help, Jane," he replied matter of factly.

"I know that," I replied sarcastically, and then I began to cry.

"Jane, I didn't mean to make you cry. Listen, I have a patient who is a social worker. I'll call her and see if she has any ideas of what we can do to help Grace."

"Thank you, and I'm sorry for losing it. I am a mess today. I feel lousy and all I want to do is stay in bed."

"Why don't you do that? Just take it easy today and I'll check in with you later."

I managed to sleep for a couple of hours and felt better as the day went on. Ted called me and gave me some information, but I wasn't encouraged. Basically, Grace had to make the decision to get help, and all I could do was try to steer her in the right direction. I also had to be careful in my suggestions so she wouldn't pull away from me any more. I decided to call her and see if she could meet me for lunch.

I was surprised when she answered the phone, and I said, "Grace, I didn't think I'd get you."

"I thought it was Derek. He left his cell phone home," she stated coldly.

"I wanted to see if you could have lunch with me this week. Maybe we could do a little shopping, too." She hesitated, and I scrambled to think of a way it would be beneficial to Derek. "Or maybe, we could get a makeover. I've been wanting to get some make-up advice. You can surprise Derek. What do you say?"

"I don't think so. Besides why would you want me to do anything nice for Derek?"

"I'm sorry about last night, Grace," I lied. "Mom and I both worry about you, and I know that sometimes I go overboard. I will really try and give you both some space. Just don't shut me out completely."

Again, she paused and then she said, "I don't know."

"Just give me chance, please. It will be my treat."

"I don't need your charity, Jane."

"It wasn't meant as charity," I replied softly. "I just want to spend some time with you."

"All right," she said, relenting. "When do you want to go?"

Relief washed over me, but I was careful not to sound too eager. "Can you go tomorrow?" I asked hopefully. "I could pick you up around eleven."

"All right, Jane."

"Do you have anything planned for today?" I asked trying to engage her in more conversation.

"No. Just the usual cleaning and laundry," she said blankly.

"How about for the weekend?"

"We don't have any plans," she answered in that same detached tone.

"Ted and I are taking Emma to Near Beach on Sunday night. They are having a concert and fireworks. Would you and Derek like to join us?"

"Probably not. Derek isn't much for the beach."

Again, there was silence, and I realized I should be happy with the lunch date, so I said, "I'd better get some things done. I'll see you tomorrow."

~ * ~

I arrived promptly at eleven at Grace's house. It had been months since I had been to her home, and I was anxious to check it out. I rang the bell, and Grace appeared with her purse. Before I could even get a foot inside, Grace was out of the door.

"Hey there," I said as I awkwardly gave her a hug.

"Hi," she replied coolly.

I apparently still had some ground to make up with Grace. As we settled ourselves in the car, I asked, "Are you hungry? I thought maybe we'd go to that new make-up superstore first and then relax over lunch."

"Sure. That sounds fine."

"I want to get a new look for summer. I've been feeling so run-down lately, and I want something to brighten my face up. What about you?"

"Derek doesn't like me to wear a lot of make-up," she confessed. "But I could use some help, too."

"Well, you can ask for a natural look. You have lovely skin, so you probably don't need much."

Grace smiled, and I was relieved that my response didn't upset her. I had made up my mind to keep my negative comments about Derek to myself, hoping that would help open up conversation between us. The remainder of our drive was somewhat strained, but we had a blast in the store with all of the different makeup. When we were finished, we each had a new look and a bag of goodies to help us replicate our new "face" at home. For lunch, we sat outside at a small café that had salads and sandwiches.

"I am so hungry, I'm about to get irritable," I said.

"Look out," Grace joked. "I better get the waiter to bring some bread, because I've seen you when you're hungry and it isn't pretty."

I laughed and said, "A loaf of bread ought to do it." I sat back in my chair and relaxed. The old Grace was resurfacing, and the tension between us was gone. We placed our orders, and the waiter returned with the much needed bread and our iced teas.

"How are things with Ted?" she asked.

"Things are good. Really good. I'd love for you two to get to know each other better."

Then hastily added, "Derek, too."

"He seems like a very nice man, and Emma is a doll."

"They both are very special. I'm just scared, you know. I made a lot of mistakes in relationships, and I don't know if I can handle another."

"You're tough, Jane. Besides, I can tell that Ted really cares about you. I saw him at Mom's, and he is totally taken with you. Don't let him get away," she added as a look of sadness came over her.

Once again, Derek had clouded our time together. I reached over and grabbed her hand and said, "Thanks, Grace."

I looked up to see our waiter with our salads, and when he placed the dish in front of me, I suddenly lost my appetite and excused myself as I headed to the restroom. My stomach was churning and in an attempt to calm it, I splashed cold water on my face. I took a few deep breaths, and my stomach started to settle down. I wet a paper towel and placed it on the back of my neck as I sat. Just then Grace walked in with a concerned look on her face.

"What's going on? Are you all right?" she questioned.

"I'm okay. I must have some sort of bug. It's been going on for a few days now. I'm sure I am recovering from the end of school and all of the stress I had. I'll be fine." I stood and was forced back down by dizziness.

"You're not okay. Stay here a minute, and I'll take care of the check and get the car."

"But, I want to pay for lunch."

"Jane, just let me do this. I'll be right back."

After a few minutes I felt better and met Grace at the door to the restaurant. She had parked the car right up front and protested when I told her I was much better and could drive.

"Let me drive you to your place and you can rest awhile," Grace ordered.

Though I felt better, I was tired and in no mood to argue.

"Thanks, Grace."

On the ride home, Grace asked, "How long have you been feeling ill?"

"I don't know. Just a couple of days. I'm sure it's nothing."

"What have you been experiencing exactly?" she continued.

"Just an upset stomach and I've been feeling worn out. It hasn't been bad. Today was the worst. I just need to rest more," I replied as I closed my eyes.

I slept the rest of the way home, and when we arrived at my apartment, I felt fine. I yawned and told Grace, "Let's go in and eat. I'm better."

Grace had asked the waiter to box up our meals. Once we were inside, I asked Grace to set them on the table while I got some plates. We sat down and, this time, I had no trouble eating my salad.

"That's more like it," I said filling my mouth with another forkful.

"Do you think you and Ted might get married?" Grace asked out of the blue.

"He has mentioned it, but there's so much to consider. I would have an instant family. I love Emma and she's great, but sometimes she gets very possessive of Ted. And then there's Annie. That was Ted's first wife. It's hard to compete with a memory."

"There's no competition. She's gone and you're here. I think you're making excuses."

I didn't respond at first and then said, "You're probably right. He's different than anyone I've ever been with... I'm just scared." Tears welled in my eyes, and I began to cry. "I don't know what's wrong with me."

Grace handed me a napkin and said, "I didn't mean to upset you. Let's talk about something else, like do you think Mom and Lawrence will get married?"

"Who knows. Did she tell you that they are going on a cruise together? I wonder if they'll have separate rooms?"

"Jane, now my stomach is upset," she said laughing.

After we finished eating, I drove Grace home, and we sat in her driveway and talked for a while.

"Thank you for coming out today, Grace. I'm sorry I ruined our lunch, though. It's the craziest virus. Now I'm fine."

Grace looked at me pensively and said, "Don't freak out on me, but do you think you could be pregnant?"

"Pregnant? No way," I answered, but my palms instantly started to sweat and my heart began to beat wildly. My mind raced as I tried to remember when I had my last period. I was startled to see Derek's face outside my window and let out a small scream.

I opened the window, and said, "You scared me half to death, Derek."

He laughed and said, "Jane, don't be so dramatic. I just wanted to see why Grace wasn't coming in. Were you talking about me?"

"No, Derek," Grace replied quickly. "Jane hasn't been feeling well, and I was just telling her to see a doctor if she doesn't feel better in a few days. I had a nice time, Jane. I'll talk to you soon," she said as she hastily left the car.

Derek looked at me and raised an eyebrow, then winked. My nausea returned, and when I was out of their view, I pulled over and got my calendar out of my purse.

"Shit," I said aloud as I realized that I was two weeks late.

Thirty-three

I stopped at a drug store and bought a home pregnancy test. At first I just left it on the counter of my bathroom. I was tired and scared and I just wanted to escape. I slept for a couple of hours and was awakened by the ringing of the phone.

It was Ted who asked, "Did I wake you?"

"Yes. I haven't been feeling well so I laid down and must have fallen asleep."

"What's the matter? Did you see a doctor?"

"I'm fine. I think I'm just worn out." I lied.

"Do you need anything? I can be there in fifteen minutes," Ted offered.

"That's sweet, but I think I'll be fine."

"I wanted to take you out tomorrow night. Mattie can watch Emma. Do you think you'll be up for it?"

"Sure. That sounds great."

I slept fitfully that night and was relieved when the clock read 5:34 and I could get up and do the test. I had to wait two minutes—a period of time that normally flies by without notice, but not now. My hand shook so badly I put the test on the counter and focused on the second hand of my watch. I closed my eyes and recalled the doctor who told me the first time. I'd begun to cry; he stood and said, "Think about what you want to do." Then he left me all alone in that cold, white room. I shook the memory from my mind and saw that only forty-five seconds had passed. It didn't matter though. A bright blue plus sign had appeared in the test window. I was definitely pregnant.

"Not again," I said aloud.

I sat for the longest time and thought I should call Ted, but we were going to see each other that night. Besides, I didn't want to tell him over the phone. I needed to talk to someone, so I called Grace.

Derek answered. I was in no mood for his bullshit, so I said, "Derek, is Grace at home? I need to speak with her right now, so don't give me any of your smart ass remarks."

He must have been caught off guard because all he said was, "Hold on." But then I heard him say, "It's your sister and she sounds whacked out."

"What's wrong?" Grace asked immediately.

"Can you come over? I need to talk to you, and I don't want Derek to hear. Please, Grace. I need you."

~ * ~

Fifteen minutes later, Grace was at my door, and I began sobbing as soon as I saw her.

"You're scaring me, Jane. What's the matter?" she asked.

"I'm pregnant," I replied numbly.

"I thought so."

"I can't believe I did this again. What was I thinking?"

"Were you using anything?" she asked gently.

"Yes, but nothing is foolproof. What am I going to do, Grace. I feel like a child again."

"Did you tell Ted yet?"

"No, you're the only one who knows, and you have to promise you won't tell Derek."

"I won't, but you need to talk to Ted soon."

"We're having dinner tonight, and I figured I'd tell him then."

"Jane, he loves you. He'll probably be thrilled. You said he had already mentioned marriage." She paused and then asked, "You are going to keep the baby, aren't you?"

"Yes. This just isn't how I planned for things to work out."

"Sometimes, things are out of our control. And we're talking about a baby. What could be better than bringing a new life into the world? It will all work out fine, Jane."

I smiled and said, "You're right. Do you think you could tell Mom for me?"

Grace laughed and said, "You're on your own on that one, kid."

~ * ~

I must have changed my clothes five times while waiting for Ted to arrive at my apartment. I couldn't focus on anything longer than three or four minutes and had managed to empty the trash and clean out the refrigerator. I kept debating on when I should tell him. Part of me just wanted to tell him right as he walked in the door, but when he arrived he said he'd planned a special evening for us. I decided to wait.

As we drove, I made a conscious effort to act as normally as possible. When we passed the signs for Boston, I began to get curious as to our destination.

"Where are we going tonight?"

"Do you remember where we went on our first official date?"

I reached for his hand and responded, "How could I forget? That was the best lobster I ever ate." Along with the memory, came a wave of queasiness. *Please let me get through dinner without getting sick,* I bargained with no one in particular.

As we pulled into the parking lot, I said, "This is so romantic, Ted. Sometimes, I can't get over how thoughtful you are."

Ted turned off the car and said, "Jane, I want this to be a night to remember."

We were seated at the same table as our first date. Ted ordered some wine. After it was served, Ted shifted in his seat uncomfortably, so I asked, "What's wrong?"

Ted smiled and reached for my hand. "I had planned to wait to do this, but I am so nervous I thought I was going to wreck the car."

"Do what?"

"Give me a minute. Jane, when Annie died, part of me died, too. I resigned myself to the fact that I had had my one chance at love, but then you came along and all that changed." He reached into his jacket pocket and pulled out a black, velvet box and said, "I love you with all of my heart, Jane, and I want to spend the rest of my life with you." He paused, then added, "Will you marry me?"

I burst into tears, and Ted got a panicked look on his face.

"I want to marry, you, Ted, but..."

"But what?" he asked in a guarded tone.

"I'm pregnant," I stated simply.

Ted's eyes grew large, and my heart fell when he asked, "Are you kidding?"

I shook my head and he ran his hand through his hair. "Wow. I mean... I'm speechless. How far along?"

He couldn't seem to finish a thought, and I was growing more despondent. It must have shown on my face, because he came and knelt down next to me.

"I'm sorry, Jane. I'm just blown away by the news. How are you?"

"I'm... scared... happy..."

"Me, too," he admitted. Then he looked me in the eyes as he put his hand on my belly and said, "We'll work it out."

Thirty-four

Ted and I had so much to discuss, and I wanted to do it in a more private setting, so we left the restaurant and headed back to my place. We picked up a pizza along the way, and after I finished eating, I was better able to discuss our situation with Ted.

"You're really happy, then?" I asked, needing a final reassurance of his devotion to me.

"Yes, Jane, I am." He paused and quickly added, "You are going to marry me, aren't you?"

Now he was the insecure one. "Of course, I'm going to marry you. I just wish... I just wish the timing were better."

"Jane, we're going to have a baby. What could be better than that?"

"I know, but..." and with that the tears returned, and I sat there crying uncontrollably.

Ted held me and said, "It's going to be an emotional nine months, isn't it?"

I smiled and relaxed a bit.

"I want to get married right away, Jane. Let's get settled in our new life before Emma goes back to school."

"Oh, Emma. How do you think she's going to take the news? A stepmother and a new baby!" I exclaimed.

"Let's just deal with the wedding first and then we'll tell everyone about the baby. By then Emma will be used to our new family and she'll be ready for the new baby."

"You certainly are an optimist. I'm not sure it's going to be that easy. I'd like to talk to Emma before we tell her about the wedding, and then I need to face my mom. I'm not sure how much I want to tell her."

"You're not afraid to tell your mom, are you?" he asked with a smirk.

"It's complicated," was all I could manage as I was immediately taken back to the first time I told my mother I was pregnant. I was so frightened, and her outrage and disappointment had left me even more alienated. *This time it's going to be different*, I told myself.

~ * ~

The next afternoon, I picked Emma up from camp and we went grocery shopping for dinner. When we arrived at Ted's house, Emma put the groceries away and I got things ready so that we could make a cake. While we mixed up some batter, I wanted to get a feel for how Emma would take the news about the wedding.

"I like spending time with you, Em," I said before kissing her on top of her head.

"Me, too. I wish you lived with us," she said while she unloaded silverware from the dishwasher.

I decided not to go any further because I didn't want to tell Emma anything until Ted was with us. We had a lovely dinner and had established a ritual of telling the best thing about our day.

After Emma had told her story about getting to the top of the rock climbing wall, Ted said, "Emma, the best part of my day is right now. I have something special to tell you. Miss Richards and I are getting married, and the three of us are going to be a family."

Emma just stared at her father and said nothing.

My stomach began to knot up, but I summoned up my courage and said, "Emma, let's go for a walk. Just the two of us." Ted looked crestfallen, but I smiled and said, "It'll be fine."

We walked down the street. Emma remained tight-lipped, so I initiated our conversation.

"Emma, remember when we talked about my dad?" She nodded her head, and I was grateful for the response. "I told you that my mom has a friend Lawrence and I hoped they would get married, remember?" Again she nodded. "Do you remember why I said I wanted her to get married?"

"Because you didn't want her to be lonely," she replied sullenly.

"That's right. When you're married, you have someone to do things with, and that is always more fun. Your dad and I want to get married because without each other, we would be lonely. Do you know the other reason?" She shrugged her shoulders. I stopped walking and bent down to her meet her gaze. "I want to marry your dad because I love you and I want to be part of your family. When you have a family, you always have someone to take care of you. Plus, I would be lonely without you, too."

Her bottom lip began to quiver, and she grabbed me around the neck. Tears and relief washed over me as I hugged Emma close. I sat on the curb and pulled her onto my lap.

"Okay," she said.

"Okay to being a family?" I asked.

"Yes," she replied, and I hugged her again. She pulled back and said, "So, that means you're going to be my mom, right?"

"I guess so," I replied, not sure of what she was trying to say.

There was still something troubling her, but she was holding back.

"What do you want to say me, Emma? You can ask me anything."

"What am I supposed to call you now?"

"I haven't thought about it. Do you have any suggestions?"

"Can I call you Mom?" she asked anxiously.

"I would love that, but only if you're sure."

"I'm sure. Can I ask you something else?"

"Sure, Emma."

"Can we go home and have dessert?"

I laughed as I stood and pulled Emma up. We walked back hand in hand, and when we arrived back home, Ted was pacing the floor. I smiled and nodded that all was well. I gave Ted and Emma some time to talk in private while I went to the kitchen to get us some ice cream and call my mother. I asked if I could come by, and as I drove over, I wasn't sure I would tell her about the baby. Part of me felt like it wasn't anyone's business, yet part of me wanted to tell her in a confident way to prove that I wasn't that teenager anymore who almost ruined her life.

~ * ~

I took a deep breath before I went into the house and found my mom sitting on the sofa watching a news program.

My mother was one to get right to the point. She asked, "What do you need to talk to me about?"

"A few things. First Ted asked me to marry him."

"Jane, that is the best news ever. I have to confess that Ted called and asked my permission. He's a wonderful man, Jane, and Emma is adorable." She paused, then added, "They're blessed to have you, too."

Compliments were not easy for my mother, and I was so moved that tears began again.

"There's something else." I paused, but I just couldn't do it. "The wedding will be small and soon. We don't want to wait."

~ * ~

As I drove home, the fear and isolation resurfaced. I pulled over and sobbed in my car. My cell phone rang. It was Ted.

"What's wrong, Jane?"

"I just told my mother."

"Was she upset?"

"No, she's happy, but I didn't tell her everything."

"So, what's wrong?"

I wasn't ready to tell Ted about my past. "I'm just an emotional mess today."

"Come over and spend the night here. I'll take care of you," he offered.

That was all I needed to hear.

Thirty-five

Ted and I had made all of the arrangements for the wedding, and I stopped by Grace's house to fill her in. I knocked on the door, and Derek answered with a smug look on his face.

"Look who's here. The blushing bride."

I did not react to his remarks. "Hello, Derek. Where's Grace?"

"She's in the kitchen."

As I passed through the living room, I noticed there were no photographs—not even from their wedding. Grace was making some iced tea in the kitchen, which was equally as bare. It had a sterile quality, and a feeling of sadness washed over me. Grace smiled and kissed my cheek when she saw me.

"I have so much to tell you. The wedding is a week from Friday. It's going to be small—just family and a few friends. Father Flaherty is going to marry us at Holy Family, and then we are going to dinner at The Chateau. We have a private room reserved. I can't believe we were able to get it put together so fast."

"Gee, Jane," Derek interrupted. "What's the rush? People are going to think you're knocked up." He laughed.

Grace looked alarmed, and I shot Derek a look just daring him to keep talking. He got the message and mumbled, "I'm going out. I've had enough of this wedding talk."

When we heard the door close, Grace apologized for Derek.

"He really didn't know, Jane."

"I know, and thank you for keeping my confidence. We are going to wait to tell everyone about the baby. I don't want any drama surrounding this pregnancy."

"Have you told Ted, yet?" she inquired gently.

"No," I admitted. "I feel like I should tell him everything, but I'm scared. I know I have to do it before the wedding."

"Jane, you were very young, and Ted certainly won't hold it against you."

"I still struggle with it, Grace. I haven't forgiven myself. How can I ask him to accept it? I just don't know."

"Ted is a special man, Jane. I think you just need to be upfront and it will all be fine."

"I'm going to tell him tonight. It's been weighing on me pretty heavily, and I want to thoroughly enjoy every minute of my wedding. Speaking of which, would you be my matron of honor?"

Grace's face lit up and then fell just as quickly. "I don't have a lot of money to spend on a dress now that I'm not working," she admitted.

"I'm paying for it. We have to go shopping for both of our dresses, though, and you have the task of helping me choose them."

~ * ~

That night, I had dinner at Ted's, and after we had put Emma to bed, Ted said he had wanted to talk to me about something. "With the wedding coming up so fast, we have to plan to move your stuff in here. If you call the movers, I'll take care of the rest. I want them to do all of the packing. You are not to lift anything," he ordered.

I didn't say anything because I hadn't even thought about where we would live. What an idiot I was. Of course we would have to live in Ted's house. Not just Ted's house—Annie's house with all of her things still hanging on the walls. Her furniture, her dishes. Ted interrupted my mental tirade.

"What's the matter, Jane?"

"I never thought about the moving part. I guess we can't move into my loft, can we?"

"No," he replied gently, "but we can redecorate and change whatever you want."

"Thank you for understanding. Now I need to tell you something. I want us to start our married life without any secrets."

Ted looked panicked and said, "This sounds serious."

"It's something from my past that I want you to know. When I was seventeen, I was dating a guy, and we were pretty serious. The night of our prom I told my parents we were going to an all-night party at my friend's house and we spent the night together at a cheesy motel in Hartsville. I ended up pregnant and thought Mike and I would marry and live happily ever after, but that wasn't the case. Mike wanted no part of a wife and a baby. He had a baseball scholarship, and he wasn't going to let me sabotage the 'best time of his life.'"

"What did your parents say?" he asked.

"My dad was gone by then, but my mother had plenty to say. She was livid. *'How could I be so stupid? I hope it was worth it'* were just a few of the comments aimed at me. We met with Mike and his parents, and his father accused me of trying to trap their son into marriage. We were so young and..."

I remember waking up and seeing my sister's face.

"Is it over?" I asked weakly.

Grace nodded, and I shut my eyes, but not before the tears escaped.

I began to weep quietly, unable to finish my sentence.

"Did you put the baby up for adoption?" Ted prodded.

"No," I answered through my sobs. Before I could continue, Ted stood and walked out of the room, leaving me alone.

I was heartbroken at his rejection, but didn't go after him. I would wait as long as necessary, and then I would tell him the rest. After what seemed like hours, but was probably less than ten minutes, Ted returned.

"I'm sorry I walked away. I needed to remove myself and think. It's all so much—the wedding, the baby... this." He paused and sat next to me. "Whatever happened in the past is over. Let's focus on the wedding and getting you moved in here. Then we'll get ready for our baby. I'm going to look up some movers."

And with that declaration, I could tell that Ted had already put my confession behind him and was moving on to the next thing. I could not compartmentalize my feelings that easily. Some scars took longer to fade.

Thirty-six

The days before the wedding flew by. I spent most of my time packing, and before I felt even close to ready, it was the day before the wedding. Ted was having a small gathering at his house so that I could meet his parents and siblings. My mother and Lawrence were coming as well, but Derek was working and Grace didn't want to come without him. I have to admit I was relieved. Derek could be a time bomb, and I never knew when he was about to explode. I was nervous enough without having to worry about him.

I bought a new dress, and as I put it on I was pleased to see that my belly was still flat. I was still uncomfortable with the idea of being a pregnant bride, but was too busy to give it much thought.

I arrived at Ted's place before his family, and he was surprisingly relaxed. The caterers had everything under control, and Ted was sitting with Emma reading a book.

"Look at you two!" I said proudly. "About to have a houseful of guests and you are all ready for them."

Ted rose and kissed me, and Emma pretty much ignored me.

"Hi, Emma. I can't wait to meet everybody. Will you help me remember their names?"

She shrugged her shoulders, and Ted said, "Emma, please answer Jane."

"I guess so," she replied, not meaning it. She got up and went to the window to watch for arriving guests.

Ted pulled me close and kissed me again.

"Come sit a minute." He motioned to the sofa, and I sat beside him. "Annie's parents are coming by tonight."

I must have looked horror-struck, because he immediately followed up with, "They know about the wedding. I invited them, but they declined. This has been awkward, and I just thought the sooner we face it, the sooner we can move past it. It's been hard for Liz, but David said they would stop by to wish us well."

"I... I... I don't know if I can do this." I willed myself not to cry.

"Please, just do it for me. David and Liz are Emma's grandparents, and they will always be a part of our lives. I can't change that and, besides, I wouldn't want to."

I don't know why I felt betrayed by his words, but I did. We were interrupted by the door bell as the Manning clan descended upon us. Ted's three brothers and his sister arrived with their spouses and a throng of kids. I was introduced to all of them, and then Ted's parents arrived. His dad was an older version of Ted and very handsome. Short blonde hair with strands of gray and vibrant blue eyes. His smile was warm and familiar, and he gave me a gentle hug as we met.

"I'm Jack Manning, Jane. We are so happy to have you join our family."

"Thank you, Jack. Everyone has been so gracious and welcoming."

My mother and Lawrence arrived, and the house was filled with laughter and children squealing. The doorbell rang and my heart sank, because the only guests that hadn't arrived were Liz and David. Ted answered the door and led them in. They approached the group timidly, and I noticed that David looked tired and Liz's eyes were red around the edges. I was immediately remorseful for resenting their presence in our life and was relieved when Bonnie embraced them and brought them into the fold.

I gathered all of my courage and walked over to them. I smiled and said, "Thank you both for coming. It means a lot to all of us."

David smiled and said, "We wish you all the best."

Liz's eyes began to fill, and she excused herself to the restroom.

"I'm sorry," David said. "I thought maybe this would help her move on. I'd better go check on her."

"Let me," I volunteered as I wanted to face this situation sooner than later.

I waited outside of the bathroom door, and Liz was surprised and a little startled to see me there.

"Come into Emma's room for a minute," I suggested.

We sat together on the bed, and I said, "I just want you to know that I will do my best to make sure that Ted and Emma are happy and well taken care of. I cannot even begin to understand how hard this is for you, but I hope in time you will feel more comfortable around me. I know Ted and Emma want you to continue to be a big part of Emma's life. I want that, too."

Liz dabbed at her eyes and said, "Thank you, Jane. This has been extremely difficult for me, but I have no animosity toward you. I'm glad that Ted and Emma found you. I just miss my daughter, and sometimes it's feels so unfair that life is going on without her."

I had no response, so I put my arm around her and gently patted her shoulder.

"Let's go back to the party. David and I will be leaving shortly—we're meeting some friends for dinner," Liz said as she stood to check her makeup in the mirror.

Ted gave me a curious look when we returned, but I smiled to let him know it was under control. I joined my mother and Bonnie, who were talking about cruises.

When they were finished, Bonnie turned her attention to me. "I saw you talking to Liz. How are you holding up?"

"Fine, thanks. It's just an uncomfortable situation, and there's really no way to fix it. Hopefully over time, it will get easier."

"David and Liz are good people, and I'm sure they will come around. I don't want you to worry about it, though. You need to take care of yourself... and my new grandbaby," she whispered loudly enough for my mom to hear.

My mother looked as though she had been slapped in the face. I opened my mouth to speak and she just walked away.

Thirty-seven

I managed to make it cheerfully throughout the rest of the night and was extremely relieved when it was over. Everyone had gone, except for my mother and Lawrence. My plan had been to spend the night at my mother's house, but now I was dreading it. I started to clean up some glasses in order to stall, but Ted gently removed them from my hands.

"Tomorrow a cleaning company is coming, so just leave everything. Besides, I want you to get plenty of rest. We've got a big day tomorrow."

I smiled and reached out to hug him. "So, we're really going to do this, huh?"

"I don't know about you, but I'm getting married tomorrow."

"I love you and Emma very much, Ted, and I'm going to do my best to take care of you and our family."

"Jane, I love you, too. Everything is going to work out just fine."

My mother and Lawrence were waiting patiently, so I said, "I'd better be on my way. I'll see you at the church."

~ * ~

My mother was unusually quiet on the ride home. Lawrence was none the wiser, though, so that made the trip a little less stressful. I said good night to them both, and after I had changed into an old pair of comfy pajamas, I went downstairs to make a cup of tea and talk with my mother.

She joined me in the kitchen wearing her blue Chenille bathrobe. She'd had that robe for as long as I could remember, and just the sight of her in it was comforting.

I poured us both a cup of chamomile mint tea and said, "I'm sorry I didn't tell you about the baby."

"Is that why you are getting married?" she asked.

"No," I replied curtly.

"I'm sorry, too, Jane. It's just that..."

"It's just that with my track record, one could only assume that we had to get married?" I challenged.

"Jane, don't be so dramatic. I didn't mean to imply anything. Just let me ask one question—would you have married him anyway?"

"Yes. In fact, he asked me to marry him before he knew about the baby."

"Thank you for telling me, Jane." She reached for my hand and said, "I just want you to be happy."

"I am, Mom. I'm scared, too," I admitted.

"Jane, I have no doubt that you will be a wonderful wife and mother. I'm very proud of you."

My mother's words hit me hard, and before I could respond, my eyes filled with tears. "I am so emotional. I don't know if I can stand nine months of this."

My mother chuckled and said, "This is just the beginning."

~ * ~

I slept surprisingly well and busied myself until the early afternoon when my mom, Grace and myself all had appointments to get our nails, hair and makeup done. Grace was supposed to be at Mom's by one o'clock. At one thirty, I picked up the phone to call her when I heard her car in the drive way.

She came in and said, "Sorry, I'm late. I just couldn't get it together today."

I stared at her left cheek where the remnants of a bruise were still visible. She had tried to conceal it with makeup, but that just made it more evident.

"What happened to your cheek?"

"Oh, it's nothing. A stupid accident really. I was in the laundry room and didn't realize that the cabinet door was open, and I banged into it."

Just then my mother walked in, and as she went to kiss Grace she stopped and asked, "What happened to you?"

"Nothing," she replied obviously irritated. "It was an accident. This is Jane's big day, so can we stop focusing on me?"

While I knew she was lying, I knew that if I pushed, Grace would leave and I wanted her with me more than anything on my wedding day.

"Let's go to the salon, then," I ordered.

~ * ~

The moment every little girl dreams of was upon me, yet it was not the wedding I had always pictured. Everything had happened so fast, and many of the special touches I had hoped for were forgotten. I smiled, though, because despite it all, I was marrying a wonderful man and I felt a joy so intense, it almost hurt. The priest spoke, and while I knew that I should pay more attention to his words, I found myself missing my dad and replaying this day with him there. He would have looked so handsome in his tuxedo, trying not to cry as he walked me down the aisle. Then he would say to Ted, "You better be good to my little girl," as he slapped Ted on the back.

I looked over at Grace. The forty-dollar makeover still didn't cover the damage Derek had inflicted on her fragile face. That would be different, too, if my dad were still alive.

My thoughts were interrupted by Grace saying, "Give me your bouquet."

I handed it to her, and Ted and I repeated our vows. When I had finished placing the ring on Ted's finger, the priest pronounced us husband and wife. I melted in Ted's embrace, and we had our first kiss as a married couple. Our friends and family gave us thundering applause, and instead of departing at that moment, the priest called Emma up on the altar.

"Emma, this is a special day and your parents wanted you to know how much they love you. Now that they have taken their wedding vows, the three of you are going to take a family vow. Do you promise to be a family and love each other and take care of each other?"

In unison, the three of us replied, "We do."

"Jane, do you have something for Emma?"

Grace handed me a necklace with a gold medallion that I had inscribed with the word *family*.

"Emma, from now on the three of us are a family," I said as I carefully put the chain around her neck.

"By the power vested in me, I now pronounce you a family. Ladies and gentleman, I present to you the Manning family."

Everyone clapped as the three of us embraced. Ted lifted up Emma, and the three of us exited the church as if we were floating. This truly was the happiest time of my life, and I was overflowing with emotion. Ted, Emma and I greeted guests as they exited the church. As we were about to get into the car, Derek approached us.

It was obvious that he had been drinking, so I said, "Emma, would you please go over there and tell Grandma Ruth that I need her?"

"Gee, Jane. I'm not going to hurt you. No need to call big, bad Ruth over to defend you. I just wanted to congratulate Ted. Buddy, you certainly got the better sister. Not like that nagging hag I'm married to. If only..."

Before he could finish, Ted grabbed Derek by the tie and pulled him close. "Listen, you shut your mouth and keep your hands to yourself. Everyone knows what you did to your wife, and if it happens again, I'll come after you myself."

Ted released him with a shove, and Derek just walked away, but not before muttering, "Bastard."

My mother appeared at my side, and asked, "What's wrong?"

"It's all right now. Will you do me a favor, though? Tell the bartender at the restaurant to only put a splash of alcohol in Derek's drinks tonight. He's so drunk, he'll never know the difference and, hopefully, he'll sober up a little."

My mother sighed and said, "I wish he would just get out of our lives for good." Then she shuddered as if she had not intended to say that aloud.

I hugged her and said, "Me, too."

Thirty-eight

Ted and I went away for two nights after the wedding, and it was a relaxing, romantic time. We talked and went for walks on the beach and just enjoyed each other's company. I had always dreamt of honeymooning in a villa in Tuscany, but with such short notice a weekend trip was the best we could do. I squashed my pangs of regret and focused on the blessings that lay ahead.

On the ride home, the reality of our new life together began to hit me, and I confessed, "I'm nervous."

"About what?" Ted asked.

"Everything. Emma, the baby, the house. And I start school in a couple of weeks."

"School?" he challenged. "I didn't think you'd be going back."

"Why would you think that?"

"Well, I don't know. I guess because Annie stayed home with Emma, I just figured you'd want to do the same. We don't need the money and the baby will be here in March. You won't be able to finish the school year anyway."

I could feel the pressure begin to swell inside of me. *Why am I the one who has to make all of the sacrifices? I moved into Annie's house, and now I'm expected to act like her, too.*

It was too much to think about, so I said, "I'm not sure what I'm doing, but I fully expect you to support me and whatever I decision I make."

"Whoa, Jane. I didn't mean to upset you. I just thought..."

He never finished his sentence and I never asked him to. We rode the next hour in silence, and I was extremely relieved to be 'home'.

He stopped me before I got out of the car and said, "I'm sorry, Jane. I know you've been under a lot of stress, and I'll help you in any way. As soon as you're settled in, we can talk about redecorating."

I kissed him and said, "Thank you."

Just then we saw Emma, Bonnie and Jack come out to greet us. Emma came running over to Ted and immediately jumped up into his arms.

"Daddy, I'm so glad you're home. I missed you so much. Did you bring me anything?"

"I missed you too, Em. Aren't you going to say hi to Mom?"

"Hi," she whispered as she buried her head in his chest.

"Did you have a nice time?" Bonnie asked after giving me a hug.

"We had a lovely time and thanks for taking care of Emma."

Jack put his arm around me as we walked into the house and said, "It was our pleasure. We're very happy... about everything."

"Thanks, Jack. That means more than you know," I replied.

As we walked into the house, the angst returned as the photos of Annie glared at me as if to say, 'you don't belong here.' I felt like I was in someone else's house, yet I was home. Thankfully Bonnie had made dinner because I was feeling very out of sorts and would not have known where to begin.

~ * ~

Dinner was filled with a lot of laughs, and I enjoyed getting to know my new family. Jack was funny and silly and Bonnie more serious. She playfully admonished him during dinner, but I could tell there was a strong connection between the two of them. I was sad to see them go, but Jack had to work the next day, and it was time for the three of us to get used to being our own family.

When it was time for Emma to go to bed, I volunteered to help her.

"I want Daddy to do it," she whined.

"I want to spend a little time with you first, and then Daddy can come in." I didn't wait for a response and added, "Besides, I have another present for you."

I grabbed a bag from my suitcase and went to Emma's room and sat on her bed.

"This is kind of silly, but I thought it would be fun, too. I got us matching pajamas!"

Emma's face lit up. Thankfully I could still appeal to the kid in her.

"We can surprise Daddy," she offered.

"Come here and sit with me, Emma. It's going to be different with me living here, huh?"

"Yes."

"I know I'm going to like being your mom, though. I know we talked about you calling me mom—is that still okay?" I prodded gently.

"Yes, but..." she stammered.

"But, what? Just say it. You won't hurt my feelings."

"It feels weird. I go to say it and it comes out all messed up," she admitted.

"I think it will get easier the more you say it, so just say it—mom."

"Mom."

"Again," I ordered.

"Mom." She laughed.

We did that about ten times, and finally we collapsed on the bed in a fit of giggles.

"I love you, Emma, and everything is going to be great. I don't want you to worry about a thing. Let's put on our new pajamas and surprise Dad."

~ * ~

After Emma was in bed, I went into 'our' bedroom and began to look through my stuff. Everything was still in boxes, and I began to feel overwhelmed. I sat on the edge of the bed, and the uneasiness returned. I wondered if Ted had kept the bed he and Annie shared. I knew it was childish, but I wanted a new bed with all new sheets, pillows and comforters. I also wanted to put some of my furniture in the house, too.

I stood and walked over to Ted's dresser and picked up a photo of him, Annie and Emma at the beach. Just then Ted came into the room and said, "I'm sorry I didn't put that away. Everything happened so fast, I didn't get a chance to do some of the things I had intended."

"It's fine. I don't think it would be good for Emma if you removed all traces of Annie from the house. I just would like to have some stuff of my own. Do you think we could get a new bed?"

"Sure. Let's go shopping tomorrow and pick one out. Then we can get your stuff out of storage and start rearranging things around here. Pretty soon, you'll feel like you lived here all your life."

Pretty soon. Is that when I'll stop seeing Annie in every corner of the house?

Thirty-nine

In the end, I agreed with Ted that I would not return to work. I cried when I told Mattie, but she assured me that this was the best move for my family, and I knew in my heart that I was doing the right thing. Emma returned to school as a first grader, and I spent my days painting and going through the boxes of my things. I totally redecorated the master bedroom and bath, and it was there that I felt totally at ease. That was not the case in the rest of the house. Any changes I made were severely scrutinized by Emma, and I had to tread lightly.

Now that the morning sickness had subsided, my pregnancy was happily uneventful and I felt reborn again. I had a lot more energy, and the small bump was a beautiful reminder of the exciting changes that lay ahead. It was time to tell Emma about the baby, and I was dreading it with all my being. She had adapted fairly well to all of the changes, but I was not sure how she would react to this.

I decided to call Grace to help bolster my confidence in preparation for our talk with Emma tonight. When she answered, she sounded like she had been sleeping.

"Hi, Grace. It's me. Did I wake you?"

"What time is it?" she asked groggily.

"Noon. Are you sick?"

"No. I've just been really tired lately. I've been having trouble sleeping. It's nothing. How are you feeling?"

"I'm fine. I feel much better now that I'm not nauseated all the time. I'm nervous because we are telling Emma about the baby tonight. Any suggestions?" I asked hopefully.

"Gosh, Jane. I don't know. Just be quick and matter of fact. Try not to make a big deal out of it."

"I'm not sure how she'll take the news," I confessed.

"Has she been giving you trouble?"

"Not really. She gives me attitude sometimes, but nothing I haven't been able to handle. I feel like I'm waiting for a bomb to explode, and I hope this doesn't set her off."

"You'll never know until you tell her. Just do it, because you don't want her hearing about it from someone else."

"You're right, Grace. I always feel better after we talk. Why don't you come over for lunch tomorrow? I get so bored during the day."

"I can't. I have a doctor's appointment."

A thought hit me, and before I could stop myself I blurted out, "Are you pregnant? Maybe that's why you're so tired."

Grace was quiet and said, "No, I'm not pregnant. I've got to go."

She hung up and I was left staring at the handset. I wondered if I should call my mother about Grace, but decided there was no fixing this situation so there was no need to worry her.

~ * ~

That night after dinner, the three of us went for a walk. I wanted Ted to be the one to tell her because I thought it would be easier coming from him. We went to the neighborhood park and sat on the swings. Emma sat on Ted's lap, and since we were alone, the time seemed right.

"Emma, we've got something exciting to tell you. We're going to have a baby," he blurted.

"I don't want a baby. I want a dog," she replied.

Ted looked mortified, but I laughed.

"Well, right now, we're having a baby," he reiterated, "and you are going to be a big sister."

"It's not going to sleep in my room, is it?"

"No, honey," I answered. "You will keep your room and the baby will have its own room. We will make the guest room into a nursery for the baby. Maybe you can help us decorate it."

"That's the room Grandma and Papa sleep in! Where will they sleep?" She began to cry.

"Emma, this is ridiculous," Ted scolded, and she began to cry harder.

Then I began to tear up, and when Emma saw, she looked frightened.

"Emma, we'll work it out. We will always have room for your grandparents. We can make the office up for them when they come," I offered as I wiped a tear from my cheek.

"Everything is changing, and I hate it," she said as she buried her face in Ted's chest.

He looked at me as if to say, "What now?"

I shrugged my shoulders because I really didn't have an answer for him.

Forty

Our little announcement to Emma unleashed an unpredictable firestorm of rebellion in her. It seemed that I could do nothing right with her, and she had no qualms about letting me know. Sometimes it was just small things. One day when she returned from school and I cleaned out her lunchbox, I found her sandwich had not been eaten. When I questioned her about it, she replied, "You cut it wrong and I couldn't eat it." I never knew what kind of a mood she was going to be in when she came home from school, and I began to wonder if I would survive her teenage years.

I was picking Emma up after school and we were going to visit Grace. I was hosting Thanksgiving this year and I thought maybe she would be less resistant if I invited her in person. I even made a special invitation for her and Derek. I hadn't seen her since the wedding; it seemed that the harder I tried to connect with her, the more she retreated. I called and told her I was stopping by just to drop something off and didn't really give her a chance to say no.

I waited for Emma in the carpool lane, and I could tell from the scowl that she did not have a good day.

I tried to ignore her expression and said, "Hi, kiddo. We're going to see Grace today."

"I don't want to go. Just take me home," she ordered.

"I can't do that because I have to bring something to Grace. Here's some juice and cookies," I said handing her a brown lunch sack.

"I'm not hungry."

We rode the rest of the way in silence. I was tired and didn't have the energy to try and coax her into conversation. I pulled into Grace's driveway and waited outside the car for Emma to join me. When she didn't, I opened her door and waited again.

"Emma, please get out of the car now."

She just closed her eyes and lay down on the seat.

"Fine, just stay here," I replied, hoping a little reverse psychology would work.

I walked to the front door and, sure enough, heard the car door close. Emma ran to catch me. She grabbed for my hand, and I accepted it gratefully, taking any positive responses from Emma that were offered.

After I rang the doorbell, we waited and waited for Grace to answer.

"Maybe she's not home," Emma offered.

"Her car's in the garage."

Finally the door opened and there stood a fragile-looking Grace with her left arm in a cast and sling. She opened the door but did not let us in. She stepped out instead and said, "Derek is sleeping or I'd invite you in."

"What happened to your arm?" I asked bluntly.

"Nothing. I fell down some steps. It was a stupid accident. What did you need to give me?" she asked, changing the subject.

I was dumbfounded, but decided not to confront her. "It's an invitation to Thanksgiving. It's my first attempt at a holiday, and I want you and Derek to be there. Please say you'll come."

She took the invitation and replied, "I don't know. I'll talk to Derek about it," as she turned to go back into the house.

"Wait, Grace." I was desperate to keep her talking but realized that she was out in the cold with no coat.

She smiled sadly and said, "Jane, I'm okay. We'll see you on Thanksgiving."

As she closed the door, I looked down at Emma and felt the sting of tears.

"Don't cry, Mom. Her arm will get better."

Yes, but will the rest of her ever recover?

~ * ~

Thanksgiving Day was cold and crisp with a clear, sunny sky. I was hopeful that Grace would show up, but I did have my doubts. I didn't share my thoughts with anyone and just prayed that it would all work out.

My mother and Lawrence arrived precisely at 4 p.m., and the men settled down in front of the television to watch football while my mother helped me in the kitchen.

She grabbed an apron from the pantry and said, "Tell me what to do."

"The turkey will be done in an hour, and I have a couple of casseroles ready to put in the oven. You can chop some celery and onions for the dressing."

I handed her a cutting board and knife, and she chopped while I melted some butter in the frying pan.

"Have you been to the doctor lately?" my mom asked with a glance at my growing belly.

"I go next week and I am dreading getting on that scale," I laughed. "It should be against the law to weigh a pregnant woman the week after Thanksgiving."

She laughed and asked, "Are you feeling good, though?"

"I am. I have more energy now and I need it. Emma keeps me hopping."

"Kids are a lot of work."

"It's not just that, Mom. I can handle the physical stuff. It's the moodiness that throws me. Some days Emma and I are in a great groove, and then she freaks out at me because I put her peas too close to her mashed potatoes."

"Does she act that way with Ted, too?"

"Sometimes, but I'm with her the most these days. Do you have any advice?"

"Jane, just be patient and try not to react to her. I guarantee that if she doesn't get a rise out of you, she'll stop."

"You're right," I admitted. "I try and appease her and it gets me nowhere."

"Just be consistent," she recommended. "Over time, she'll settle down."

"And then the baby will get here and we'll all be one happy family, right?" I snickered.

"No one said it would be easy, Jane, but most people would agree that it's definitely worth all of the aggravation."

I transferred the dressing into a baking dish and glanced at my watch.

My mom immediately asked, "When was Grace supposed to be here?"

"Same as you, but you know how she is. I'll bet they get here any minute now."

"I don't feel good about this, Jane. Let's call her."

I grabbed the phone and dialed Grace's number.

Derek answered, "Speak."

How charming! "Derek, this is Jane."

"Hey, Sis. What can I do for you?" he slurred.

"We were wondering when you and Grace would be getting here for dinner?"

"I didn't know we were invited. I'd have been there early just to see you again."

I swallowed hard to suppress the gagging in my throat and replied, "I dropped off an invitation with Grace, and I assumed you were both coming because I never heard any different from her."

"Gee, I never saw any invitation, and Grace isn't home. She went out somewhere. She must be shopping. She can find more ways to waste my hard-earned money. I bet you don't do that to your precious Ted, do you Janey?"

"It's Thanksgiving," I snapped back. "All the stores are closed. Put Grace on the phone, Derek!"

I heard Derek laugh and the sound of the phone hitting the floor. I waited in the hopes that Grace would pick up, but eventually someone placed the phone on the receiver and the call was disconnected.

I sat at the kitchen table and motioned my mother to join me.

She looked worried and asked, "What's wrong? They're not coming, are they?"

I shook my head. "No. Derek claims that Grace never told him about dinner. He also said she wasn't home. And there's something else. I made an invitation to dinner today and went to her house to deliver it thinking that she couldn't refuse me in person. When she came to the door, I saw that she had a broken arm. She told me she fell, but I don't believe her."

My mother burst into tears. I was so rattled, I was unsure as to what I should do. I reached for her hand and was relieved when Lawrence appeared.

"Ruth, honey, what's wrong?" he asked as he knelt down beside her.

My mother immediately dried her eyes and answered, "I'm fine, really. Just more problems with Grace."

"They're not coming," I informed him.

I filled him in on the rest of the details and left them alone while I went to tell Ted what was going on. I stopped a second, though, and watched Lawrence embrace my mother and added him to my list of people I was thankful for. If only Grace had someone to be thankful for.

Forty-one

I never heard from Grace after Thanksgiving, and I was becoming increasingly fearful for her safety. I had tried to call her numerous times; she either didn't answer or never returned my message. Once Derek answered and I just hung up. Lawrence had confided in me that he left a message for Grace and asked her to please call her mother—it was urgent. Even that didn't reach Grace. She had definitely slipped away from us, and I desperately needed someone outside of the family to talk to. I called Jillian and asked her to come over for lunch that weekend.

I was so excited to catch up with Jillian, and I was eager to have another adult to talk to. Our worlds had gone in different directions, but we made a special effort to keep in touch. When the doorbell rang, I felt like a kid waiting for a playmate to show up.

"I'm so glad to see you," I said, giving her a big hug.

"Look at you," she exclaimed. "You really are glowing."

I laughed and said, "And growing. I feel huge now. I can't imagine what I'll feel like in a couple of months."

We walked to the kitchen and I motioned for Jillian to sit at the table while I finished adding some nuts and chopped apples to our salads.

"Fill me in on everything that's going on at school," I urged as I placed our salads down.

"My class is great this year, but I really miss having you next door. The woman who took your place is nice, but we don't have a lot in common. She's been teaching for thirty years and so she's pretty set in her ways."

"Mattie says she likes working with her, but she's thinking about retiring at the end of the school year."

"She misses you, too. Oh, and Lauren said to say hello."

"What's she up to?"

"The usual—she's dating a guy she met through an online service. His description of himself was not very accurate, but he has a job and no prison record, which is more that she can say about the last guy."

I chuckled and added, "It's good that some things haven't changed. What about you? Seeing anyone?"

She smiled and replied coyly, "As a matter of fact, I am. I met him at a training seminar. His name is Mark, and he teaches art at Wilmington High. We've gone out a few times, and we seem to have a lot in common."

"I'm so happy for you. I can't wait to meet him."

"Give it some time, okay? What's new with you? How's married life?"

I paused, then answered, "It's great, but it's taking some getting used to. Most people get married and have time before the kids come. Not me—I'm getting it all at once."

"Yes, you certainly are on the fast track. How's Emma?"

"For the most part, she's been great. She gives me grief about things, especially when I don't see it coming. Yesterday, she refused to eat breakfast because I made pancakes without asking her if that was what she wanted. I try to ignore her, but yesterday I called her a brat. How's that for great mothering skills?"

"You didn't mean it," Jillian said.

"I know, but it was still wrong so I apologize for yelling at her and she gets away with acting like a brat. I still have so much to learn."

"You'll get the hang of it, Jane. She really loves you, you know. Just give her time."

"That's what everyone says, so I'm trying. My patience is just wearing thin these days."

"You've got a lot on your plate. It looks like you've settled into the house, though. That's something," she offered.

"Well, that's weird, too. I still feel like I'm living in someone else's home. I totally redecorated the bedroom, but haven't touched anything else really. If I try and put something in a different spot, Emma has a fit and tells me it doesn't go there. I tried a few times, but it's a battle I'm not up for fighting. I'm sorry to go on about everything. I must sound like a miserable, old hag."

"No, you don't. You have a lot going on and you just need to vent."

"I miss our lunch talks each day. I have to admit it's boring being home alone all day. There's only so much shopping I can do."

"What about your sister? Do you see her much?"

"That's what I really wanted to talk to you about. Actually, I haven't seen her in such a long time. She's a mess, Jillian. She doesn't call or visit. She never showed up to Thanksgiving dinner."

"Have you gone over there?" she asked.

"I went to her house to give her an invitation to Thanksgiving, and she wouldn't even let me in. She had a broken arm," I said quietly.

"And you think he did it?"

"I'd bet my life on it. The day of my wedding, she had a black eye and claimed she ran into a door. This time, she said she fell. I could tell she was lying."

"Maybe you need to go back over there and try again. Take your mom with you, too. It's hard to lie to your mother, so maybe she'll come clean."

~ * ~

I thought about Jillian's advice, and later that night I called my mother.

"Mom, I think we should come up with a plan and go see Grace."

"And, what? Kidnap her?" she asked dryly.

"I wish. I just feel like we need to keep the lines of communication open or we're going to lose her for good."

"I'm willing to try," she replied. "But, I think she's gone already."

Forty-two

I never heard from Grace. As Christmas neared, her absence weighed heavily on me. On the morning of Christmas Eve, I gathered up the presents I had purchased for Grace and picked up my mother. As we drove, I could see my mother wringing her hands out of the corner of my eye.

"Relax, Mom. It will work out fine."

"You don't know that, Jane. She may refuse to see us."

"I won't let her. And I certainly won't let Derek keep us from her."

"It's easy to talk a good game, but he's dangerous. You need to be careful. You have the baby to think about."

"I know. I just hate him so much... I wish he would just go away."

We rode the rest of the way in silence. As I turned onto Grace's street, I immediately saw her getting the mail.

"She's home. That's something."

I pulled the car into her driveway and she looked at us as if trying to figure out who we were. I put the car in park, and as recognition spread across her face, she ran for the front door. I quickly threw the gear into park and opened the door to catch up with her.

"Grace," I called. "Grace, we're not leaving."

She stopped at the door, and when I reached her, I pleaded, "Grace, please let us in. We are worried sick about you and it's killing Mom. Please let us in... for her sake," I added, hoping the guilt would reach her.

"Come in, but Derek will be home soon. I don't need you to cause any trouble for me."

I motioned for Mom and assured her, "I'll be on my best behavior."

As we walked in the living room, I put the packages on a table and immediately noticed there were no Christmas decorations. Grace was no longer in a sling, but she had a cut above her lip and she looked as though she hadn't combed her hair in days.

Mom handed Grace a platter of cookies, and said, "I brought some of your favorites."

Grace meekly replied, "Thank you." After an awkward silence, she asked, "Would you like some coffee?"

"Sure, let me help you," I offered.

"I've got it. You two just sit," Grace said as she disappeared into the kitchen.

I looked at my mother, who had tears in her eyes, and said, "At least, she's seeing us. This is a great first step."

"But look at this place. Have you ever seen such a depressing looking room? Grace loved Christmas and you'd never know it's tomorrow from looking around here. It's so barren... like a prison."

"I know, but let's focus on the positive. It's Christmas Eve and we are spending time with Grace."

Just then Grace reappeared and said, "The coffee will be ready in a few minutes."

Again, the quiet was deafening, so I reached for a package and handed to it to Grace.

"Open up this present, while we wait."

Grace's face flushed with embarrassment. "I don't have anything for you. I'm sorry."

"Grace, we're just happy to see you and spend time with you."

She opened the gift; inside was a picture of the three of us on my wedding day.

"I love it," she said softly. "I haven't gotten around to decorating this place, yet, so this will get me started. Let me get the coffee."

When she left, I asked my mother if she was all right.

"I just don't know what I'm feeling, Jane. It's just upsetting on so many levels."

A few minutes later, Grace reappeared with the coffee and we opened up the cookies.

"These are great, Mom. Thanks for bringing them," Grace said.

"Where's Derek?" I asked.

"He's working. He should be home soon."

"What are you doing for Christmas?" I questioned.

"Nothing really. Christmas brings back bad memories for Derek."

"Grace, please some over to my house for dinner. We'll all be together and it will be fun. We missed you so much at Thanksgiving. Please come to dinner tomorrow."

"I don't know. I'd have to talk to Derek."

"Can you call him?" I urged gently.

"No. He's working and I don't want to disturb him. I'll call you after I talk to him."

My mother, who had been uncharacteristically silent, finally spoke up. "You'll call us? Like you returned our previous calls? Do you know how many times we have called you? What is going on with you, Grace?" my mother shouted as she burst into tears.

Grace became flustered, and answered, "Nothing is going on. Why can't you accept the fact that I am married and my husband comes first?"

"I can accept that, but I can't stand by and watch this man beat you and berate you and cut you off from everyone who loves you."

"Derek loves me," she shouted.

"He has a funny way of showing it, Grace. If he loves you, why is he stopping you from spending time with your family?" My mother stood and began pacing the floor.

"Derek has never kept me from you," she challenged.

"Then why didn't you come to Thanksgiving? Why didn't you return our calls?"

"I'm sorry. I'll try harder, but right now I need you both to leave." She stood and walked toward the door.

My mother followed her and grabbed her by the arm. "Why? Because you don't want Derek to know we were here, or is it because I'm telling you the truth?"

Grace's head dropped, "You just need to go. It will be better that way."

My mother walked out of the door without her coat, and as I retrieved it, I tried once last time and said, "I know you aren't strong enough to leave on your own, but we can help. Please, if you won't do it for yourself, do it for Mom."

I lifted Grace's chin so I could look her in the eye, but she pulled away and pointed to the door. There really was nothing we could do.

Forty-three

Despite the absence of Grace, our first Christmas together was pretty perfect. Ted and I spent Christmas Eve in front of the fireplace talking about how our lives had come together in such a short period of time. Emma was wide eyed and totally taken with the magic of the holiday. Santa brought her the exact dollhouse she had asked for, and not much could pry her away from it. My mother and Lawrence joined us for dinner after they spent the afternoon with his son. My thoughts continually went back to Grace, but I was determined not to let it show. I had my own family to think of, and at least with them, I could make a difference. I had tried to call Grace on Christmas without success, so I continued to try every few days.

Again, I dialed her number, and this time, I decided to leave a message. After the beep, I said, "Hi, Grace, it's me. Just wanted to say Happy New Year. Well, Happy New Year's Eve anyway. I'm thinking about you and I love you."

If I couldn't have a conversation with her, the answering machine would have to suffice. It was really all

I could do, so after I made the call, I drove over to the farmer's market to get some fresh mushrooms and spinach. Emma was spending the night with Liz and David, and I was planning a special dinner with Ted to celebrate the anniversary of our first date.

I loved just wandering around the market because they had foods from all over the world. It also felt good to get some exercise, as I was getting larger by the minute and still had three months to go.

I gathered up the things I needed plus a few extras and was standing at the juice bar trying to decide what I was in the mood for, when I felt someone staring at me. I looked over to see a man staring at me. He looked familiar and as I scrutinized his face, I realized it was Mike. He was heavier and had less hair, but it was definitely him. I wasn't sure I wanted to talk with him, but when he saw the look of recognition on my face, he took it as an invitation to approach.

"Jane?" he asked cautiously.

"Hi, Mike," I replied as my head began to spin. The last time we saw each other I was pregnant as well. Pregnant with a child that he wanted nothing to do with. So young and selfish. Now I was angry. All of the rage I had felt toward him was coming to the surface and I wanted nothing more than to tell him how I felt, but this wasn't the time or the place so I turned and walked away.

"Hey, where are you going? I just wanted to know how you were doing—you know, catch up."

Maybe this was the time. I slowly walked back in his direction, and said, "I'm great. I'm married to a wonderful man who is thrilled that I am having his baby."

"That's great," he replied. He obviously didn't get my message because he asked, "Is this your first?" I stared at him as he realized his error. I was not about to let him off the hook.

"No," I answered slowly.

"I'm sorry, Jane," he stammered.

"Did you ever wonder what happened to our baby, Mike? You went off to college without a care in the world, and I was left all alone. Did your father tell you I had a miscarriage?" Mike gazed at me blankly. "Did he? Because that's what I told everyone. If you had bothered to even call me you would have known the truth."

Now he tried to walk away, but I wouldn't let him.

"Come back here. You owe me at least that much."

Slowly he faced me again and said, "I was just a kid, Jane. I'm sorry."

"So was I. That was the most awful thing that has ever happened to me, and I went through it all alone. Do you know that I think about what I did every single day? Every day. I try not to let it enter my head, and then something will trigger a memory and it all comes flooding back. Do you know how hard it is to live with that?" He just stared blankly at the ground, but I wasn't finished. "It wasn't right, Mike. A kid or not, you had a responsibility to me and our child, but because you were a coward, I thought I had no other choice. I know better than that now, but that still doesn't change what I did. So, I hope that answers your question, Mike. That is how I am."

I turned on my heels and walked out of the door to my car. I drove to the back of the market, put the car in park and began to sob. I shed tears that I had suppressed for far too long, and I realized that this was a wound that would never heal.

~ * ~

I drove home, but didn't remember any of the ride. When I walked in the door, Ted was already home and had brought me a dozen red roses. I immediately began crying, and Ted assumed I forgot about our anniversary.

"It's all right, Jane."

I sat down without removing my coat and cried even harder.

"Jane, what's wrong? You're worrying me."

"I'm sorry, Ted. I saw Mike at the farmer's market."

"Mike?"

"From high school?" I reminded him, hoping I wouldn't have to go into any more detail.

"What did he say to you? Whatever it was, he had no right."

"He didn't say anything. He acted like we were nothing more than old school mates who happened to bump into each other. It was like he had totally put everything out of his mind. I couldn't believe it," I said as I rested my head on his shoulder.

"Everything will be fine. You need to just forget about it, too, and focus on our baby."

Everything was so black and white with Ted. He didn't understand that this was definitely gray.

Forty-four

The encounter with Mike left me tense and irritable. I couldn't discuss my feelings with Ted. As far as he was concerned, the situation was over and I should simply forget about it. I wasn't wired that way, but the only person who understood what I went through at the time was Grace, and I couldn't talk to her.

I still had seven weeks to go before the baby was due, and some days I felt like it would never get here. To pass the time, I threw myself into decorating the baby's room. February was a dismal month. Snow and rain and no holidays to look forward to. I painted the walls a pale green and spent hours shopping for the perfect matching bedding and curtains. I tried to get Emma to help out with the animal mural I was painting, but she wanted no part of it.

"I want to have my room painted green, too," she whined. "This baby is getting everything."

"Emma, your room was painted recently. I got you those princess sheets you wanted, didn't I?"

"I don't like princesses anymore. I want my room painted," she demanded.

I was overcome with a wave of exhaustion and just said, "Emma, please." I stood and felt a sharp pain across the lower portion of my belly. I screamed, and Emma ran from the room. After about fifteen seconds the pain subsided and then Ted appeared.

"What's wrong?"

"I think I stood up too fast, and I got a sharp pain in my stomach."

"Let's get you into bed so you can lie down," Ted ordered.

"I really don't think it's necessary, Ted."

"Just humor me, Jane."

I settled into bed and said, "Go get Emma. I think I frightened her."

A minute later she appeared but refused to look at me.

"Come sit on the bed with me, Em."

She shook her head.

"I'm fine, honey. You don't have to be scared."

Slowly she approached, and I grabbed her and hugged her. She began to cry and said, "I'm sorry."

"Sorry about what?" I asked.

"Sorry I caused your stomach to hurt."

"Oh, sweetie. You didn't make me have the pain. I just overdid it, that's all."

She smiled and said, "I'm going to go watch TV now."

Ted came in with a glass of milk and some cookies for me. "I thought this might help."

"Cookies always help," I answered.

I took a bite and felt another pain grip my belly. I grimaced, and Ted said, "I'm calling the doctor."

I kept the number by the side of the bed, and I listened as Ted relayed the details to the answering service. When he hung up he said, "We're going in." I must have looked panicked because he added, "It's just a precaution."

~ * ~

Ten minutes later, Mattie was with Emma and we were on our way to the hospital. I had had another episode of pain and it seemed that they were coming on a regular basis. I prayed silently during the car ride that the baby would wait. I was only thirty-three weeks along and knew the longer this baby could hold out, the better.

Ted pulled into the labor and delivery entrance, and as I exited the car another pain stopped me cold. I was immediately forced into a wheelchair by a nurse. They whisked me into the hospital and asked me a dozen questions before I was put into a room and asked to change. As I waited for the doctor to show up, I resumed my prayers. *Please let this baby be okay, God. Please. Please.*

The door opened, and Ted and Dr. Sampson walked in together. I immediately felt better just seeing them both. She examined me and said, "The bad news is you are in labor and you've begun to dilate. The good news is that your water hasn't broken, so I think we have a great chance of stopping the labor. I'm going to order some medication for you and the contractions should stop. I'll send a nurse in, and she'll get an I.V. started. I'll check on you in a little bit, but if you need me, just tell the nurse."

I looked at Ted and started crying. "I feel like this is my fault somehow."

"Jane, these things happen. Everything will be fine, I promise."

I knew Ted couldn't make such a promise, but I felt better anyway. Again, the door opened and a nurse entered with an I.V. and said, "We're going to give you some fluids and some medicine to stop this labor. This will relax you, too."

While she was hooking me up, I felt another pain, but it didn't last as long as the others. The doctor returned and assured me that it wasn't my fault and said she would check on me in an hour or so. The tears began again, and Ted brushed them aside.

"Jane, it's going to be all right. Look at the monitor. The baby's heartbeat is strong and steady. Please just try and relax."

I just nodded and closed my eyes. The fear of something happening to this baby overwhelmed me, and I couldn't recall ever being so scared. I longed for my mother to be with me and wondered if I was ready for motherhood.

Forty-five

I spent the next two weeks at home in bed. Ted got Emma off to school in the morning and my mother came over in the afternoon to help out until Ted came home. I was allowed to get out of bed only to shower and use the bathroom. Any other time, spending a few weeks in bed would seem like the ultimate in luxury, but not now. I was bored and restless and was tired of watching television. Jillian and Mattie came by and visited, and two of my neighbors brought us dinner. I never heard from Grace and tried again to call. I dialed and was surprised when Derek answered.

"Derek, it's Jane. How are you?" I asked hoping maybe a little small talk would open the door to Grace.

"Jane, what a surprise. It's been a long time. Have you missed me?" he asked dryly.

I ignored the question and said, "Derek, could I please talk to Grace? I've been in the hospital with early labor and now I have to stay in bed. I really need her, Derek."

"In bed, huh? I could come over and keep you company," he offered.

Again, I ignored him and asked, "Please, Derek. I'd like to speak to Grace."

He never responded, but he didn't hang up either, and a few seconds later I heard Grace's voice on the other end.

"Hi, Grace. How are you?" I prodded gently.

"I'm fine. Derek said you were in the hospital. Did you have the baby?"

"No, Grace. It's too early. I'm on bed rest and have to take this awful medication every day that makes my heart race. I feel like my heart will pound out of my chest sometimes. But, the baby is fine. I'm just going a little stir crazy is all."

There was silence on Grace's end, so I continued to talk. "What's going on with you?"

"Nothing, really." Silence again.

"Would you and Derek be able to come visit me? I'd love to see you both."

"I'm not sure."

"Mom comes by every afternoon to help. She'd really love to see you, Grace."

"We'll see, Jane."

"Grace, can't you see what is happening? Derek has cut you off from everyone who loves you. Please let us help you," I begged.

"Good-bye, Jane."

I lost her again. Tears formed in my eyes, but I forced them away. I needed to stay calm for the baby. The phone rang, and my heart leapt thinking that Grace had come to her senses.

"Grace?" I answered.

"Sorry, Jane. It's Liz."

I always seemed to say the wrong thing around her. "I'm sorry, Liz. I was hoping it was my sister. It's a long story. How are you?"

"I'm fine. I was wondering if Emma could spend the weekend with us? I know it's short notice..."

"I think that would be great, and I'm sure Emma would agree. It's pretty boring around here these days for all of us."

"Ted told us that you're stuck in bed. When Annie was pregnant with Emma she had to stay in bed, too. She would call me twenty times a day. She was the worst patient." I heard her sigh, and then she said, "I'm sorry, Jane. How are you?"

"I'm fine, and please don't be sorry. It's nice to know I'm not the only one. And taking Emma will help because I know she'll be having fun with you and David."

"Thanks, Jane. How about we pick her up at four?"

"Great. We'll see you then."

I hung up and closed my eyes to rest a moment when I heard a knock on the front door and my mother's key in the lock.

"Jane, it's just me," she called out.

I smiled because she said the same thing every time she came in. She came in and sat next to me on the bed and asked, "What's new?"

I laughed and said, "Well, I took a shower today. That's new." Then I got serious and said, "I talked to Grace today, too."

My mother started to get excited, then she figured out from my expression that nothing had changed.

"At least she spoke to me. Derek answered the phone and he let me talk to her. At first I tried to be non-judgmental and asked for them both to come visit, but I got nowhere and ended up telling her she needed help. She hung up on me."

"You know what's worse, Jane? I can't even cry any more. I feel like I've got nothing left to give where Grace is concerned. I just pray for her every day. That's all I can do."

"I know, Mom. Let's talk about something happier. How's Lawrence?"

"Lawrence is wonderful. He asked me to marry him," she stated as if she was telling me the weather forecast.

"When? Why didn't you tell me sooner? Did you say yes?" I hounded excitedly.

"Gee, Jane. Calm down. He asked me a few days ago, and I didn't tell you because I needed time to think."

"Think about what?" I exclaimed.

"I've been on my own for a long time, Jane. I'm pretty set in my ways and it's been so long since I shared my life with someone. It's a big step, and I needed some time to decide."

"Have you made up your mind?" I asked.

"Yes, I have," she answered coyly.

"Well?"

"I said yes."

I squealed, "Yes. Mom, that's the best news ever."

I hugged her tightly. After a moment, she pulled away and said, "It's time for Emma's bus."

My mom was so private, but her joy was evident. She was radiant as she spoke about marrying Lawrence, and I was grateful she let him into her life. I wanted to hold onto this moment, but I could tell my mother was beginning to get a little uncomfortable, so I decided to get up and go to the bathroom. When I did, a stabbing pain stopped me cold. This was not like the others. I felt a warm trickle running down my leg. It was blood.

Forty-six

The paramedics arrived within minutes after my mother called, and I would have totally lost my mind on the ambulance ride had she not been with me. The technicians were talking to me, trying to keep me alert while taking vital signs and communicating with the hospital. My mother just rubbed my arm while she prayed silently. I prayed, not knowing what to ask for the baby, for me. My head was spinning. When I got there, a nurse put me in a room and hooked me up to a monitor. A doctor came in and did an ultrasound.

He looked at me and said, "We need to take the baby now. The heartbeat is strong, but the placenta is dislodging and you are losing a lot of blood. Dr. Sampson is on her way. We'll try and wait for her, but I'm not going to put you or the baby at risk."

"I'll be having a C-section?" I whimpered.

"Yes. We'll wait about five minutes. In the meantime, a nurse will come in and prep you."

"But my husband isn't here," I cried.

Just then Ted and my mother came in and a bit of relief washed over me.

A nurse came in and said, "I'm Geneva. Dr. Sampson said she'll see you in the operating room. She also said not to worry. I'm going to get you ready for surgery. Now, Grandma, you need to go to the waiting room and, Dad, you go out to the nurses' station and ask for Sheila. She'll get you ready. You're not squeamish, are you? I can only handle one patient at a time." Her laugh put me more at ease.

My mother kissed me and said, "I'll be praying for all of you."

Ted kissed me, too and said, "I'll see you in a few minutes. I love you, Jane."

"I love you, too."

~ * ~

The tears were flowing as Ted and I watched our son make his entrance into the world, and I learned that there is nothing more heart-stopping than waiting for your baby's first cry. He was small, but feisty. His lungs were strong, as evidenced by his wails.

"When can I hold him?" I asked.

The nurse answered, "Not until after we get him examined by the neo-natal team. We'll bring him to you in the recovery room."

"Ted, you have to go with him."

I could see he was torn about leaving me. "I'm fine. Dr. Sampson?"

"She's good," the doctor concurred. "The bleeding has stopped. I'm just going to finish up here and she'll be in the recovery room."

Ted kissed me and said, "You did a beautiful job, hon."

I smiled and said, "Thanks. Now go be with our boy."

~ * ~

I must have fallen asleep because the next thing I remember, Ted gently kissed me on the forehead.

Ted was beaming and said, "He's doing really well, Jane." He brought the baby to me and placed him in my arms. "He's perfect. He's small, but everything is working just the way it should be."

He was the most beautiful baby I had ever seen, and I instantly fell head over heels in love. I ran my fingers over his blond peach fuzz. I counted his fingers and toes, and after my inspection I brought him close and nuzzled him. Nothing could compare to the bliss I felt at that moment.

I heard a knock on the door, and my mother stuck her head in. "Can we come in?"

"Sure. You want to meet your grandson, don't you?" I teased.

Lawrence held the door open for my mother and Emma. She was practically dragging Emma in, so Ted went over and scooped her up into his arms.

"Hi, Emma. There's somebody we'd like you to meet."

"I don't want to," Emma said as she buried her face in Ted's shoulder.

"Emma, please. Just take a look," Ted urged.

I held the baby up and said, "Everyone, this is Emma's brother, Joseph."

"Oh, Jane. Your dad would have been thrilled." My mother beamed.

"He's beautiful," Lawrence added.

"It's a boy?" Emma asked incredulously. "I wanted a sister."

"Maybe next time, kiddo. Do you want to hold him, Em?" I asked.

She nodded, and Ted helped her cradle Joseph's head in her small arms.

My mother took a bunch of pictures and then said, "I forgot. Liz and David are here. They were wondering if you still wanted Emma to spend the weekend with them."

"Sure. Do you want to ask them to come in?"

"I think they'd prefer to stay in the waiting room," my mother admitted.

"I'll take Emma out there. Are you ready to go, Em?" Ted asked.

"I guess, but when can I hold him again?"

"When he comes home, you can hold him all you want, okay? First, come give me a hug. I'm going to miss you," I said.

"You are?" she asked curiously.

"Of course, you're my girl, and nothing will ever change that."

She smiled and was appeased for the moment. Lawrence stepped out with Ted and Emma to give my mom and me some time alone.

"Isn't he beautiful?" I asked as my mother held him.

"I didn't know you were planning on naming him after your father. He would have been the best grandfather. I hate that he is missing this," she admitted as she dried her eyes. "Thank you for giving him Dad's name."

"I still miss him so much, and now I feel like he's back with us." I leaned back and closed my eyes for a minute. "Did you call Grace?" I asked sleepily.

"I left her a message."

I nodded and we both understood. Certain things were out of our control, and right now there was too much happiness in our world to think of anything else.

Forty-seven

I had no idea how a baby would change our lives. The joy and fulfillment were more than I ever anticipated. So were the exhaustion, the depression and the pain from my incision. I had never in my life felt so totally inadequate.

After three weeks, though, we were settling into a routine. Joe, as Emma had decided he would be called, was doing well. He stayed in the hospital three extra days in order to be monitored, and we took him for a check-up once a week. He was a sweet-natured baby, and sometimes I found myself just staring at him, picturing him at different ages. I had never experienced a love like this. It sometimes frightened me and made me cry. My mom said it was the hormones, and I hoped it would soon pass.

Ted was in heaven with our new addition and after all he had been through, he was truly happy. He sometimes came home at lunch just to spend a few minutes with us, and thanks to him, Joe had quite the collection of sports equipment. At night, after Emma was asleep, the three of us would gather in our bed. Even though I was worn out, I cherished that time we spent together. Ted and I would talk about our day and the kids, and marvel how our lives had changed in such a short time.

Emma loved holding Joe and reading him books, but she was extremely jealous when anyone else paid attention to him. When she came home from school one day, my mom and I had planned a special afternoon just for her.

"Hi, Emma. We're going to have a party," I announced proudly.

Her face lit up as she asked, "What for?"

"Just because I love you, that's what for."

She threw herself into my arms and hugged me tightly. My life was truly blessed.

"Grandma went to the store, and she bought all kinds of fun stuff for ice cream sundaes. Wash your hands, and we'll put out all the stuff."

Emma chatted about school and her friends, and it was clear that she was thriving with the attention.

"I have two best friends now," she boasted.

"Two? Who are they?"

"Well, Gina, of course."

"Of course," I echoed.

"And there's this new girl named Alexandra. Except, she likes to be called Alex. Isn't that a cool name?"

"It is."

"The three of us have lunch together every day, and we play four square at recess."

My mind began to wander as Emma kept on chatting away. That old familiar longing to share all of my happiness with Grace resurfaced. I had left several messages for her, but never heard back. As soon as I was able to drive, I would take Joe over to her house. If only she realized what a void she left in my life. Would she ever know how much she was valued?

"Mom? Are you listening to me?" Emma whined.

"Of course, I am," I lied. "Do you have a lot of homework today?"

"I have to write out my spelling words three times each."

"Why don't you wash up and start your assignment," I suggested.

Just then, my mother walked in with Joe.

"Someone needs to be fed," she announced.

"I don't want to do my homework. I want you to play a game with me."

"I have to feed the baby, Emma."

"I'll play with you, honey," my mom offered.

"No. I want my mom to play with me," she cried.

"Emma," I stated calmly. "Right now I have to feed Joe, but as soon as I am done I'll play with you."

"This was supposed to be my party and I don't want him here. I want him to go away. I hate having a brother," she yelled. She ran to her room and slammed the door.

Mom looked at me and said, "Take a deep breath."

I felt tears form in my eyes, and said, "I'm not sure I'm cut out for this."

"You don't have a choice, my dear. Feed the baby, and I'll go talk to Emma."

I took Joe into my arms. We settled into my favorite overstuffed chair and he began to nurse. I looked at him and said, "She didn't mean it, you know. She really loves you."

I closed my eyes, savoring the peace and quiet, I the phone rang.

"Hello?"

"Jane, it's Grace."

"Oh, I am so happy you called me. I miss you so much, Grace. Did you hear? I have a son."

"I got the message. I'm really happy for you."

Her voice was so flat, as if she had no life left in her. "His name is Joseph. Joe. He'd really like to meet his aunt Grace."

"I'd like to meet him, too."

"Mom is here. She can come get you. When do you want to come?"

"I'm not sure. I have to check with Derek, but I'll come soon."

"I want you to be his godmother, Grace. Please say yes. The baptism is in a few weeks."

"Oh, Jane. I'd love to, but..."

"But what? There is no one else I'd even consider asking."

"Jane, it's too much responsibility. I would hate to let you or him down."

"You'd never do that. Don't you realize how much you are loved and needed? I have a huge hole in my life without you, Grace. Mom does, too. Do you know that Lawrence asked her to marry him?" She was silent, so I continued. "We want to share all of these things with you. You just have to let us."

"It's not that simple. I've got to go. I love you, Jane. Don't forget it."

She hung up. Again, I had failed to reach her. My mother came and sat on the sofa.

"Emma's fine. She just needs some time to get used to everything. Who was on the phone?"

"It was Grace. She called about Joe."

"Did she say anything else?" She asked hopefully.

"I asked her to be the baby's godmother, but she said no."

My mother sighed. "So nothing's changed."

"No, but we're doing all that we can." And for now, that would have to suffice.

Forty-eight

The day of the baptism was upon us and I was stressed to my limit. Ted's family was coming and his parents were staying with us. As happy as I was to see them, I was exhausted. Physically, I was almost back to normal, but two months of interrupted sleep had taken its toll and my patience was wearing thin. Our guests had arrived at the house, and I still had to get my makeup on and then dress Joe.

Bonnie must have sensed my anxiety because she sprang into action. "Ted, make sure Emma is dressed and ready. I'll change Joe and, Jane, you finish getting ready."

I smiled at her and retreated to my room. I sat on the edge of my bed and stared a minute at the phone. I picked it up to try Grace one more time, but replaced the receiver. I had to accept the fact that Grace was not able to be a part of my life right now. Maybe she'd come back to us one day, but for today she was gone.

I put on some makeup and surprised myself because I looked good. It had been so long since I put any effort into my appearance, and I was glad I could still get it together. I rejoined our family, and Ted's face lit up when he saw me.

He came over and kissed me and said, "You look beautiful."

"Thanks, Ted. I needed that," I smiled.

"It's the truth. Now let's get going."

Ted and I rode with just our kids. I was grateful for the short break from the rest of the family. Emma was singing to Joe, and I closed my eyes and tried to relax.

"You okay, Jane?"

"I'm a bit overwhelmed these days."

"It will get easier."

"I know, but right now I feel like I might break in two."

"Please, just try and relax and enjoy the day. We have so much to be thankful for."

Ted was right, and I made up my mind that I was going to take pleasure in the celebration.

~ * ~

There was something so comforting about having Joe baptized. The church held so many memories for me. I knew the designs in the stained glass windows by heart, and today a beautiful array of colors shone through them. All of our family was gathered around the baptismal font, and Father Flaherty reminisced about my dad as he told Joe he would have some big shoes to fill. I laughed and cried, and by the time we finished dinner afterwards, I was completely exhausted. Everyone had gone home except for Bonnie, who much to my delight, had offered to stay for a few days. I just wanted to get both kids in their beds and then collapse into my own.

"Emma, it's time for bed," I called.

"I don't want to go to bed now. I want to watch a movie," she whined.

"Emma, it's been along day and you have school," I countered. "Go brush your teeth."

She stood and turned on the television.

I sighed and tried to muster some strength. "Emma, turn off that television now or you won't watch it all week."

"Daaaddy," she wailed.

"What's the matter, Emma?" Ted asked as he entered the family room.

"I want to watch a movie."

"All right, let's pick one out."

"No!" I shouted. "Emma, I told you it was time for bed. Ted, she can't go to you every time I tell her no."

"I'm sorry. I didn't know she asked you already. Emma, no TV."

Emma proceeded to lie on the floor and scream.

"Ted, please help me. I can't do this all by myself."

Ted gave me a frustrated look and opened his mouth to speak, but stopped and bent down to pick Emma up. I watched as she tried to thrash her way out of his arms, but he calmly carried her to her room. I sat down and closed my eyes.

Bonnie sat next to me and said, "Why don't you go take a bath or do something else to relax. Ted has Emma and I'll get Joe ready for bed and then you can feed him."

"That would be wonderful. Thank you, Bonnie."

"It will get easier, Jane. Just remember that."

I retreated to our bedroom and ran a hot bubble bath. I couldn't remember the last time I had relaxed alone. I really felt like I wanted to go to sleep and not wake up for a week, but this would do for now. I slipped into the tub, and even though the water was close to scalding, I felt myself start to let go. I closed my eyes and just focused on my breathing. I must have dozed off, because the next thing I knew, there was a gentle knock at the door.

Ted poked his head in. "Is it safe to enter?" he asked with a grin. "I brought a peace offering."

He placed a mug of tea and a piece of cake on the edge of the tub.

I smiled. "Thanks." I paused then added, "I'm sorry I lost it earlier. How's Emma?"

"She's asleep already. After she calmed down, we talked about how if one of us makes a decision, she cannot go to the other to get her way. I told her if she does it again, we'll punish her."

"This parenting thing is hard," I admitted with a smile.

"It will get better, Jane. Soon Joe will be sleeping through the night and life will get back to normal. Speaking of which, how would you like to go out for dinner tomorrow?"

"You mean like a date?"

"Exactly like a date. My mom will watch the kids and we can spend an adults-only evening."

"It sounds like you have more than dinner in mind," I teased.

"If all goes as planned, I do," he shot back. He leaned over and kissed me and left me to enjoy the peace and quiet. Once again, he made everything right again. Why was I still so sad?

Forty-nine

The excitement of the day must have been too much for the baby, because he was up every hour. Exhausted couldn't even begin to cover how I felt, so I told Ted that I didn't want to go out that night, but he and Bonnie insisted it would be good for me. I took a three-hour nap and felt much better—especially when I saw that Bonnie had straightened up the house, too. She also offered to stay with Joe so I could go get a haircut and buy some new clothes, and I happily took her up on the offer. When I had finished, I checked my watch and saw that I still had some time before the baby had to eat again so I drove to Grace's house. I was surprised to see her working in the yard. I guess I assumed she never left her house.

I got out of the car and approached cautiously because she made no move toward me.

"Hi, Grace. I was just in the neighborhood..."

"Hi. Is the baby with you?" she asked while she continued to plant her flowers.

"No. My mother-in-law is with him. She was here for the christening, and she offered to watch him so I could get out for a while."

I waited for a response, but she just kept her head down and raked the dirt. I reached into my purse and took out a photo.

"Here's his picture," I said as I squatted down to be on her level.

She lifted her head, and I shuddered as I saw her blackened eye. It was swollen and her eyeball was bloodied. I felt sick to my stomach. I instinctively reached out to touch her face, but she pulled away. She took the picture, and her face softened as she studied her new nephew.

"He's beautiful, Jane,'" she said softly. "I'm really happy for you. Can I keep the picture?"

"Of course, but why don't you come back to my house with me and meet him in person? I'll take you right back."

"No, Jane. I have a lot to do. I'll come see him soon," she promised, and with that, she turned and disappeared into her house.

I stood there a minute before I realized she wasn't coming back.

~ * ~

I tried to put my conversation with Grace out of my head and put all my effort into having a nice time with my husband, but it gnawed at me while I got ready. Bonnie was keeping the kids occupied, and I hoped the effort I had put into my appearance showed.

I joined Bonnie and the kids in the kitchen, and Emma asked, "Why are you so dressed up?"

"Daddy and I are going out tonight."

"I want to go," she whined.

"Sorry, kiddo," Bonnie answered. "I need you to stay with me and help me eat those cookies I made."

I smiled my thanks to Bonnie and was relieved when Emma didn't take it any further. I heard the front door open and was excited to see my husband.

"You look nice," he said as he kissed me hello.

"Thanks. I'm really looking forward to our night out," I said hoping to forget about the pit in my stomach that lingered since my visit with Grace.

"Give me a few minutes and we'll get going."

~ * ~

Ted and I had dinner at a small, Italian place that was owned by a mother and son who did all of the cooking. They had black and white photos of their family and different places in Italy hanging all over the stucco walls. I felt like I was in an Italian villa and as Ted and I shared a bottle of wine, I couldn't help but smile.

"What are you smiling at?"

"I'm just so relaxed and happy to spend some time with you."

"I'm glad. I know you've been stressed out lately, so I hope this helps."

"It does, Ted. Sometimes I just need to step back and take a breath."

"We've got a full life, Jane, and we just have to take time and enjoy it."

"Can you believe how much our lives have changed in one year?" I asked.

Ted laughed. "Last year at this time, we couldn't even tell anyone we were dating, and now we're married with two kids."

"I know I get overwhelmed, Ted, but I'm really happy. And I love you very much."

He grinned, and said, "Let's eat so that we can go home and you can show me how much you love me."

~ * ~

When we returned home, Joe was ready to be fed and I was excited to get him to sleep so that I could be with my husband. I was anxious, too, as this was the first time we'd made love since the baby. However, I need not have worried.

Ted and I fell right back into our groove, and afterwards, he said, "I'm glad you're back."

"Me, too."

Ted held me in his arms and began to doze. I started to get up, and Ted pulled me to him.

"Don't go."

"I was just going to check on the kids."

"They're fine. Just stay with me. Please."

He needs me, too, I thought as I relaxed and drifted off to sleep.

Fifty

"Mommy," Emma whispered, sounding oddly timid. "Mommy, Joe won't move. I tried to wake him up and play with him, and he won't move."

I looked at the clock. It read 6:43. My God, Joe never slept through the night.

"What are you talking about?"

Just then Ted woke up.

"What's wrong, Em?" he asked.

"Daddy, the baby won't wake up."

I heard what she was saying, but could not process her words. Ted ran out of the room, and a painful chill went up my spine. As if in slow motion, I got out of the bed but was so dizzy I had to hold onto the wall as I made my way to Joe's nursery.

Bonnie met me at the doorway. Ted had Joe's lifeless body and was trying to shake him awake.

"Get the phone!" Ted yelled. "He isn't breathing, Jane—he isn't breathing."

I felt a scream in the back of my throat that would not come out as I fell to my knees. Why was I paralyzed by fear?

Emma returned with the phone, and Ted yelled to me, "Call 911!"

Bonnie grabbed the phone from Emma and proceeded to dial. Ted began to breathe into him, and Emma began to cry.

Bonnie pleaded, "Please send someone—my grandson isn't breathing. What's the address here?"

"812 Hawthorne," I managed to call out as I tried to wake myself from the fog I was in.

I managed to stand while grasping onto the wall and slowly made my way over to Ted and Joe. I looked into the crib and let out a moan so primitive I could not believe it came from a human being. There was Joe, motionless. His skin had a bluish tint, and I watched with horror as Ted tried CPR. I heard banging on the door and Bonnie ran to let the paramedics in. A man and woman from the rescue service came in and immediately took over for Ted.

The woman began CPR, and the man asked, "How long has your son been unconscious?" while he unpacked a stethoscope and blood pressure cuff.

Ted answered, "I don't know. Our daughter woke us up and told us he wasn't moving."

I began to pray, "Dear God, please let him live. Please let him live."

Ted came over and held me, but I couldn't stand to have anyone comfort me so I jerked myself free. I saw Emma huddled in the doorway, crying softly, and thankfully Bonnie took her from the room.

The woman stopped CPR. She listened with the stethoscope and shook her head at her partner.

"Please," I begged the Paramedics. "Do something."

How can this be happening? I wondered to myself. *Please, God, I will do anything. Take me instead. Just let this baby live.*

The man gave Joseph a shot as the woman hooked him up to a monitor. There was no heartbeat. They took out the tiny paddles and tried to shock his heart. I watched in horror as my baby's body jumped in response to the electricity. Still no heartbeat. They continued pressing on his tiny chest with their fingers.

"Keep trying," I pleaded.

They tried the paddles again—still no response. The woman went back to trying CPR. The man spoke to the hospital on the radio and then gave Joseph another shot.

"Please, God let this work," I whispered aloud.

They tried another time with the paddles, but there was no response. The man looked at his partner and just shook his head.

"No," Ted wailed. "Try something else. There must be something you can do."

"I'm sorry," the young woman said softly. "It's been too long. He hasn't been breathing for a while." She paused, then added, "We'll give you a few moments alone with him."

I ran and vomited in the trashcan. My son was dead. My baby. Dead.

He packed up their things while she gathered up Joe and brought him to us. Ted took Joe in his arms and rocked him as he sobbed. I wanted to go to Ted, but I was in too much pain.

"I can't believe he's gone, Jane," he said through his sobs.

I had no words but began to sob uncontrollably as I fell to the floor.

After a few minutes, Ted brought Joseph to me and quietly asked "Do you want to hold him?"

"I need to be alone with him, Ted."

Ted nodded knowingly, and I stood and went over to the rocker that Ted had bought me for my birthday. I sat and buried my head in my hands and cried softly while I listened to my husband say his good-byes to our son.

Ted sobbed, "I love you, son." He walked over to me, kissed the baby on his forehead and placed him in my arms before leaving.

A moan escaped as I held him to my chest. He felt cold, but I didn't care. I knew he was gone, but I couldn't let him go just yet. After a few moments, I laid him on the changing table and undressed him one last time. I filled the bathroom sink with warm water and added my favorite baby wash, knowing I would never again be able to stand the smell of lavender. Gently I washed and dried his lifeless body. I picked out a clean pair of pajamas so it would seem as if he were just sleeping. As I dressed him, I thought back to the joy I felt when I held him in my arms for the first time. Tears escaped and rolled down my cheeks. I then combed his hair, paying special attention to the cowlick that was developing in the back of his head. He looked so peaceful and sweet, and at that moment I felt my heart shatter. I wrapped him in my favorite blanket, the one my mother knit for him. I cradled him in my arms knowing, but not accepting, that it was for the last time. I sat in our rocker and let the tears flow.

The door to the nursery opened, and Ted, red-eyed and on the verge of more tears, said, "It's time."

Fifty-one

How I became the mother of a dead son was beyond my comprehension. As I sat in the church waiting for the coffin I picked out to be brought in, I felt as if I was living someone else's life. People had been in and out of my house bringing food. All of them wanted to reach out to me, but I wanted absolutely no physical contact. I wanted the warmth of my baby Joe, and nothing else would satisfy me.

Ted was inconsolable and each time he asked for comfort, I responded with an embrace or a touch but would not allow myself to be comforted. In private, my tears flowed freely, but I didn't want to share this grief with anyone. I guess it was a sort of penance.

The tiny casket was wheeled into the church, and Ted grabbed my hand with such force that under ordinary circumstances it would have caused me to flinch. Today it somehow felt good. Father Flaherty went through the mass as usual, and as the hymns were sung, I broke down. I'd picked some of my favorites knowing the sadness they would impart, yet somehow I needed the pain once more.

When it was time for the homily, Father Flaherty began with, "Ted and Jane, I cannot begin to imagine what you are going through right now. Death is never easy, and the death of a child, well, that seems cruel and unfair. You may be asking why. Why did Joseph leave us? Why am I still here? Perhaps instead of asking why, ask what does God want me to do because I am still here? Whatever God's purpose, we must trust in His wisdom and make use of the brief time that we have on this earth. Find comfort in knowing that Joe is one of God's angels, and when the pain becomes too much, ask God for His help. I ask you all to pray for this family's strength. Pray that they will find peace. It is hardest for those left behind, but rejoice in knowing that Joseph is back with God and one day you will all be reunited."

Ted was openly sobbing, and instead of sadness, I began to feel anger. What kind of God would do this? Was this payback for my sins? I took a deep breath and forced myself to calm down. The service was over, and as we made our way out of the church, I spotted Grace in the back row. She mouthed, "I'm sorry," and the dam that had been holding back the tears let loose. Ted pulled me to him as I sobbed, and he quickly ushered me into the waiting limousine.

After a moment, I composed myself and just let myself relax into Ted's arms. We didn't say one word to each other, and when we arrived at the cemetery, Ted broke down.

"I can't do this, Jane. I can't watch them lower him into the ground."

My anger returned, but this time it was directed at Ted. "Please don't leave me alone. I can't do this by myself."

He nodded, so we got out and slowly walked to the seats under the green tent. It was a sunny day with clear, blue skies. A perfect day. How unfair that the world kept going when ours had come to a screeching halt.

Ted's parents and my mother and Lawrence were the only family members or friends that I wanted at the grave site. Father Flaherty gave a brief blessing, and when it was over Ted put a hand on the smooth white box and wailed, "What am I going to do with out you? I had so many plans for us? Why did He take you from me?"

This was the most devastating scene I had ever witnessed, yet I could not go to Ted. Bonnie and Jack, one on each side, supported Ted as he made his way to the limousine.

The moment I had been dreading was upon me. It was time to lower the coffin into the ground. My mother began to cry hysterically, and Lawrence looked to me. I nodded, letting Lawrence know he should take her away. This left Father Flaherty and the two cemetery workers to join me in the final goodbye. Father approached me but I just shook my head. This was my pain to absorb, and I didn't want anyone to try and lessen it.

Slowly the two men lowered Joe into the ground. I felt bile rise in my throat and fought bitterly to control the wrenching of my stomach. The two men slowly began to shovel dirt on top of the casket, and I could no longer breathe. I was gasping for air in between my sobs, and Father Flaherty grabbed me by the arm to try and lead me away.

"No," I screamed. "I can't leave him. Joe, Mommy's here. She'll never leave you."

"Jane, let me take you back to the car. You need to sit down," Father said.

"I can't do it."

"I'm here. I'll help you."

"If I leave, he'll be gone for good."

Fifty-two

I felt as if I would come out of my skin at the reception following the funeral. I just wanted to escape, and although I was grateful to our family and friends, I had had enough. I couldn't stand for one more person to touch me and tell me how sorry they were, how they knew what I was going through.

When we finally went home, I locked myself up in my bedroom. I changed into an old sweatshirt and sweatpants, and crawled into bed. I heard people talking and dishes clanging together. I knew that I was being rude by not greeting our visitors, but I didn't care. I welcomed sleep, and though it was fitful, it provided some much needed escape. I awoke to a knock on my door. When I didn't answer, my mother poked her head in and gently called my name. She came and sat on the edge of the bed.

"Jane, you really should get up."

"I don't want to. I'm really tired," I said, feeling like a child trying to stay home from school.

"It's dinner time, and Emma is back. I think it would be good for her to spend some time with you."

"I can't."

"Jane, I know how hard this is for you, but you have to try."

I felt my anger rise to a boil. "You know how hard this is for me?" I asked indignantly. "I'm glad you know how I feel, because I sure as hell don't. My baby is dead. After only six weeks, he is gone forever, and you know what I am going through."

My mother looked wounded, and I enjoyed it. I wanted her to suffer, just like I was.

"Jane, I didn't mean it that way. It's just that we are all grieving, and we need to pull together. Ted has been out there all afternoon by himself, and I'm sure he wants to be with you. And poor Emma. She is scared and tired, and if she could just talk to you a little, I think that would help."

I rolled over and didn't answer her. I felt her get off the bed and stand over me for a moment.

"Jane, I can't even begin to know the pain you are in, but you have to realize that the rest of us are hurting, too." I heard a sob escape as she continued, "I loved that baby with all of my heart, and right now I am so angry with God for taking him that I can't think straight. But I realize that everyone is torn apart by Joe's death and it's about getting through this together."

"I don't want to get through this," I wailed. "I want my baby back."

~ * ~

I did get out of bed. Ted, Emma, my mother, Bonnie and Jack were gathered in the dining room finishing the many dishes brought to us by friends and neighbors. Ted looked at me and smiled as tears brimmed in his eyes. My mother nodded in recognition of my effort. Emma caught my gaze and immediately looked away. I pulled up a chair next to her and kissed her on top of her head. I saw her relax, and Bonnie stood to get me a plate.

"Thanks, Bonnie, but I'm not hungry."

"Please just try and eat something, Jane. You haven't eaten all day," Ted reminded me.

I got up and put a piece of ham on my dish and added a few vegetables.

"Jane, Bonnie and I were just saying that we are going to leave in the morning."

"Unless you need me to stay," Bonnie added. "Jack can go back by himself."

I shook my head and moved the food around on my plate.

"We'll be back soon, though," Bonnie added. She looked at me and wept. She left the table, and we again sat in the silence that had come to hover over the strained conversation.

The silence was painful, and I thought maybe holding Emma would take away some of the edge away.

"Come sit with me, Emma." She hesitated so I added, "It's all right."

She approached cautiously, and sat stiffly in my lap. I wrapped my arms around her and said, "I'm glad you're home, Em."

"I thought you'd be mad at me," she whispered.

"Why would I be mad at you?"

Her lip quivered as she answered, "I didn't do anything, I promise."

My tears returned. "To Joe?"

She nodded.

"Oh, Emma. It's not your fault that Joe died. It's nobody's fault."

I looked up to find all eyes at the table on me, but was grateful when Emma, apparently content with my answer, said, "Guess what I got from Grandma and Grandpa?"

Ted asked, "What?"

The conversation continued; however, I wasn't listening. I was replaying the funeral in my head, and I kept picturing that small, white casket being wheeled into the church and then lowered into the ground. I shuddered and felt Ted's hand on my back. He was standing behind me, and as he gave my shoulders a squeeze, I covered his hands with mine. For now, this was all I could do.

Fifty-three

As though the pain in my heart wasn't enough, my breasts were swollen and painful from not nursing. Every part of my body ached for my Joe, and there was nothing that would make it go away. Ted tried to bring our lives back to some sense of normalcy, but I wasn't ready and spent most of my time in bed. He and Emma went to the grocery store, did laundry and cleaned up the house.

"Let's go get something to eat tonight," Ted suggested.

"I'm not feeling up to it, Ted."

"Jane, I really need to get out of the house. It would be good for you, too."

"I can't," I admitted.

"I can't stay in any longer. Emma and I will be back soon."

~ * ~

I watched the clock and grew anxious as I watched the minutes tick by. Even though I wanted to be alone, I was comforted by knowing Ted and Emma were in the house. I was in bed when I heard them come home and was able to calm down, even though it was some time before Ted joined me.

When he got in bed, he turned to me and announced, "I'm going back to work tomorrow, Jane."

I began to panic. "No, Ted, please stay home a little longer."

"It's time, babe. I'm going crazy just sitting around here, and I think Emma needs to get back in a routine. We all do."

"What's that supposed to mean?" I challenged.

"You need to try harder, Jane. Do you realize that you haven't showered in three days?" he asked gently. When I didn't answer, he continued, "I want you to get up tomorrow and shower before Emma goes to school."

I nodded and rolled over.

~ * ~

The next morning, I waited until Ted was gone before I showered. The hot water stung at first, but it helped ease the swelling in my breasts. I thought back to the last time that I nursed my baby. I'd gently hurried Joe because Ted was waiting for me. If I could only have those few minutes back.

I finished my shower and was dressed when I woke Emma for school. She was quiet, but I could tell she was happy to be going back. I felt a little lighter, too, and I held her hand as we walked to the bus stop. As we approached, I saw the moms start to shuffle uncomfortably and a feeling of dread came over me. We joined the group, and Emma left me and ran to her friends.

My neighbor Anna approached me and asked, "How are you, Jane?"

"I'm fine," I answered quickly. *Fine for someone who just buried her infant son.*

"Can I do anything?"

I just shook my head and fought back the tears. Thankfully the bus arrived and took the attention off me.

Emma hugged me and asked, "You're going to be here when I get back from school, aren't you?"

"Of course, I will. Have fun today," I added as I kissed both of her cheeks and watched her get on the bus.

After it pulled away, Abby came over to me and asked, "Do you want to go get a cup of coffee? We could talk about anything or nothing. Whatever you like."

I shook my head and said, "I have a lot to do, but thanks anyway."

I started to walk away, and she grabbed my arm. "I lost a child, too, Jane."

I must have looked startled, and she continued, "It's all right, Jane. It was six years ago. I just want you to know that I'm here if you want to talk. I go to a meeting once a month for people who have lost a child. I have the name of a great counselor, too. It saved me, Jane. She can help you, too. Just say the word, and I'll set up an appointment for you."

It was so overwhelming, I just shook my head and impulsively hugged her before I ran back home. It felt good to run, yet the minute I arrived at my front door, I began to crumble. I had eight hours until Emma would be coming home. *What am I going to do with myself?* I wondered. I went in and immediately cleaned up the breakfast dishes and then I changed the sheets on our bed. I got some chicken out of the freezer for dinner and looked around for something else to do, but there wasn't anything. I looked at my watch, and I still had six hours until Emma's return. I felt so tired, and although I had promised myself I would not go back to bed, I didn't care anymore. I was ready to escape and sleep was my ally; however, as I walked by the closed door to Joe's room it drew me in. I opened the door and just looked around. Nothing had changed since that morning. It was less than one week ago, yet a lifetime had passed. I wanted to go inside, and rock in the chair and pretend he was still here. Oh, God, I wanted my baby back in my arms. I sat in the doorway and cried and cried, and when my supply of tears seemed exhausted, I shut the door and climbed into my bed. The phone ran, and the caller ID let me know it was Ted. I answered, trying to sound as normal as possible.

"Hi, hon. I was just checking in."

"I'm fine," I lied, "and Emma got off to school without a hitch."

"Good. I knew it would help us all to get back to our old routine."

I thought, *What about me? My routine was all about taking care of Joe. What am I supposed to do now?* But I just answered, "You were right, Ted."

Fifty-four

It had been a month, and the anguish I felt was still as raw as the day Joe died. Ted and Emma seemed to be making the transition, but I had no desire to move on. Last week we'd cleaned out his room, and the finality of my baby's death hit me hard. So hard that if I had indeed made any progress on my grieving process, it was gone now. I had become a good actress, though. Each day I got dressed, but the minute Emma got on the bus, I crawled back in bed. The weekends were harder—Ted wanted to go to the movies or out to dinner, and I couldn't do it. Part of me felt disloyal to Joe and the other part of me felt guilty. Somehow Joe's death was related to my past sins, and I just couldn't get over it. I thought I was doing a good job of hiding my pain, but Ted saw through me and finally confronted me.

"Jane, we need to talk. I know you don't like to discuss Joe's death, but we can't keep ignoring it." I had nothing to say, so he continued. "I think we need to see somebody, a professional who can help us through this. We need to talk to someone, Jane. Both of us."

"I'm scared, Ted."

"Tell me what you're afraid of," he probed gently.

I started to cry, and my sobs became uncontrollable. I feared that I would forget Joe if I continued on with my life. I felt like it was my fault that he died. Why didn't I check on him that night? I wanted to punish myself, and keeping the pain alive was a sort of penance. I felt like I was crazy with all of these thoughts running through my head, and I didn't want anyone to find out about them. I couldn't tell Ted. I couldn't tell anyone. It was easier to cry and get it out that way.

When I calmed down, Ted tried a different approach. "Jillian called and wants you to go out for lunch with her and Mattie on Saturday. I told her you would go."

As I opened my mouth to protest, Ted interrupted. "I want you to go. Do this for me."

I nodded and felt a surge of admiration for my husband. He had been dealt two devastating losses and, yet, he was doing his best to carry on. And with that came anger. Hadn't he lost enough? He was such a good man who didn't deserve the heartbreak he had been forced to endure. So yes, I would do this for him. It was the least I could do.

~ * ~

When Saturday arrived, I was filled with dread. I thought about feigning a headache, but Ted was so happy to see me getting ready that I couldn't disappoint him. Mattie had offered to pick me up, but I declined. The lunch was going to be hard enough to get through. I didn't want to add two car rides to that. I arrived at this little café that was an old house. Inside the wooden floors and plaster walls gave it a homey feel. Jillian was waiting inside, and when she saw me, her face turned from nervousness to pity.

She hugged me tight and said, "You look great, Jane. I'm so happy you came. Mattie should be here any minute."

Sure enough, Mattie walked in and the three of us were seated at a table by a window. I was surprised to see that the irises and daffodils had bloomed. Spring had arrived with all of its glory, yet I had missed it.

We spent a few minutes in silence staring at the menu, and after we had ordered, I could see that they were both a little uncomfortable, especially Jillian.

"Jillian, what's been going on with you?" I asked hoping to engage them in some mindless conversation. I wanted to steer clear of Joe and was hopeful for the diversion.

"I'm still dating Mark, and it's going really well. I've met his parents, and he's coming to my folks' place as soon as school gets out. We're going to visit them at their condo in Florida."

"That's great. Are you ready for summer?" I asked.

"I am. I love the kids, but I'm getting tired. Another six weeks and we're done. Do you think you'll come back to work now that..."

There it was. The elephant in the room that had yet to be addressed. Jillian looked panicked and said, "I'm so sorry, Jane. I didn't mean anything by it."

Tears welled in my eyes, and I said, "I know you didn't." Mattie reached over and rubbed my hand. I was determined not to have a breakdown at our lunch. "Are you still planning to retire this year, Mattie?" I asked trying to change the subject.

"Jane, I want to talk about you," Mattie insisted. "How are you handling Joe's death?"

Jillian shifted uncomfortably in her chair, so I replied, "You don't need to hear my sad story. I'd like to think about something else for a while."

Jillian sat back, visibly relaxed as our food arrived.

"Jim and I are going to Italy this summer. We are renting a villa in a small town in Tuscany, and we're going to spend two weeks just living among the locals."

"I'm dying to go to Europe," Jillian chimed in as my mind began to wander back to the night Joe died. *Was God punishing me for killing my baby in high school? Is that why my son was taken from me?*

Mattie interrupted my thoughts. "Jane, you seem tired."

"I am," I lied. What I really wanted was to get back home and make sure Joe's blanket was still there. I felt anxiety wash over me as I thought that something might happen to it. "I need to get going. This was nice, though," I added, though I surely didn't mean it. I had to get out of there.

Jillian looked somewhat relieved that our visit was over, but I could tell Mattie wanted to talk. "I need a ride home, Jane. Would you mind?"

Yes, I mind. I need to get home. "Not at all. Let's take care of the bill and we can go."

"No, Jane. Mattie and I are paying. It's the least we can do," Jillian said.

"Thank you, both," I said rising.

Jillian hugged me and said, "Let's do this again, soon. Summer will be here, and we can spend more time together. I'd love for you to meet Mark."

"Me, too. I'll call you." *Don't wait by the phone.*

Mattie and I walked out to the car, and as we did she grabbed my arm and said, "I'm worried about you, Jane."

"Please, don't be," I said as we got into the car.

"You need to talk about it."

"I can't, Mattie. It's too much."

"Honey, you have to or it's going to eat you up."

I began to cry. "I'm sorry. I didn't want to do this."

"Stop being sorry. You have to let it out."

I cried harder and said, "I miss him so much."

Mattie held me and said, "Just let go, Jane."

As I did, I wondered if I would ever be able to stop.

Fifty-five

The nights were the worst. The darkness brought back all of the painful memories. Holding Joe's cold body, having the paramedic take him from my arms, watching him being lowered into the ground. When the sun began to rise, that was when sleep usually came. It seemed as though I was now totally out of sync with the world around me. I was awake all night and slept most of the day. Besides Ted and Emma, the only other person I saw was my mother. They all tried to get me to go to a movie or shopping, but I couldn't bring myself to do it. I wanted to be dead, too, so I was slowly removing myself from life. Ted was not about to lose another wife, though.

"Jane, get dressed," he demanded. "We are going to dinner, just the two of us."

"I can't, Ted."

"It's been over two months, Jane. All you do is sit in this house. Emma and I need you to come back to us. Get dressed, please."

"What about Emma?"

"Your mother and Lawrence are here to take care of her." He paused, then added, "Don't make me beg."

I nodded and said, "Okay. Give me some time to get ready."

I slowly got out of bed and splashed some warm water on my face. As I dried it off, I looked at myself in the mirror and was shocked. I had dark circles under my eyes and I needed a haircut, badly. I put on some make-up and dried my hair. It helped a little, but when I put on my favorite dress, I realized how much weight I had lost. I took a deep breath and headed to the door, but then felt the pull toward Joe's blanket. I sat on the bed and took it out from under my pillow. I held it to my face and tried to conjure up his scent. It was faint, but it was still there, and reluctantly I put it back. I sighed, wondering if I would ever be normal again.

I went into the living room, and my mom's face lit up when she saw me.

"Hi, honey. You look nice," she said.

"Thanks," I replied, even though I knew she was lying.

"Don't worry about Emma. Stay out as late as you like."

I just wanted to crawl back into bed but smiled as if I appreciated her offer.

"Emma, come say goodbye to your mom and dad," my mother called.

Emma ignored the request and kept her eyes fixed on the television.

"Emma," Ted shouted.

She jumped and slowly made her way over to us.

"What?" she asked sounding like an angry teenager.

"Mom and I are going out. Come say goodbye."

Emma stood there as we kissed her, and it hit me that I had no idea what was going on in her life anymore. I felt a pang of guilt, yet at this point I wasn't sure I would be able to do anything about it.

Ted and I walked outside, and the cool air against my face gave me a burst of energy. A small part of me felt happy to be out of the house, and I decided to try and have as normal a night as possible, though I wasn't quite sure what that would mean. I was at loss as to how to talk with my husband, and a wave of anxiety washed over me. Was this how it was going to be? I leaned back and closed my eyes.

"Are you all right?" Ted asked.

"Yes, just a little tired."

"We'll make it an early evening. I hope you don't mind, but I thought we'd go to The Piazza. I've been wanting Italian."

"That sounds good."

We rode the rest of the way in silence, and I was relieved when we arrived at the restaurant. We were seated and Ted ordered us a bottle of Cabernet. After a few sips, I felt myself relax.

"I'm glad we did this, Jane. I've missed you."

I smiled and answered, "I know." My mind began to wander, and panic set in as I thought about the blanket. *Please don't let anything happen to it.*

"Jane, you're a million miles away. I wish you would let me in."

"I'm just not ready, Ted."

"What can I do to help?"

Nothing will ever help. "Just give me time."

"I feel like the longer I wait, the harder it will be for us to come back together."

"I don't know what to say." *I just want to be left alone.*

"I need you, and so does Emma. Her teacher called me at work today. She said she left a message last week and never heard back from us. Emma has been disruptive in class and has been picking on a boy. She calls him names, and the other day she hit him."

"I'll talk to her, Ted."

"It's going to take more than that, Jane. We need to get some help. I made an appointment for us to see a counselor together tomorrow. I cleared my schedule at work, and I want you to meet me there."

I nodded in agreement, knowing that this was something I had to do. I was sinking fast, but I still wasn't sure I wanted to be saved. I took another sip of wine and saw an older woman approach our table.

"Hi, Dr. Manning. My husband and I were finishing our dinner and I told him I had to come over and see how that new baby of yours was doing?" She turned to me and said, "I just knew it was going to be a boy. How old is he now?"

Shut up! Shut up! I was horrified and watched as her mouth just kept on moving. I stood and practically shoved her aside as I ran out of the restaurant. I gasped for air as I leaned against our car. I wanted to cry, but the tears wouldn't come. I slammed my hand on the hood of the car. It felt cathartic so I did it again. And again. And again. My hand began to throb, but I didn't care. I stopped only when Ted grabbed my arm.

"Jane, she didn't know." He grabbed my face and held it between his hands. "She didn't know." I collapsed in his arms and cried. "It's going to be all right, Jane."

If only wishing made it so.

Fifty-six

I guess I knew deep down that I wasn't going to meet Ted at the counselor's office. I pretended to myself the entire day, and when the time came, I got in my car and drove to the cemetery. I had not been back since the funeral and found myself oddly excited at the prospect, as if Joe would be there waiting for me. I knew in my head that he was gone forever, but my heart still held out a bit of hope.

He was buried with my dad so I found the grave site easily and sat next to the headstone. I had not seen it before and smiled at the simplicity of the message—"Our Joe." I rubbed my hand along the top of the stone and sat on the grass facing it.

"Hi, Joe. It's Mommy. It's a beautiful day today. I wish you were here with me."

I sat in silence and played with the grass. "Joe, I can't seem to go on without you. It hurts so bad, like nothing I've ever felt before. I don't know how to act or what I'm supposed to do. Nothing makes sense anymore."

I laid down and let the sun wash over my face as the tears slid off my face. I rested awhile and reluctantly got ready to leave. Emma was due home, and I was going to be in enough trouble for not going to the therapist with Ted. I didn't need to add forgetting Emma to the list.

"I love you, Joe. I'll be back soon," I said as my hand lingered over the rough marble of his headstone. I slowly walked back to my car and took one last glance at Joe and smiled. I felt better after this visit. That was until I saw the five missed calls on my cell phone.

~ * ~

Emma and I went to the grocery store after school. It seemed that whenever I left the house, I felt the need to avoid anyone I knew. I just didn't want to talk to people. Friends, neighbors—they all meant well, but I just couldn't stand their pitying looks. I also hated to hear them say Joe's name. It had become sacred to me, and to hear them utter it made me want to scream.

Luckily, we made it in and out of there without running into anyone. When we got home, Ted's car was in the garage. Emma and I carried the groceries in, and she ran up to him and announced, "We got ice cream."

"Great, Em. Go in your room and do your homework. Mom and I need to talk."

When she was gone, Ted said, "Sit down."

"I have to put these groceries away."

"Stop it, Jane. I don't give a damn about that. We need to talk."

I sat at the table although I wanted to run away.

"Where were you?"

I didn't answer and just looked down. I felt like a child.

"Jane, I'm trying to be patient, but I'm at the end of my rope here. Why didn't you meet me at the doctor's office?"

"I tried, really I did, but I just couldn't."

"I don't understand. We need help, Jane, but I can't do it alone."

"I don't want to talk to a stranger about Joe. I'll get through this on my own," I said, knowing that I might never make it.

"Jane, you can't do this alone. Dr. Whitford said that we need to talk about Joe together. We need to be able to mention his name without falling apart, and I need his guidance."

"Ted, I can't ever picture a time when I won't feel a stabbing pain when I say his name."

"I know it feels so raw now, but it will get easier. Dr. Whitford has ways to help us cope, but you need to go with me."

Just then the doorbell rang. I wondered who it could be and remembered that Emma was spending the weekend with her grandparents.

"That must be Liz. I totally forgot to help Emma pack," I admitted.

"You go let her in and I'll get Emma ready."

"Thanks," I said as I went to answer the door. Liz was standing there with a sweet smile on her face.

"Hi, Jane," she said as I opened the door for her.

"Hi, Liz. I'm sorry Emma's not ready. Ted and I got to talking, and I forgot about getting her overnight bag ready."

"I know this is a dumb question, but how are you doing, Jane?"

"Honestly, it depends. I take it day by day."

"For me, it sometimes was minute to minute."

I smiled.

"If you ever need to talk... I've been there."

Before I could answer, Emma bounded into the room and almost knocked Liz over as she hugged her. She was so excited, and I realized it had been a long time since I had seen her this happy. I felt a pang of guilt as Ted joined us.

"Have a great time, kiddo. Give me a kiss before you go."

I bent down so I could look her in the eyes. "I love you very much, Emma."

She beamed as she grabbed me around the neck and squeezed. "I love you, too," she whispered. "I'll be back tomorrow. Will you be okay while I'm gone?"

I nodded and said, "Go and have fun. Thanks, Liz."

"We'll see you tomorrow afternoon sometime."

Emma hugged Ted and they were off.

"Well, it's just you and me. Let's go to a movie."

"All right," I replied even though I wanted nothing more than to crawl into bed. At least in the darkness of the theater, no one could see me cry.

~ * ~

I made it through the movie, but couldn't begin to tell anyone what it was about because my mind kept wandering back to Joe. Now, I was dreading being alone with my husband. He was craving physical contact with me, and I wasn't sure that I ever wanted to be touched again. When I came out of the bathroom, I had hoped that Ted would be asleep, but he was waiting for me. I slipped under the covers, and he reached for me. I tried to relax as he held me in his arms.

Ted must have sensed my anxiety and said, "Just let me hold you."

We laid there for awhile, and then he leaned over and kissed me. "Jane, I love you so much. I need you."

There was nothing I could say, so I just gave myself to him. He was tender and gentle and it was more than I deserved. The mix of emotions was overwhelming: sadness, guilt, desperation. My mind was a whirlwind, and when it was over, I wiped the tears from my eyes so Ted wouldn't see.

Fifty-seven

I didn't sleep that night. I wanted to go to the cemetery. I wanted to be alone. I wanted to escape so I quietly got out of bed and dressed, hoping not to wake Ted. I grabbed Joe's blanket from under my pillow and went to the kitchen. I got a piece of paper and a pen and wrote, *"Ted, I need to be alone for awhile and sort some things out. I love you and Emma very much. Jane."*

I grabbed the car keys and my purse and went out the front door to my car. I sat for a few moments and contemplated what I was about to do and knew it was what I needed. As I drove toward the cemetery, I felt myself loosen up. The sun was coming up. It was going to be a beautiful day, and I was content. I was going to be with my Joe.

I took my place on the grass. "Hi, Joe. Mommy's back. I don't seem to be doing so well, baby. I just left Dad and Emma, and I have no idea where I'm going or what I'm doing."

I hugged my knees to my chest and continued, "I used to be so strong, Joe. I don't even recognize myself anymore. Is this what the rest of my life is going to be like? I don't know if I can go on like this."

I stood and wiped some blades of grass off the headstone and slowly walked back to my car.

Where was I going to go? I dialed my mom's number.

~ * ~

I pulled my car into the driveway and Ted pulled in right behind me.

He got out of the car and ran toward me. "What's going on? Are you leaving me?"

"Ted, let's not discuss it here."

"Let's go inside and talk about it then," he demanded.

"No, I'm..."

"Then where? Just tell me where we can go so we can work this out."

"I'm not ready."

"Jane, it's been two months. When will you be ready?"

"I don't know."

"Jane, what am I supposed to do?"

"Just let me have some time. Please."

"Am I just supposed to wait around and hope that one day you'll be ready to come back to me and Emma? Have you thought about her, Jane? She's already lost one mother—are you going to explain this to her?"

"I can't help it. Nothing is right anymore, and I don't know how to handle it."

"That's why I wanted you to see the counselor with me. You need help."

"I need to do this my way."

Ted looked furious as he yelled, "What about me, Jane? What about what I need? How can you leave me like this? Haven't I suffered enough?" he asked as his eyes welled up.

His words stung me. "Yes, you have, and I am not doing this to hurt you. I just don't know what else to do."

"Come home," he begged softly. "Come home and let me help you. Joe died, but we didn't. Me and you and Emma—we're all still alive. We have to start living again."

"I don't know if I can. I haven't been any kind of wife or mother since Joe died. You and Emma should have someone who is there for you—mentally and physically. I have been there in body, but my attention has not been on either of you. That's not right, Ted."

"I don't care," he replied through his sobs.

"I do," I whispered. "Just give me time."

I hugged him and felt a piercing in my heart as I calmly walked into my mother's house.

Fifty-eight

For the first week, my mother left me alone. I spent most of my time in my old room. I did shower and dress each day, and besides my daily trip to the cemetery, that was about all that I could muster the strength for. Ted had called each day; however, I was not up to talking with him, yet. On day number seven, my mother had had enough and called me into the kitchen.

"Jane, sit down." I did as instructed, and she continued, "Honey, you have to get some help. You can't go on like this."

"Mom, you don't understand what I'm going through."

"I know I don't, but I know that what you are doing is not healthy. It's not going to help you get over this."

"I'm not sure I want to get over it," I admitted.

"Then that's even more reason to get help, Jane. What about Ted and Emma?"

"Maybe they're better off without me."

"Do you think that this added suffering is good for them? Don't be so selfish, Jane."

"Selfish?" I spat. "My son is dead, and you're calling me selfish. Both of your children are still alive, so when

you really know what I'm going through, then we'll talk."
I felt such hatred for her at that moment—hatred for all
mothers who still had their children. I stood and walked
toward the front door, and when I opened it, Grace was
standing there. She looked like an old woman—barely
resembling her old self. Seeing her softened my anger,
though, so I asked, "What are you doing here?"

"Mom called and said you were in a bad way. I'm so
sorry about Joe."

"I have to get out of here," I said. "Let's go for a
walk."

We walked in silence down to the corner and sat on a
bench in the park.

"Remember how Mom always made you take me here?
You hated waiting around while I played on the swings.
I'd give anything to go back to that time," I said wistfully.

"What's going on, Jane? Why are you living with Mom
instead of Ted and Emma?"

"I just couldn't take it anymore, Grace. Losing Joe was
like nothing I'd ever experienced. My heart is so broken, I
don't know if I can go on."

She put her arm around me, and I rested my head on
her shoulder. Quietly she said, "I lost a baby, too."

I looked at her, and we both were crying. "What
happened?"

"I was four months along and I fell down the steps.
When I went to the hospital, she didn't have a heartbeat
anymore."

Fell down the steps. That bastard Derek must have
pushed her. "You fell?" I asked incredulously. "What
were you doing?"

"It's not important. I just told you so that you would know that I've been there, too."

"It is important. How did the fall happen, Grace?"

"Derek and I were arguing and I got mad and wasn't paying attention. It was my fault."

"Grace, when are you going to stop covering for Derek? It's bad enough that he treats you like shit and uses you for a human punching bag, but he took your baby away. How can you stand him?"

"You don't know anything about my life, Jane."

"I know that your husband beats up on you. I know that if he didn't push you down those steps, it would have happened eventually."

"I didn't come here to get a lecture from you."

"Then why did you come, Grace? Why after all this time? After all the pleading Mom and I have done, why now?"

"Because I know what that loss feels like, and I wanted you to see that you're about to lose so much more if you walk away from Ted and Emma."

"Do you really think you're in any position to give me advice, Grace?" I asked sarcastically. "You're choosing to stay with a man who physically abuses you and caused you to lose your baby. Would you like to tell me how I should manage my life?"

She stood and looked right through me. "You're no different than me, Jane. You can help yourself and find a way to move on, but you're choosing not to. At least, you have a husband and child who love you. Some of us aren't so fortunate."

Fifty-nine

My conversation with Grace left me rattled. I felt bad for lashing out at her. She didn't deserve my tirade. Half of me thought maybe I could shock her into leaving him. The other half of me was wondering about us not being so different. I just didn't know.

I took my time walking back to my mom's house and was relieved when I realized her car was gone. I felt wiped out and headed straight for my bed when I noticed a letter addressed to me from Liz. I wasn't sure that I had the stamina to read it, but in the end my curiosity got the better of me. I opened the letter, and a business card fell into my lap. I fingered it a moment before seeing that it was for a grief counselor.

Dear Jane,

I realize that this letter from me may surprise you as we have a unique sort of relationship. When you first came into our lives, I'll confess I resented you. After all, you were living my daughter's life and my place in it was tenuous, at best. In my eyes, having you marry Ted and become Emma's mother was almost as difficult to bear as when Annie died. David, however, knew better. He would point out subtle, but positive changes in Ted and Emma. They smiled more and their spirits were lighter. David never let up on me, and soon I began to see their joy for myself. With a counselor's help, I also had to admit that you were the reason they were so happy.

Now I see sadness in all of your eyes and I want more than anything to make it go away. I know firsthand what it is like to lose a child. When Annie died I felt a pain so intense, it was indescribable. I felt so lost, like I didn't know my purpose in life anymore. Tears rolled down my cheeks as I continued to read. *I can only assume from your current circumstances that you are feeling the same. I'm asking you to get some help, Jane. Please don't be like me. I cut myself off from everyone and now I regret it. Luckily, David stood by me because I didn't see a counselor until Ted married you. So you see, I have you to thank for getting me the help I needed. I realized that I wasted so much time. I know Annie would have been so disappointed in me—not only for mourning her like I did, but also for not wanting Ted and Emma to move on.*

I know I have no right to ask this, but please don't shut out Ted and Emma. They suffered a loss, too. And now, all three of you are hurting, but you're all alone. They lost Annie and Joe, too, but they have each other. It would be easier for everyone if they had you, too.

I've enclosed my doctor's card and I hope you will give her a call. I know the heartbreak you are going through, but it's time to start living again.

With love,

Liz

I reread the letter and then picked up the card. I grabbed the phone and dialed.

"Ted, it's me. I'm ready to start living again."

Epilogue

It's been over three years since Joe died, and I have finally achieved some sense of normalcy. With the help of a wonderful therapist, Ted and I got back together. We moved into a new house—the other held too many painful memories of both Annie and Joe. Getting pregnant again was one of the most difficult decisions I ever made and the most stressful, but Abigail Elizabeth has brought all of us incredible joy. It was an uneventful pregnancy, and once Abby passed that six-week mark, my anxiety began to wane.

Emma loves her sister and is growing up so fast. I made a wonderful friend in Liz, Annie's mother. We talk frequently, and she has helped fill some of the void that Grace left. I speak to Grace every few months, but have not seen her since we had the fight at Mom's over Derek. Nothing has changed for her, and I have accepted the fact that I can't help her. My mother and Lawrence are a large part of our lives, and for that I am extremely grateful.

As for Ted—he continues to amaze me with his strength and optimism. He enjoys life each day and doesn't look back. For me, it's not that easy. I still miss

Joe terribly, though the pain has lessened. There have been days when I haven't thought about him, and that makes me both happy and sad. It's progress, yet I feel like I am abandoning him when he is an afterthought. I still see my therapist monthly and probably will for a long time. I've realized that I'm not going to be one of those women who overcome tragedy by starting a foundation in their child's name. That's not me. The pain I experienced was so private and so deep, it was hard enough to deal with let alone share it with others. I know I have a lot to be thankful for, and on the days when Joe is heavy in my heart, I try to remember that. It doesn't always work, but I do the best I can. Choosing to live again was the best decision I ever made. Life does go on—you just have to choose to be a part of it.

Meet

Robyn Sheridan

Facing Forward is Robyn Sheridan's first novel. She lives near Atlanta with her husband and three children and is currently at work on her next book.